Summer at
Green
Valley
Vineyard

Lucy Coleman

embla
books

First published in Great Britain in 2023 by

embla
books

Bonnier Books UK Limited
4th Floor, Victoria House, Bloomsbury Square, London, WC1B 4DA
Owned by Bonnier Books
Sveavägen 56, Stockholm, Sweden

A CIP catalogue record for this book is available from the British Library.

ISBN: 9781471413582

This book is typeset using Atomik ePublisher

Embla Books is an imprint of Bonnier Books UK
www.bonnierbooks.co.uk

Summer at
Green
Valley
Vineyard

Having walked barefoot among the vines and felt a powerful connection, this is dedicated to those who regularly ground themselves in nature.

July

Linzi

1.

The Dawn of a New Era

'Linzi? Linzi! Hang on a sec . . . me legs won't go any faster.'

I turn my head, surprised to see Gwyn Davies hurrying towards me. His face is glowing with exertion. Setting down the wheelbarrow, I idly kick some stray gravel off the path and back onto the border while I wait for him to catch up.

Gwyn manages the forestry team here at the vineyard and he also oversees site security. His time is split between juggling work schedules and whizzing around the extensive grounds on his quad bike managing the crew and making inspections.

'I got . . . somethin'. . . ya need ta . . . hear.' Gwyn huffs and puffs as he draws to a halt, pausing for a second or two while he composes himself. He mutters something in Welsh beneath his breath, before fixing his gaze on me. 'I thought you were . . . in the Forestry Outpost,' he bemoans. 'I'd have driven up if I'd realised you were out and about.'

No one talks about Gwyn's limp, or the fact that it's getting steadily worse. He's a proud man and at sixty-one he's as keen as any thirty-year-old, but a car accident in his early fifties damaged his knee. For a while now, walking long distances over uneven ground has taken a visible toll on him. If his dear wife were still alive, she'd have laid down the law to him, but he refuses to ease up.

'Oh, so you're not chasing after me to give a hand with the weeding?' I jest, unable to suppress a broad smile.

5

'Like you'd trust me near those vines.' Gwyn leans in close, lowering his voice as his eyes scope out the swathe of tall trees surrounding us. Up here, looking down onto the lake, sound does travel, as demonstrated by the constant low rumble from motorway traffic way off in the distance, but there's no one even remotely within earshot. 'This is from the old man himself, but it's not common knowledge. There's goin' ta be an announcement.'

I glance at him, frowning. 'Then maybe you should keep that information to yourself until he's ready to tell the rest of us, Gwyn,' I remark.

'You don't understand . . . he told me because he wants me to give you the heads-up.'

Ah, so that's why Gwyn has gone to some trouble to track me down. I'm a good mile away from the main buildings that make up the hub of The Green Valley Vineyard hotel and restaurant complex. I can't imagine what's so important that it can't wait until I'm back at lunchtime though.

'The boss is handin' over the runnin' of the place to his grandson, Elliot,' he blurts out.

I stare at him, shocked. 'I thought something was going on – Thomas hasn't been out and about much lately. But are you sure you have that right? I mean, in all the time I've been here I've never once clapped eyes on this Elliot. I hope he understands exactly what he's taking on.'

'Made a bit of a name for himself in London as an investment analyst, by all accounts.'

It's not just the glitzy shows that attract Thomas Montgomery, and his wife, Katherine, on their regular jaunts to the city then. 'Oh well . . . hopefully he'll do what he does best and leave the rest of us to get on with our jobs. We might have to kit him out when he does the tour of the estate, though. An expensive suit and leather shoes won't stay clean for long.'

Gwyn chuckles, but it's a nervous reaction more than an appreciation for my humour.

'Thomas will no doubt give him a warnin' not to upset you. There ain't anyone else around here willin' to talk to the precious grapevines,' Gwyn states, quite matter-of-factly.

When I joined the vineyard forestry team nine years ago, I was a twenty-three-year-old, desperate for work. I'd recently moved back to the UK after five years living and working in Tuscany. Through a mutual acquaintance, Thomas approached me to come here to this beautiful spot in the verdant countryside of the Welsh valleys, to nurse some sickly vines back to good health. However, when I arrived, there was a level of scepticism among my colleagues about my ability to do the job; not least because people tend to equate age with experience. The fact that I also talk to the plants didn't help my credibility either.

It was a tight-knit team headed up by Thomas's son Robert, and Gwyn could see I was struggling to fit in. He kept an eye on me, looking on with interest and then awe as my hard work began to pay off. The bonus of what has become an enduring friendship with Gwyn is that we can speak frankly to each other, and that's useful because when I'm upset I tend to withdraw. While I have a lot of patience for the plants, I can't always say the same for people.

Gwyn's voice breaks my chain of thought.

'Elliot is bein' brought in ta manage the restaurant and the hotel, and once he understands the way the entire operation works, Thomas will do a full handover. The boss said he'd be takin' you to one side for a chat about that, but—'

'But he wanted you to forewarn me so it could sink in.'

'Thomas won't entrust his precious vines to someone who doesn't have a clue about viticulture, or winemakin', Linzi. That goes without sayin' and he laboured that point. He just wanted me to . . . pave the way for the conversation so you're ready when you get the call. Things are about to change, but he's goin' ta keep an eye ta smooth out any wrinkles.'

As Gwyn is talking to me, my thoughts are whirling. Family connections, as I've learnt to my detriment in the past, count for everything. You forgive your own what you wouldn't forgive a stranger, no matter how loyal they are, or how hard they work for you.

Initially, Thomas employed me on a one-year contract with the sole aim of increasing the annual yield of the vines. When he saw the results, he appointed me as his head gardener, reporting directly to him. We spent hours together, either inspecting the vines or drawing up plans to landscape the grounds. He said I had a natural ability and he valued that above all else: it gave me a sense of belief in myself. Often, he'd pull on his welly boots and come in search of me just to spend an hour tying up the vines or pruning. He's always treated me more like a friend than an employee and said working alongside me was cathartic.

I'm also a good listener, and Thomas enjoys talking about the past. He once told me that, as a strapping young man, Gwyn could fell a substantial tree in less than a dozen swipes of an axe. But that was back in the early eighties, when Thomas and his small team of groundsmen were working tirelessly to clear the heavily forested land he'd inherited from his maternal grandfather. It was no mean feat to turn it into the magnificent vineyard it is today, and that doesn't happen unless you put your heart and soul into it.

'Should I be concerned?'

Gwyn shrugs his shoulders. 'I knew Elliot as a lad when his dad brought him here durin' the school holidays. Bit of a serious boy, as I recall. Clever like, there was no mistakin' that. He traipsed around after Robert and did as he were told, but he ain't the sort to enjoy gettin' his hands dirty. Biggest loss ever to the family, was losin' Robert. Now he had a love for the land in the way that you do, Linzi. He didn't talk to the vines, but the business wouldn't be where it is today if it weren't for him.'

I let out a dejected sigh. 'I miss Robert too, Gwyn.' Even though we didn't hit it off at first for a variety of different reasons, over time we came to appreciate each other's views and mutual respect resulted in a blending of ideas. His heart was in the right place; we simply got off on the wrong foot because Thomas hadn't consulted him before bringing me in.

Gwyn and I exchange an uneasy glance as we remember the day fourteen months ago when Thomas broke the news that his only son had been killed in a car crash. A devastating event that was followed by a huge drop in staff morale. Overnight we'd lost our managing director, a man with an ambitious vision that was still a work in progress.

Thomas was forced to put his personal tragedy to one side and come out of retirement to oversee the extensive building work that was underway. But even he found it hard to pick up the reins as so much had changed since he'd stepped away from the business.

In a way, immersing himself in work was the worst thing for Thomas to do as it gave him an excuse not to deal with his grief. The effect on him was heart-rending. The satisfaction of knowing he'd created something special and that his son would continue his legacy had been tragically wrenched from him. The inner spark that always lit him up was growing dimmer with each passing day.

The irony is that as Robert's hard work was coming to fruition, the vineyard went through a succession of general managers who struggled to understand Thomas's ethos here. He became even more dispirited, and it took a toll on him emotionally and physically at a time when he should be taking life easy. A serious health scare isn't something you can simply ignore; it's a wake-up call.

'I know, Linzi, me too. But we both know that things can't go on as they are. It's obvious now why Thomas has been a bit more like his old self recently. Elliot takin' over the vineyard assures our future. It's a good thing, you mark my words, but we need to brace ourselves for a period of settlin' in.'

I can't argue with that. 'Well, as long as Elliot has a healthy respect for the land and the vines, then he won't hear a peep from me.'

The look on Gwyn's face tells me that he didn't walk all this way, breaking into a sweat, because our worries about the longer-term future are about to magically disappear.

'Just don't go . . .' He pauses. His left eyebrow begins to twitch, which means he's about to say something he thinks I might not want to hear. 'Don't go judgin' the guy before he's had a chance to get his feet under the table. Everyone makes mistakes at the start – even you. We're friends and friends talk straight to one another. For a quiet life, and because it would please Thomas, I'm askin' ya to be diplomatic and cut Elliot some slack. You know it makes sense, Linzi.'

'I'll walk him around and answer his questions, but I'll expect him to listen and take what I'm saying on board. I don't suffer fools gladly when it comes to viticulture, Gwyn. And I'm not going to bend like a willow just to pander to his ego, even if he is going to be our boss. If he starts trying to change the way we do things and doesn't understand the implications, I'll put him straight every time.'

Gwyn shakes his head, rolling his eyes at me. I turn away, grabbing the handles of the wheelbarrow, and glance over my shoulder, raising a smile. 'Thanks for the advance warning. You know I appreciate it. And don't worry, forewarned is forearmed. There's no way I want to upset Thomas and I'll do my best to keep my cool. But I won't let a newcomer, even if he is Thomas's grandson, impact our reputation for producing world-class wines. Now, you'd better get back to work and I need to get on.'

Things are about to change and who knows what's coming? Thomas put his trust in me to deliver what I promised, and I did. In return, he didn't just give me a permanent job, he gave me a home here at the vineyard. I saved his precious vines and he saved me from myself. I owe him, and that's the truth.

'I hope you enjoyed the introductory video tutorials yesterday, but I'm sure you're all eager to get hands-on. Before we head out, I can't stress enough how important it is to know when to listen, and when to ask questions,' I inform this summer's batch of eager trainees.

As I glance around the room, I'm glad to see that we have at least two notetakers. Usually, it doesn't take long to suss out who will last the entire summer and who the quitters will be. Out of the nine people who joined us yesterday, the first of July, for the four-month-long residential course, I wouldn't be surprised if we lose a couple of them before we're halfway through.

'There are only two rules to remember.' I stop, taking a moment to make eye contact with each and every one of them. 'The first is that when we're outside and I'm talking, you should be listening.' The silence weighs heavily in the room and I know I have their full attention. 'The second is that if there's anything you're unsure about, you ask the question *before* you touch the plant. Am I making myself clear?'

Heads nod. It's almost time to let them loose. But only on the weeds, until they've earned my trust. And anyone who isn't interested in going back to basics doesn't have the right mindset for a course entitled 'A Holistic Approach to the Natural Way to Grow Grapevines'.

There's a loud tapping sound as the door opens and Gwyn peers in.

'Sorry to interrupt, Linzi. Can I have a quick word?'

'Sure. Right, guys, if you want to grab a coffee first, we'll meet over in the outer car park to load up the trailer at ten-thirty on the dot.'

As I make my way out into the corridor, there's a buzz of chatter in the background. Even so, I hear a lone voice above the others, uttering a loud grumble. 'I think I've already mastered the art of weeding.' A ripple of laughter ensues.

'What's up, Gwyn?'

'Thomas has asked if you'd be kind enough ta join him for coffee. He knows you're teachin' and said to tell ya that it won't take long. He asked me to keep an eye on the group until you get back. After their break I'll get them ta load up the hoes and the buckets.'

I'm dreading this conversation, but Gwyn gives me a reassuring smile. 'Thomas is determined ta make it work, Linzi. Just keep an open mind.'

Getting a new boss is like starting a new job; there are no guarantees you'll fit in to their overall plan. It was different with the new managers because they didn't own the place. One day soon Elliot will, but filling Thomas's shoes isn't easy. Robert had one major thing in common with his father – a love and appreciation for the land. They were growers first and foremost. That isn't the case for Elliot and will be a concern for Thomas.

As I stride along the glass-enclosed walkway, past the little row of cottages the other side of a limestone-paved courtyard, I know I'm lucky to live in one of them. *Bwthyn y Robin Goch*, Red Robin Cottage, is my sanctuary. *Steel yourself, Linzi*, I tell myself as I head into the large annexe and make my way to Thomas's office. *Don't make waves, because you have a lot to lose.*

Giving a sharp rap on the door, I gingerly push it open. On the far wall, the bi-fold glass doors are pushed back, and Thomas is sitting on the balcony. He beckons me to join him, standing to greet me with a warm hug.

'It's good to see you, m'dear. I haven't been avoiding you, I've just been busy and haven't had time to get outside. It all looks perfect from here and I can relax knowing that you're on top of everything. Anyway, I figured that even the tutor is allowed to have a coffee break.' He grins at me and it's the old Thomas, the one who smiled more than he frowned. 'Make yourself comfortable. This vista never grows old, does it?'

Ever the gentleman, Thomas doesn't sit until I'm settled, and we turn our attention to the view. The long rows of vines seem to stretch out forever and seeing the vineyard from this elevated vantage point makes my heart swell with pride. All those tender new spring shoots are now in leaf and it's down to the sun and the rain to swell the budding fruits. Beyond that, the sheep grazing in the adjoining farmer's fields bleat to one another, as if in conversation. It's the sort of vista you see in a painting and I stare at it, seeing in my mind's eye the delightful changes throughout the seasons. Each bringing the landscape to life in a unique way. Today there's a velvety green shimmer, as the breeze blows gently through the vines, the shrubs and the trees. It's heavenly.

I turn to look at Thomas, watching as he draws in a slow and worryingly deep breath before speaking.

'In building this annexe Robert had a real vision, didn't he?'

I'm surprised he frames it as a question, as if he's looking for confirmation. It was a massive investment, but now the disruption of the building work is finally out of the way it's onwards and upwards from here.

'He did. He made his mark, Thomas.' With the extra guest rooms, the new offices, and the extended restaurant, what better showcase for the wonderful wines we produce?

Thomas settles back, looking content.

'It's been quite a journey since the day you arrived, hasn't it, Linzi? It's almost a decade now, can you believe it?' Thomas slides a cup and saucer closer to me. 'Cappuccino, no sugar and your favourite lemon biscotti.'

'You're right – the time has flown!' As our eyes meet, memories come flooding back of things I haven't dwelt on for a while. Like sitting on a terrace in Tuscany with my former boss and Thomas, on the last of a series of trips he made spanning eighteen months. Back then, I had no reason to believe our paths would cross again, or that Thomas would reach out to me.

'I probably ate my weight in biscotti when I was working in Italy,' I joke, eliciting a chuckle from Thomas. 'A lot has happened since then.' It's impossible to keep a hint of sadness from creeping into my voice.

'It has. And it wasn't only you who turned your back on Italy. Raffaele eventually followed you here.'

Thomas is teasing me; he knows Raffaele Conti and I are close, but we're just good friends.

'It wasn't me who enticed him here. The Black Ridge Vineyard needed an expert wine taster and I simply mentioned there was a job going.'

'Well, it strengthened the links between the two vineyards and I'm grateful to you for that.' Thomas pauses and I wonder where this is going. 'Are you still happy living here, Linzi? No thoughts of returning to Italy?'

My reaction is instant. 'This is my home now, Thomas. The only place I've ever lived where I felt I made a real difference.' In Italy I was merely the protégée, as was Raffaele. I wanted it to be my forever home – however, wanting and getting are two very different things.

'That's good to hear, Linzi. Life isn't fair, we both know that, but Robert would be so proud knowing that I've finally convinced Elliot to get involved.' Thomas looks at me intently.

The way Thomas said *convinced* sends a little shiver down my spine, despite the warmth of the sun's rays shining down on us. Feeling nervous, I nibble on the biscotti, trying hard to push away memories of the past I disciplined myself long ago not to dwell on.

As if reading my mind, Thomas continues. 'Do you still have any contact with Castello di Ilaria?'

I shake my head, pausing to pick up the coffee cup and savour a mouthful. Caffeine is exactly what I need right now to fortify me. 'No. It feels like a lifetime ago, but I'm grateful for every single moment of the five years I spent there. It was a steep learning curve and the most intense period of my life, but also the most wonderful.'

Thomas closes his eyes for the briefest of moments, no doubt transported back to the day we first met. Umberto Leone, the owner of the medieval vineyard in Greve, Tuscany, introduced me to Thomas as *la donna che sussurra alle vigne* – the vine whisperer. Thomas was amused, thinking it was some sort of quaint tradition, but Umberto was serious.

As an eighteen-year-old backpacker, a casual job picking grapes to fund my travels ended up as an apprenticeship learning from one of the greatest wine growers in Italy. It was only then I realised why my life had always felt so empty: it had been devoid of passion. Italy, the grapevines and Umberto changed that, for a while.

'I'm happy you've found a way to secure the future of the vineyard, Thomas. I really am.'

Thomas gives me a coy smile, knowing that he's prepared the ground.

'Gwyn's loyalty means a lot to me. And you know that my love for this place will be with me until the day I die, but it needs a vitality I can't bring to it anymore. However . . .' His hesitation is telling. 'My grandson, Elliot, is dynamic. There will be no worries on the financial front and that's crucial at this stage in our development. We've come too far to overextend ourselves and put it all in jeopardy. Elliot understands the importance of valuing each person's contribution. But his expertise is heavily weighted towards the commercial aspects of running a business.'

Pushing away nostalgic thoughts, I'm firmly back in the moment.

'You've surrounded yourself with a good team, Thomas, we won't let you – or Elliot – down. I promise not to upset—'

'I want you to teach him, Linzi. Introduce him to the land and the grapevines. Show him why what you do is so important. Make him understand, because without that insight he's at a real disadvantage.'

Thomas's words make me almost choke on my coffee. 'You are joking . . . I hope. We both know that sort of connection only comes from spending time out in the open and rolling up your sleeves. Each to their own, as they say. Anyway, he'll be much too busy to allocate time to that. I can give him an introductory tour and answer whatever questions he might have, no problem at all.'

'As you so rightly point out, Linzi, it's something he must learn for himself. He'll be seeking you out to please me and his viticultural education can begin. I'm going to give you a new job title and job description to put a little more weight behind your role. It's just tidying up loose ends.'

My expression is one of confusion. 'Why?'

'Trust me, it's a necessary detail I should have remedied before now and you'll get a corresponding rise in salary. It will also avoid any misunderstandings when it comes to the decisions made regarding the care of the vines.'

'That's not necessary, Thomas. You've been very good to—'

'Listen, in the big wide world it's all about job titles and pay grades. You were good enough to take on the mentoring programme Robert pushed through. I know it takes you outside of your comfort zone, but it's knowledge we need to share if we want to influence the future of the industry. People like the label "organic", but it's so much more than jumping through hoops to get certified. What you do is on a different spectrum altogether.'

Recalling my first day here, and the look on Thomas's face as I kicked off my shoes and walked barefoot alongside him when we inspected the vines, still makes me smile. He had no idea that the over-application of chemical fertilisers they were using to protect the plants was actually damaging them. All around me the spring growth was starting to yellow and scorch. A wave of sadness washed over me as I picked up on their struggle and my inner voice was strong. *I'm here to help*, I reassured them. *It's not too late.*

'I still tell the story of your arrival to anyone who shows an interest in the vineyard,' Thomas continues, chuckling to himself. 'You successfully influenced Robert's point of view when he saw the results of your efforts, even though he never really understood the bond you have with the plants.'

'But it's true to say that he had green fingers . . . like you, Thomas.'

'It wasn't enough though, Linzi, was it? And I fear it's not an interest we've passed down the line. While my grandson will do his homework, I want him to spend some actual time among the vines. It's crucial he understands it's not simply about the bottom-line figure on a spreadsheet.'

'You're worried that Elliot will interfere with what I do?'

Thomas shifts uneasily in his chair. 'I know he won't understand it to begin with. He'll focus on the finances because that's his strength and, my, do we need that right now to keep us on track! But having said that, as the viticulture and training manager, the true nature of your role will be formally recognised.'

I can feel the blood draining from my face. 'What?'

Thomas holds up his hands, staring back at me sheepishly. 'I know it sounds pretentious, but head gardener belies your true role. You still won't be managing staff; I promise you that. Gwyn will continue to allocate the team and ensure you have the manpower you need. But Elliot will respect the title and the role you have to play. My wish is that you set aside time to show him what you do and gain his trust. He's the financier and you're the viticulturalist. They are two entirely different disciplines, but both are equally vital to the continuing success of our vineyard. Robert was in synch with the land, but the business side overwhelmed him at times. Now we have Elliot and it's an about-turn. He'll make sure the business is profitable; when it comes to the vines and the landscaping, I want you to make sure our standards don't slip. You're in charge of that side of things until he's fully up to speed and I expect you to stand your ground if the occasion warrants it.'

He said 'our' vineyard, and while that isn't true, on another level it is. But only Thomas and I can appreciate that. A vine whisperer can feel when the plants aren't happy; it's a physical thing like a psychic medium sensing a spirit. Nature talks to us all the time but, sadly, people have forgotten how to listen and that breaks my heart.

'Are you saying he's coming into this thinking I'm not the right person for the job?' I try to keep my voice even.

'Of course not.' Thomas dismisses my comment without even pausing to think about it. 'I'm asking you to do this as a favour to me, Linzi. It's important that my grandson understands we are merely caretakers of the land. That's a huge responsibility because it will be here long after we're gone. While I'm alive I'll be an ongoing influence, but it will be in the background, as that's the deal I've made with my grandson. If you can gain his confidence, then he'll trust your judgement. One day he'll settle down and I'm not simply handing him a business he can sell on at a profit – it's so much more than that. Everyone who works here has been hand-picked and deserves job security. Each is an expert at what they do; from our wonderful chefs to the waiting staff who welcome our guests to make their experience here memorable, to our forestry team and . . . you – the keeper of the vines, the person at the heart of our operation.'

It's my unofficial title and I'm aware that people use it behind my back. Thomas often refers to me in that way, and the truth is that's how I see myself.

'It's a circle, isn't it? We all need each other to succeed.' I lower my eyes, wondering whether this is a bright new beginning, or the start of changes I won't be able to accept.

'Precisely. It's something that Elliot must take on board because his career up to this point has been focused on a different sort of pruning to yield success. I want to avoid that scenario and I'm unleashing my secret weapon.'

A huge lump begins to rise in my throat as I realise Thomas's concern is real. 'Which is?'

'*You*, Linzi. There won't be a single criticism he can raise about our working practices that you can't justify. He's a good man and he won't argue if you can back up what you say with facts and figures. The nature of his previous job was to dig deep to expose the flaws in a business, the inconvenient truths that often remain hidden. I like to think that we don't work that way, but if he finds anything that doesn't add up, he'll want to address it.'

'What makes you think he'll be prepared to listen to me?'

Thomas starts laughing. 'I didn't say it was going to be easy, but in you he will have met his match. You've never backed down from an argument when you know you're right, Linzi, have you? The ethos we have when it comes to our growing practices is why we've been able to expand so rapidly. We have a product of which we can be proud. I need you to challenge any changes you think will be detrimental going forward, in the same way that I trust Michael, as hotel and restaurant manager, to defend his corner.'

It sounds like Thomas is expecting an all-out war.

'I'd do that anyway because I believe in speaking the truth.' But even as I say the words, a little tremor of hesitation courses through me.

Two years ago, when I hit thirty it made me sit back and appraise my life. Because my family and I aren't close, what I have now seems even more precious; the respect for what I do from my colleagues, some of whom are now good friends, job security, and comfort. I'm not sure I could start over again from scratch. Maybe this willow is prepared to bend a little. But how far? Everything has a snapping point.

'And to be clear,' Thomas states quite firmly, 'I don't intend to interfere with the running of this place. Having said that, I'm a phone call away if you have any concerns now that you're stepping up into a new role, Linzi. I'll get an enhanced job description drawn up for you to approve and sign prior to Elliot's arrival. It'll clip his wings a little, but for all the right reasons. Can I count on you to have my back on this?'

How can I refuse Thomas anything? Without him I don't know where I'd be right now. Having hit rock bottom once, I'm not sure I could cope with it a second time.

2.

What, No Fireworks?

The following day, as I lead the trainees into the main restaurant, spirits are high. We're joining the welcome party to meet the new boss for the first time.

'Please grab a glass and gather around for the toast!' Gwyn announces, and we hurry over to the buffet table. You can't have a celebration in a vineyard without a glass of wine, and under the eagle eyes of head chef Deron Trahern, our culinary team has also done us proud. There is a whole array of bite-size appetisers and no expense has been spared. Even at eleven o'clock in the morning I can't resist a caramelised scallop on a swathe of what turns out to be a lemon butter sauce. It's been hours since breakfast and we're all hungry.

My best friend, Sienna Freeman, hurries over to me. She was an admin assistant when I first arrived, and now she's the office manager. We hit it off immediately and she's been a big part of the new life I've built for myself here. Having reached a crossroads, this was my fresh start and I left behind a period of my life I'd rather forget.

'I was worried you'd been held up,' Sienna whispers, leaning in to grab a tiny cracker topped with a sliver of rare roast beef with a pearl of horseradish mousse piped on the top. She pops it into her mouth, rolling her eyes as I watch her reach out for another one.

'It was a long walk. Is Thomas around?'

'No. He told me he won't be in for a while. Katherine

surprised him this morning and they're heading off to visit some old friends for a well-deserved break.' She leans in even closer. 'Elliot is nervous. He doesn't look it, but he's wired on caffeine. In my humble opinion, downing three double espressos in quick succession isn't a great idea. I guess there are worse things to be hooked on, though.'

The look we exchange reflects how we feel – anxious about what's to come.

'Gather round, everyone. Today is a special 'un as we welcome Elliot Montgomery, our new managing director.' Gwyn's voice encourages everyone to draw closer.

Sienna and I follow the stragglers, making our way into the main body of the restaurant as Elliot appears right on cue. He has a glass in his hand and he certainly looks the part, exuding confidence. Most of us in the audience are juggling a small plate for the irresistible canapés as well as a wine glass, so the handclapping is awkward. It doesn't seem to faze Elliot at all, and he steps forward with an air of eager enthusiasm, all smiles. My, is that man buzzing. I glance at Sienna, and she raises her eyebrows at me. He is wired.

As far as first impressions go, Elliot is a little younger than I expected; he's probably in his early thirties but he has that same commanding presence his late father had. He's also extremely handsome. The sort of man who makes heads turn, with his confident stride and that effortlessly engaging smile, but that, too, is in his genes. There isn't a hair out of place, and he looks every inch the businessman in his exquisitely tailored suit. If only he'd slipped off that jacket, or loosened his tie a little, he'd look more relaxed. Instead, it's like he's stepped straight out of the boardroom. Gwyn raises his hand to quieten the background chatter.

Thomas's grandson clears his throat nervously, and a growing hush falls over the crowd. Now he's looking a bit jittery, and I find myself feeling sorry for him. Thomas obviously decided there was no reason to insist that he postpone his holiday to be here, but perhaps Elliot might have appreciated the moral support.

'This is quite a day for me,' he begins, sounding nostalgic, which is a surprise. 'Most of you knew my late father, Robert. I can't express how honoured I feel to follow in the footsteps of the two greatest influences in my life. My grandfather, Thomas, inherited some land and a farmhouse and many years later it has grown into a thriving enterprise.' He pauses, making overt eye contact as he glances around the room. 'I'm here to learn from all of you because the future is something we'll build together. I can assure you that I'm not coming into this with any preconceived ideas. My office door is always open, and as I get to know you individually, I hope you will entrust me with your ideas to ensure our future is one of growth and the pursuit of excellence. Here's to the start of a new adventure. And what better way to toast that than with last year's award-winning Green Valley Vineyard Sparkling Blush!'

He raises his glass and all around me staff begin to whistle and hoot, but I'm disappointed. That's corporate talk, it's a boost before the proverbial hits the fan and people will soon cotton on to that. Oh, Thomas . . . now I understand why you had that little chat with me. It was Elliot, or yet another unknown manager whose CV would blow you away, but when their feet hit the ground they probably wouldn't last any longer than the others. Good people at that level are head-hunted, the rest shamelessly hype themselves up when it's time to move on.

As a first impression, what do we know about Elliot now that we didn't before? Nothing. That was a lazy speech, harking back to what his family has achieved and pledging nothing at all other than the fact he'll be asking for our ideas going forward. I gulp down a huge mouthful of what I must admit, with great satisfaction, is a delicately balanced wine, but I'm feeling miserable. If that speech was meant to be a call to action, we're sunk.

* * *

After an intensive afternoon in the classroom going into the fine detail of how to cut back the grapevines at the end of the season to promote healthy regrowth for the following year, we wrap up early. The trainees are all heading into Cardiff this evening to see a film: living on site Monday to Friday, little excursions like this are an important team-building exercise.

'We can't change your mind about joining us?' Gracie asks, as I close down my laptop. 'It'll be fun.'

'Sadly, it's my turn to do the soil testing and I didn't get around to it this morning. Have a great time, though.'

'Oh, we will.' She smiles.

After gathering my things together, I make my way to the door and spot another of my students, Adam, loitering outside in the corridor.

'Did you have a question?' I ask and he flashes me a nervous look.

'It's not about the session . . . I was wondering what the staff turnover is like here. I mean, how often do jobs come up?'

Adam is paying for his attendance on this course himself and it's quite a commitment when you don't have a sponsor.

'Not very often, I'm afraid. But if you pop along to the office and ask for Sienna, tell her I sent you. Give her your contact details and say you'd like to go on the circulation list for future vacancies on the forestry team.'

His face brightens. 'Thanks, Linzi. I'll do that now. Have a great evening.'

I watch as he hurries along the corridor. Now that's the sort of trainee who inspires me to share what I know. Too many people follow the pack these days. It's like they aren't capable of thinking for themselves and expect everything to fall into their laps because life owes them something. My upbringing was overshadowed by parents who were over-achievers and expected the same from their offspring. Where there should have been unconditional love, there was pressure. I was lucky. I escaped, and my eyes were opened to a whole new world. One that gave me the confidence to believe in myself and go in search of something that would inspire me.

'Linzi!'

Elliot's unmistakeably confident voice makes me instantly turn around and I give him a welcoming smile.

'Hi, Elliot, how are you settling in?'

He proffers his hand and, as we shake, his eyes flick over my face.

'Good, thank you. And I must apologise, as the day has run away from me. I'm so glad to have caught you. I gather you've been teaching?'

'I have, but it's an early finish today. Yesterday was a long one and my trainees are off on a little trip to Cardiff.'

'You aren't joining them?' His brow wrinkles, but my eyes wander up to his hairline. That's some serious styling going on there. I bet he spends more time looking in the mirror each morning than I spend in an entire week, and, to my shame, a smirk begins to etch itself onto my face.

'Oh, no. I'm um . . . running a bit behind and have a few things to do outside before I quit for the day.'

'A late finish for you then. Would it hamper you if I tag along?' I glance down at his highly polished leather shoes. 'Suitably attired, of course,' he continues, genially. 'It'll only take me ten minutes to change.'

'OK. I'll meet you in Reception in about fifteen minutes?'

'Perfect.' And with that, off he strides as I let out a gentle sigh. I was so looking forward to some time alone with the vines.

As I make my way to the cottage to drop off my laptop, I pop into the office and am delighted to see Gwyn. 'Are you busy?'

'I'm headin' up to the compound but it's nothin' important. I've been supervisin' the takin' down of that big old cedar tree, the one that got hit by lightnin' last winter. Why?'

'Would you have time to take a few soil samples before you head home? Elliot has decided he'd like to accompany me as I finish up for the day. I can hardly refuse. Rather than bore him with the science, I'll take him on a little tour to get a feel for what he's taking on.' There's a hint of exasperation in my tone.

'No worries, I'm on it. Remember, first impressions are important, Linzi. You got this.'

'Thanks, Gwyn. Duly noted and I owe you one.'

I arrive in Reception and do a double take when I realise that the person talking to Bethan, who is manning the desk, is Elliot. From the back I initially mistook him for a guest. He's wearing a long-sleeved check cotton shirt, navy cargo trousers and a pair of pristine walking boots. When he spots me, his smile is engaging. He turns back to say something, making Bethan laugh, before he strides over to me.

'I had to take a slight detour,' I explain, in case he thinks I purposely kept him waiting.

We both take a step forward to grab the handle of the glass entrance door and there's an awkward moment when it becomes obvious that I wasn't expecting him to open it for me.

'Sorry, you lead the way,' he says, stepping back. 'I suspect your daily routine is pretty rigid.'

'Surprisingly, no. The rotas for the forestry team are fluid, too. During the summer a lot depends on where the trainees are working each day and what the priorities are. And each season is different.'

'It's encouraging to hear that everyone works together. I was a little surprised when I saw on the chart that the forestry team leader reports to Gwyn and not to you. Does that ever cause any issues?'

I lead Elliot around to the path that skirts the main guest car park as we head for the woods.

'No. Three members of the forestry team are purely ground

and land management. The others are on a rota for the daily maintenance schedules I pass to Gwyn.'

'But you inspect their work? I hear your standards are high.' He turns to grin at me.

A little laugh escapes my lips as I glance at him. 'I do, and they are. We'll head up to the forestry office, which is affectionately known as the Outpost. There's a short cut we can take over the stile' – I point in the direction of the far corner – 'or we can take the scenic route up past the lake. I'm not sure how much time you have.'

Those jade-green eyes search my face before he glances at his watch. 'I have all the time in the world, but it's entirely up to you. And I owe you an apology because I didn't realise it was gone five already. I don't want to eat into your evening.'

'Oh, it's fine. It's easier for me to disappear for a couple of hours now than try to fit my schedule around a tour during the day. It'll be a week or two before I'll feel comfortable leaving my trainees to carry out a task unsupervised.'

We step off the tarmac path to follow the trail up through the woods and the light breeze is refreshing. Elliot stops to look at a tiny stream that wends its way to our left, down to an area we call the Woodpile. A heap of fresh wood chippings is the result of a hard day's work.

'The smell is amazing,' Elliot remarks, stepping off the trail to wander over to the huge pile of logs still waiting to be chipped. He seems entranced.

'It's cedar. They finally took down a tree that was badly damaged last winter. It'll certainly make a great mulch for some of the flowerbeds at the entrance to the hotel.'

'That's quite an impressive machine.' Elliot tilts his head in the direction of the chipper.

'It's noisy, that's for sure, but it is a beast. They'll be here again tomorrow morning clearing this lot up. You should drop by; they'd love to give you a demonstration. There's only so much you can see on foot unless you have a couple of hours to spare,' I explain as we set off again.

'It all looks completely different to the last time I was here. I'm not even sure I have my bearings yet.'

'Gwyn will take you on a tour of the boundary on the quad bikes and that will help orientate you. At the top of this incline the forest thins out and there's a lake in the clearing. It was created shortly after I came here. The forest trail has become quite an attraction for visitors to the hotel and the restaurant. It's a perfect after-dinner walk.'

'Ah, yes. I remember my f-father . . .' He pauses to clear his throat and I wonder if that was an emotional reaction. 'I remember talk about it during the construction phase. Is there still a panoramic view of the vineyard from up top, or do the trees obscure it now?'

'No, it's still visible, although they've doubled in size in the last ten years since they were thinned out.' And then I realise that the last time he trod this ground it would have been with his father, Robert, next to him. I'm not good at dealing with other people's emotional baggage as I still struggle to deal with my own. However, that doesn't mean I'm not empathetic – just that I can't handle it.

'It's funny,' Elliot concedes, almost talking to himself as he scans around. 'Every time I planned a trip here something would crop up. Now it's my biggest regret, not making time to see for myself the changes my father and grandfather often discussed at the dinner table . . .' His words trail off.

I'm not one for filling awkward silences but I feel it's the polite thing to do. 'I should imagine it's a lot to take in.'

As we reach a fork in the path, I steer him to the right, but he pauses for a moment.

'Yes. Is this the Outpost? I remember it being used to store some old farming equipment in the past.'

'It made sense to move the team's office away from the core buildings. As Gwyn says, "The muddy boot brigade is best heard but not seen." Not least because people are a little intimidated by chainsaw-wielding employees.'

Elliot starts laughing and it instantly diffuses any

awkwardness. 'I'm impressed by the changes. I remember this spot as a murky place; tall trees tightly packed together and hardly any light getting through. Now it's been managed properly it's a wonderful walk. It's areas like this that add to the overall experience for our guests. I'm sure it was labour intensive, but a clever use of resources given the return.'

Given the return? It's nature doing what it does best. It relaxes people as they wander around, taking a brief respite from their stressed lives. Oh, Thomas . . . you've dropped me in it at the deep end, haven't you? There's a reason why Elliot's walking boots are so shiny. They're new, as I suspected, and this might even be the first time he's worn them. His roots might be anchored in the countryside, but his adult life has been spent in the city. What happens when he pushes aside those whimsical memories of his childhood visits and gets down to business?

As we recommence our walk up to the ridge, I plaster a congenial smile on my face every time Elliot stops to look at something. I'm not here to hold his hand while he comes to terms with what haunts him from the past. I have no idea what his relationship was like with his father, but the fact that it's been so long since he's been here tells me it wasn't great.

I can only hope that doesn't affect his decisions going forward.

3.

Dinner For Two

Elliot is transfixed by the view, but I'm eager to move on. 'Do you intend to settle here in Wales permanently?' I throw the question out there in general conversation.

'I'll be living on site until I'm fully up to speed, then I'll probably split my time between here and London.'

'Really?' I blurt out. My involuntary reaction causes him to frown.

'You don't think that's a good idea?'

'Oh . . . no. I . . . um . . . thought you might be considering buying something nearby.' Now I've put my foot in it. I assumed he'd find somewhere close to his mother, Eve's, house, which is only a forty-minute drive away. Even so, Robert often stayed here overnight rather than driving back through the narrow country lanes late, when he was tired. His wife constantly worried about him and, as it turned out, she was right to do so.

'I don't think it will warrant me spending all my time here once things are running smoothly. I have no intention of upsetting everyone's routine when it obviously works well.'

As much as I don't want him interfering in what I do, I sincerely hope he isn't underestimating what running this place entails.

'You're happy with everything you've seen so far?' I check, trying not to sound at all surprised.

'Pretty much. There might be room for a couple of little

tweaks here and there. Unless you're about to reveal a major problem, of course. I'm surprised you don't have a bespoke team assigned to you, or even an assistant. I'm here to listen, as well as to observe, so you can talk to me quite frankly.'

Listen? Observe? What is this . . . some sort of evaluation? I wouldn't be surprised if he yanked out his phone to dictate a few bullet points to pick up on later.

'Gwyn runs a great team and he keeps on top of the rotas to ensure all of the important jobs get done in a timely manner.'

'Ultimately, he answers to you though, as the viticulture and training manager?'

'N-no. That's not how it works.'

'So, who exactly do you manage?'

I knew that pretentious job title was going to cause problems. So much for Thomas's theory that it would impress Elliot.

'I manage myself, the vines and the summer trainees.'

His expression makes me stifle a rueful smile as he's clearly underwhelmed.

'Oh . . . I . . . see,' he mutters, as we lapse into silence.

It's all uphill from here to the top of the ridge and he's already beginning to struggle a little to keep up with my vigorous pace. He's competitive, that's obvious, and he is fit. But the sort of fitness that comes from lifting weights in the gym rather than racking up the miles in the open air. It's with great satisfaction I note that by the time we're standing on the highest point looking down over The Green Valley Vineyard, my breathing is level and Elliot is pretending he isn't winded.

'Wow!' he exclaims, taking a moment to catch his breath.

The bountiful green valley rolls away in front of us and, although we've only climbed a hill, looking down it's as if we've climbed a mountain. All of this is now Elliot's responsibility.

It does the exact same thing to me every single time I stand here gazing out over the luscious vines. You might give up on people out of pure frustration, but nature is a sobering reminder that as much as we continue to mess up, it simply wants to flourish.

'It's incredible, isn't it?' I reply, not to goad him into a response but because it reflects all my hard work and, occasionally, tears of frustration. Come rain, or shine, I've tended these plants like they're my own and now they're doing me proud.

'I guess this is why my grandfather told me that when it comes to the vines you call the shots. That's quite something.' Having composed himself, Elliot is clearly impressed.

'It's not rocket science, but it requires constant vigilance. The plants have a way of telling you just what they need and when. It's my job to listen and act immediately to ensure we achieve a bumper crop.'

Elliot is deep in thought as he stares out over the long straight rows of greenery. 'That's why some of the staff affectionately call you the keeper of the vines, and my grandfather warned me not to upset you.'

I shrug my shoulders. 'With me it's plants first, people second. Sorry if that sounds rude, but it's true.' There's no point beating about the bush.

'Well, whatever your methods are they're obviously working, Linzi. It's quite a relief for me, and no surprise that my grandfather has some key personnel he trusts implicitly to have his back no matter what. I only hope I can measure up to his expectations.'

Now that's a telling statement to make and I'm shocked that Elliot would voice it.

'Thomas is a great man. Someone who values other people's skills and trusts them to get on with the job.' It's not that I'm dropping hints here, of course.

Elliot presses his lips together, nodding his head in agreement as he glances at his watch. 'Chef is expecting me to appear for dinner in about forty-five minutes and I hate eating alone. Would you care to join me so we can continue this conversation? I feel like I'm coming into my new role unprepared in some ways, and that doesn't sit well with me.'

I'm torn. I owe Thomas, but I'm not sure what Elliot's agenda is – he's pumping me for information and yet it will be on my time, so I could say no. But am I better off keeping on the good side of him until he shows his true colours? Experience has taught me that people often say one thing, then do another. Although, when the new boss asks you to dinner it's not exactly an invitation you can refuse. Especially when you live on site. For me it will be cringe-making, as all the staff are obviously on edge, eager to impress Elliot. He's a stranger, but as Thomas's grandson he's about to determine our future simply because he's the next in line.

'If we head back now, that's fine. I need to get rid of the dust and the dirt of the day first,' I laugh, to lighten the moment.

'Maybe you can show me around the Outpost another time, Linzi. When it's convenient, of course.'

'No problem. Chef won't thank me if I make you late, so we'd better get moving.'

Elliot turns on his heels to make the trek back to the complex. 'Thank goodness it's all downhill,' he mutters as he walks.

I'm grinning behind his back. The hilly terrain is something he's going to have to get used to.

Standing under the shower as the water cascades down over me, I'm not sure how I feel about Elliot. He asks a lot of question but isn't giving much away. The impression I got earlier is that he's evaluating everything – me included. That's only natural, I suppose. I try to put myself in his shoes. He's coming in as virtually a stranger, even though this is his family's business. He's also walking in his late father's footsteps, but not willingly, because if that were the case, Thomas wouldn't have filled the hole himself following Robert's death. There's something off about all this but I can't quite put my finger on it.

As I step out of the shower and begin to get myself ready, I know that our talented head chef, Deron, will be eager to impress Elliot. Within twelve months of his arrival the restaurant attained its first Michelin star, which really put this place on the map.

I'm almost ready when my phone kicks into life. It's Sienna.

'I had to call . . . how was the walk-around with Elliot? I saw the two of you heading off deep in conversation as I was leaving.'

'Fine. Why? What do you know that I don't?' I tease her.

'Nothing . . . yet! He did spend a couple of hours this afternoon looking at the staff files. Afterwards, he called Gwyn in for a chat and met up briefly with Michael before he sought you out.'

'Gwyn was fine when we were talking, so obviously Elliot is just doing a general introduction. We only got up as far as the ridge. He kept stopping to look around, which is only natural, I suppose. I'm having dinner with him in the restaurant in about ten minutes. I think he has a lot of questions he wants answered.'

'Oh, really?' Sienna's voice perks up. 'You're getting a positive vibe then?'

Am I? 'Hmm . . . I'd be more concerned if he was laying down the law before he understood how things are run, but it's too soon to tell. What do you think I should wear?'

'Ooh . . . dinner with the new boss. And they'll all be on their toes wanting to make a good first impression. Nothing too fussy.'

'Me? Fussy? It's jeans, leggings, T-shirts and jumpers.'

'There must be something lingering in the back of your wardrobe, Linzi.'

I press speakerphone and start shuffling through the coat hangers. 'Oh no,' I groan. 'That awful dress I bought for the staff Christmas party last year. What was I thinking? Um . . . my little black dress isn't really appropriate.'

'How about the silver grey one you wore to your birthday bash?' she suggests.

I dig it out and hold it up against me, catching my reflection in the mirror. 'Hmm . . . that'll do.'

'And why not wear your hair down?'

'It's not a date, Sienna,' I point out.

'I know, but how often do you get to eat dinner in the restaurant?'

She's up to something, I know it.

'This isn't about pumping him for information. He's the one asking questions, remember.'

'Yes, but . . . after a glass or two of wine maybe he'll relax a little in your company. Let's face it, we're all nervous until we know what his intentions are.'

I stifle a laugh, which comes out as more of a dismissive snort. 'If you think I'm going to glam myself up and pander to him, then think again. He doesn't like eating alone and I can't blame him, especially as all the staff are going to be watching his every move.'

'So why say yes? You could have said you were busy this evening.'

Sienna knows me so well and an unbidden smirk twitches the edge of my lips. 'Let's just say that I like the idea of doing him a favour. It's not as if there's anyone else he could invite at such short notice, is there?' I'm the only employee who lives on site.

'Actually, I'm rather envious. Even with staff discount my Cam won't splash out on a romantic dinner there for me. He says we need every penny if we're going to set a date sometime soon.'

'A wedding date?' I query.

'I know, I nearly fell off my chair when he said that just now. Three years we've been engaged and saving like crazy, but never mind a wedding, I want a house. Anyway, if Elliot mentions me, put in a good word. I can't afford to lose my job, not now.'

'Don't be daft. You run the office and this place would fall apart without you.'

'I like to think so, but you never know. Anyway, have fun and order the most expensive items on the menu. And I'll expect a full debrief in the morning.'

As I click the end call button, I think that maybe Sienna is right and I should make an effort. I don't want to look out of place. Pulling the scrunchie off my hair I stare at myself in the mirror. This is going to require curling tongs . . . and a touch of makeup, I think.

The moment I walk into the restaurant I'm so glad I listened to Sienna. The atmosphere is buzzing with several family parties celebrating special occasions. The champagne corks are certainly popping this evening. But there are also a number of romantic tables for two, with couples who only have eyes for each other, and guests from the hotel, all here to enjoy a gourmet dining experience.

'Linzi!' I half turn to see Michael striding towards me. It's unusual for him to be hovering around the entrance to the dining area. 'Don't you look lovely this evening.'

We move to one side as a group of four people filter in behind me.

I lean into him, keeping my voice low. 'Thanks. I'm having dinner with the boss. I don't know if he mentioned it.'

Michael raises his eyebrows. 'He booked a table for two, but we weren't sure who to expect.'

'What are things like in the kitchen?' I venture to ask, and he gives me a sobering look.

'Deron is a bit snappy, but everyone understands he's anxious. He wants everything to be just right. I keep telling everyone to relax and treat Elliot like any of the string of general managers Thomas has hired and fired over the past fourteen months. It's not the same though and we all know it. I'll be hovering all evening and that goes some way to reassure my staff that I have their backs.' Michael gives me one of his engaging smiles. 'How did your first encounter with Elliot go?'

I pause as one of the waiters walks past, acknowledging him with a friendly nod of my head. Allan grins at me, his eyes taking in the dress and my almost perfectly curled hair.

'Looking good, Linzi. I didn't recognise you at first,' he murmurs as he walks past and I bat my eyelashes at him, laughing.

Turning back to look at Michael, I see his eyes scanning the restaurant. He isn't nervous but his staff are, and he's here to make sure everything runs smoothly as it does every night.

'Obviously he has a lot of questions. I showed him the new forest walk, the lake, and we ended up at the ridge. He was impressed, I mean who wouldn't be?'

Michael flashes his eyes at me and I turn to see Elliot approaching from the reception area.

'Good evening, Michael and Linzi. I hope we're not putting you out given the restaurant is so busy this evening, Michael. Please tell everyone it's a working dinner and not an inspection.' Elliot sounds relaxed, but he must realise his words don't change a thing.

Wearing an open-neck, crisp white cotton shirt, black tailored trousers and a pair of expensive-looking black shoes, Elliot is handsome enough for eyes to glance our way.

'Not at all. It's our pleasure to show you what we do best, Elliot. I will inform the staff not to disturb you any more than is necessary while they are serving.'

Elliot pats Michael on his shoulder. 'Appreciated. I'm looking forward to this – I'm starving.'

He's certainly putting in the effort to lessen any tension, but Thomas's wife planning a surprise trip to Scotland came at the worst possible time. If he were here to settle Elliot into his new role on his first day it would be so much easier all round, I reflect, as Michael escorts us over to our table.

He indicates a quiet spot in the far corner. 'I assumed you'd enjoy an uninterrupted view of the vineyard. However, it's nice enough to eat out on the terrace where there's a little less background noise,' Michael suggests.

When Elliot nods his head in agreement, Michael raises his forefinger in the air and I glance outside to see two waiting staff already magically laying up one of the tables. By the time we've walked along the length of the panoramic window and traversed the raised decking area, our chairs have been pulled out and we're invited to take a seat.

'Impressive. It is a lot quieter out here, Michael, thank you,' Elliot remarks as I glance around.

'Enjoy!' Michael disappears, but I know he'll be keeping a close eye from afar.

Allan has been standing discreetly to one side and he immediately steps forward to hand Elliot the wine menu. 'Would you like a few minutes to make your selection?'

I'm used to the jokey Allan, always fooling about, but tonight he's the true professional.

'I think I'll be guided by the expert. Linzi, what do you suggest?'

I had a feeling Elliot might spring that on me and I immediately pipe up, 'A bottle of the 2018 Green Valley Dry White and a bottle of the 2016 Black Ridge Rondo, thank you, Allan.'

'Perfect. I'll leave you to peruse the menu.'

There are only two other tables out here that are laid up, both seating four people, so it won't be crowded when they arrive. In terms of allowing Elliot to soak up the ambience, you can't beat this view.

'It's awkward, isn't it?' Elliot states, adjusting the cutlery which was faultlessly lined up in the first place. Is he mistaking my reverie for waiting for him to take the lead?

'Sorry, you've lost me there.'

He stares at me rather pointedly. 'Everyone is treating me as if I'm an intruder and they aren't sure whether I'm a risk, or not.'

This man isn't one for holding back, but neither am I.

'I think everyone is simply keen to make a good impression, that's all.'

'I like that you're prepared to be direct with me. My grandfather said that I need you more than you need me.' Elliot starts laughing, but I can see from the twinkle in his eye that he's serious.

I shake my head as I break out into a wide smile. 'Thomas and I go back a bit before The Green Valley Vineyard.'

'So I gather, and I'm curious to know more.'

Trust me to walk into that one.

'I just happened to be a trainee working with Umberto Leone, the owner of a medieval vineyard in Greve, Tuscany, when Thomas attended a series of one-to-one sessions.'

Two waiters arrive and, without interrupting our flow, a chilled wine bucket is placed within easy reach. We watch as a bottle of red is uncorked and I nod, indicating that we are happy to serve ourselves.

'And you are the vine whisperer. What you say holds sway here with everyone, including my grandfather. But that's not the only reason I need you on my side.'

'Surely we're all on the same side,' I point out as I pour a little white wine into each of our glasses. 'This is our second most popular seller after the sparkling blush. I'm curious to see what you think of it.'

Now that's a challenge, and he flashes me a quizzical look. 'I'm no wine buff and I don't pretend to be one.'

'Just take a sip and tell me what you think.'

I'm having fun and maybe it is a bit mean of me but, to give him his due, he swirls the wine in the glass and then raises it to his nose. 'Fresh!' he says, positively and then takes a slurp.

Oh, how pretentious are people who slurp. In my humble opinion, it isn't necessary at all unless you are the crème de la crème of sommeliers. 'Swishing the wine around your mouth for a couple of seconds will get those taste buds reacting and cleanse your palate. Then take another sip and you'll notice it will taste a little different.' If Thomas were here, he'd be highly amused.

'Citrussy, too,' Elliot continues as he places the glass back down on the table.

'Not bad,' I reply encouragingly.

'So, how would you describe it?'

I take a moment to breathe in the accent notes and then take a slow sip, letting it gently flow around my mouth. Closing my eyes, I relive the joys of a wine I know so well it's almost a part of me. 'A crisp, green fruit palate with lively overtones of citrus and a refreshing finish. I'd say it's a winner!' I declare, and he bursts out laughing.

'OK. You've asserted your authority as the wine connoisseur. My grandfather is right – I do need you. If I'm going to make this work, it'll probably require a little more help than just your obvious expertise. Allan is hovering and we really should order. What do you suggest?'

'Are you a meat eater?'

'You ordered a bottle of red wine, so I think you've already sussed me out. I think this dry white wine was a test.'

I turn my head and Allan immediately strides forward to take our order.

'We'll both go for the Welsh hand-dived scallops for starters. Our new boss would like the roasted Welsh lamb rump with pea and broad bean tart and Manchego custard. I'll have roasted spring chicken with braised cavolo nero. Awesome, thank you, Allan.'

'My pleasure, Linzi,' he replies, giving Elliot a deferential nod of his head. It's sweet how nervous he is, but it raises a sobering thought. I'm known as a rebel, pushing the boundaries because I find them claustrophobic. I need to rein myself in because this isn't merely my job at risk here – it's my whole life.

'I love the lamb, but I thought you might like to try the chicken as well. Assuming you're happy to do that, of course?'

'That sounds good to me.'

'Most of the vegetables and herbs are from the chef's

garden here in the grounds,' I add. 'Straight from the soil to the table.'

'I've never grown anything myself, but I've eaten in a lot of excellent restaurants over the years. I can say with confidence that my food-tasting skills are well honed,' Elliot replies, with a sense of amusement.

'Not even a pot plant?'

'No, I'd only forget to water it. Admittedly, when I was growing up we had a walled garden full of fruit trees and a huge vegetable patch. There was a stage when I was curious, but if my memory serves me well it was more about digging stuff up than planting things. I was always getting into trouble for it and soon lost interest.'

'That's a shame. Now all of this is yours, perhaps we can rekindle your curiosity.' As I gaze across at him, I realise he's less daunting when he's sitting down. Elliot is probably six foot four. Being almost a foot shorter, when we were out walking it gave me a crick in the neck to keep looking up at him.

'Maybe. Books were my thing and still are, so I've obviously been acquainting myself with some of the problems associated with growing vines. Let's say that I know enough to understand that it's a complex subject and I've barely scratched the surface. I think my father was relieved when I didn't show any interest in the vineyard, and yet here I am.'

As we chink glasses, his smile fades a little. Whether it's the thought of following in his grandfather's and his father's shoes I don't know, but our starters arrive and it's time for eating, not talking.

'The scallops come with locally grown baby tomatoes and a tomato consommé with lovage and cucumber,' I inform him.

'Great presentation,' Elliot observes, as he tucks in eagerly.

I have no intention of spoiling my enjoyment by making polite conversation and I simply nod my head in agreement. He gets the message and we eat in silence, enjoying the food, the view and the sound of the birds foraging in the trees which divide this section of the vineyard from a swathe of pastureland to our right. When I finish eating, he sits back in his chair, wine glass in hand.

'How's the white wine?' I ask.

'Fine. Is there any reason why the vineyard only produces white and rosé wines?'

At last, a question that delves a little deeper. 'It's mainly due to cost. The red wine you're about to sample with your lamb is produced less than ten miles away. Black Ridge Vineyard presses our grapes, then ferments and bottles our wine. The black grapes used in making our classic rosé are picked at the same time as the white, which is the most economical way to operate given the volume we produce. If we were going to consider red wine we'd leave the grapes on the vine a little longer to ripen. Maybe as long as a week, or two perhaps. Each year is different, as there are so many factors to take into account. We need rainfall and sunshine to make the fruit plump and sweet. And the timing of the pick is a crucial decision.'

Elliot sits forward, picking up the bottle of red wine to study the label on the back.

'Now that's cheating,' I remark accusingly, as he pours a little into the two broad bowl wine glasses.

He hands a glass to me, looking sheepish. 'I'd better confess now that I'm not really a great wine drinker. There – I've said it. Oh, I enjoy a nice glass with a meal, but when food isn't involved I go for a beer every time.'

It's hard not to laugh. 'The bar has a whole range of beers on tap, you know. But give it a try and see what you think. Welsh vineyards produce some truly wonderful wines and there's a great sense of pride among the growers.'

He swirls the wine in the glass like a pro, then tilts his head to take in an appreciative breath. 'Full-bodied and robust,' he states, firmly.

'Now tell me something that wasn't on the label,' I tease him, and he glances at me nervously as he takes a sip.

I do the same, letting the velvety, ruby-red liquid slowly coat my mouth while I wait for his evaluation.

'Blackberries and something deeper. Earthy?' He looks at me questioningly.

'I'm picking up flavours of dark fruits. There's a hint of smoke, a characteristic woodiness with a sprinkle of spice to finish it off.' I do another swirl and raise the glass to my nose.

'I have a lot to learn. That was almost poetic,' he declares, sounding impressed.

When I look up at him he's watching me intently. I give him an awkward smile, but he doesn't look away; he simply stares at my hair. I wonder if there's something caught in it. Fortunately, our main course arrives and is put in front of us with a flourish.

'You must try the chicken,' I encourage him as I slide my plate closer. 'The tarragon jus is simply wonderful. Chef does a staff tasting session every time they change the menu and I try to make sure I'm around to take part.' I watch as he carves off a piece and indicate for him to sample a little of everything on the plate.

'Mmm . . .' The moment the fork is in his mouth his taste buds are getting it. 'The braised cavolo nero has a real sweetness to it, and the hint of roasted garlic is tantalising. I've eaten in a lot of good restaurants, some of the best, and I must say Deron is deserving of that Michelin star. You'd better take that plate away before I eat it all.' He grins at me.

I don't want him to feel I'm being condescending, but I get the impression that he's a man who eats because he's hungry. But, as with enjoying a good wine, fine dining is an experience that shouldn't be rushed.

'You'll enjoy the roasted Welsh lamb. It's from one of the local farms. You'll find that robust red will complement it perfectly,' I reply, as I tuck in. But I can't help glancing across at Elliot and smiling to myself as he slows down to savour each mouthful of food and every sip of wine.

The sense of taste, and smell, need fine-tuning to pick

up on the tiniest of nuances. In the luxury dining and wine producing business it's crucial that the man at the top can appreciate excellence. It comes at a price, but if corners are cut even a sterling reputation can be irreparably tarnished. It's a long journey of discovery for Elliot and, honouring Thomas's wishes, tonight is the first step in his education.

4.

Is This the Calm Before the Storm?

Since my dinner with Elliot, I've had no communication at all with him. I'm taking that as a good sign and, to be honest, I've been glad not to have had any unscheduled interruptions as it's been so busy. Time has flown and I can't believe it's the eleventh of July already.

With the trainees now working among the vines every day, I'm constantly alongside them. It creates a greater bond and allows me to gently point out a better way of doing something. Which, roughly translated, means someone hasn't listened and, without singling them out, I can quickly gather everyone together to do a little demonstration. It's tiring, but each day gets a little easier and at this time of the year there are a lot of shoots to tie in or pinch out. My eyes are everywhere, because it's the first crop under Elliot's command and I'm betting he'll be expecting a bumper one to beat last year.

A loud tap on the front door has me hurrying out into the hallway. When I open it I glance down at my watch.

'What's this? You're late!'

Sienna rolls her eyes at me, dropping her bag down on the floor beneath the coat hooks and slipping off her shoes. 'Sorry, it's been one of those days.'

'Come on through to the kitchen. You can tell me all about it.'

She flops down into one of my lovingly hand-painted farmhouse chairs nestled around the distressed pine table.

'You're so lucky living on site, Linzi,' she says, as her eyes scan around. 'I just love these little cottages. This one has such a homely feel to it, though, not like the other holiday lets. I suppose that's because you furnished it yourself. The little finishing touches you've added make it unique.'

They were only built six years ago and it's true to say that I put a lot of thought into creating that cosy, country vibe.

As I pour the hot water into two coffee mugs, I half turn to glance at her.

'This would be much too small for you and Cam,' I point out. Cam is a man who is prepared to work hard to make his dreams come true and I admire that. 'And I'll never own Red Robin Cottage, so it's not really mine.'

'It's such a shame that you can't buy it, but then who knows what the future holds? And you're right. Cam has lofty ambitions, but seriously, I'm fed-up living in rented accommodation. I want something that's ours, something we can decorate together so it feels like home. I so envy you having this to come back to at the end of the day.'

I carry the mugs across to the table and pull out the seat opposite her.

'There's a huge difference, Sienna. Cam is looking at it from a longer-term perspective.' It's obvious she's come to have a rant and that's what friends are for. All I can do is listen and hope I say the right thing at the right time.

'He's trying my patience, Linzi. I gave him an ultimatum. I want the house first and then we can think about spending money on a wedding.'

Goodness, Sienna doesn't usually dig her heels in like this.

'Cam is OK with that?' I venture to ask.

'I guess I'm about to find out. We have more than enough saved to put a hefty deposit on a decent-size three-bedroom house and turn it into something special.' I can tell from her expression how exasperated Sienna is feeling.

I sit quietly, sipping my coffee, waiting for her to calm down. She's gazing out at the courtyard garden and I'm tempted to slide back the patio doors. However, if guests happen to be sitting in the garden next door they'd overhear our conversation.

'Having a good moan makes me feel better, so thanks for listening, Linzi.'

'You mentioned that it's been one of those days. Elliot doesn't seem to have been around much so far this week – I thought maybe it would allow you to catch up a little?'

'Well, he's not demanding stuff left, right and centre, but leaving Gwyn in charge has put a lot of pressure on him. And Elliot's absence means that when people can't get hold of him, they call me.'

I nod my head in agreement. 'Oh dear. I'm sorry to hear that. I know Gwyn has been stressed. On the few occasions we've crossed paths he's been tetchy and that's so not like him.'

Although we're the best of friends, there are work-related issues that Sienna obviously can't discuss and I change the subject rather diplomatically. 'I'm thinking of joining the Brecon Beacons Mountain Biking Club.'

'Really?' Sienna looks at me quizzically. 'Your bicycle is up to that, is it?'

'Not exactly, I'd have to invest in a new one. One of those all-terrain models. It might be fun.'

'What, risking life and limb riding dangerous trails? Seriously, what's up with everyone suddenly acting out of character?'

I shrug my shoulders. 'It's not like you to stress, Sienna. It's this thing with Cam, isn't it?'

'Partly, but just look around, Linzi. Some of the staff are smiling, but there are one or two who aren't.'

It's something that hasn't escaped my attention because we're all feeling that undercurrent of tension hanging in the air. Although I know that Michael and Deron are certainly singing Elliot's praises. Apparently, when Elliot and I said goodnight after our sumptuous meal, he headed straight for the kitchen to shake Deron's hand and compliment the staff.

Michael thanked me the next day for having their backs. His remark was puzzling, as it wasn't down to me. And why would Elliot have any reason to criticise either the service or the food anyway?

Sienna notices my frown. 'Did uh . . . I don't suppose Elliot mentioned a woman named Isobel . . . Isobel Weatherford, to you?'

'No, sorry. He talked a little bit about his childhood when I took him up to the ridge but in the restaurant my focus was on drawing his attention to what we offer – amazing food and awesome wines.'

'I just get this feeling . . . I don't know. Ever since he arrived he's been asking a lot of questions but saying very little, Linzi. I don't know quite what to expect next. The way he operates is in stark contrast to Thomas. He'd call me in just to run something past me and I always felt I could speak my piece, even if he didn't like the answer.'

It's weird because I know exactly what she means. Sitting with Elliot I felt I had his full attention, but since that night there's been no contact whatsoever. 'It's just the settling-in period, Sienna,' I reply, pragmatically.

'Is it? His phone is switched off and this woman keeps calling me, saying she needs to speak to him urgently. I've left messages for him and sent a dozen emails but he's not responding. What more can I do? And Gwyn is stomping around because Elliot put him in charge while he's holding his off-site informal meetings.'

'Poor Gwyn is trying to juggle the impossible. The forestry team is replacing that whole run of fencing between us and the sheep farm that they had to prop up during the winter storms. There's no signal up there and he should be with them supervising the work. We can't risk another invasion of our woolly-coated friends as the farmer won't be happy. It takes a long time to round them up when they get out.'

Sienna shakes her head, unhappily. 'It hasn't done Elliot any favours disappearing like this.'

'You don't have any idea what Elliot's itinerary is?'

'No. On Monday he asked for a list of the local suppliers to the restaurant, and directions to The Black Ridge Vineyard. When he left the next day, he said he hoped to be back by the end of the week, but it was only in passing as he was literally on his way out the door. If he's visiting local places, why isn't he coming back here at the end of the day? If he doesn't turn up tomorrow, I'm going to be fending off some very irate people. I don't suppose you've had any contact with Thomas?'

'No, not a peep.' I'm still puzzling over why Elliot feels the need to visit the vineyard's contacts in person without taking someone from here along to make the introductions. And as for suppliers for the restaurant . . . surely that's down to Michael and Chef Deron? It feels like Elliot is purposely circumventing our normal lines of communication.

'Thomas hasn't touched base with me, either. Don't you think that's a little odd?'

'Yes . . . maybe it is under the circumstances.' But I clearly remember Thomas saying that the agreement he'd made with Elliot was that he wouldn't interfere. 'Look, there's no point stressing about it. Elliot is a businessman first and foremost. Maybe he's just satisfying himself that we have a robust supply chain. He's coming into this with a fresh set of eyes and that might not be a bad thing.' I drain my coffee cup, studiously avoiding eye contact with Sienna as she lets out a huge sigh.

'Elliot's sudden and unannounced absence so soon after his arrival is causing a lot of speculation, Linzi. Given his background, what if his role here is to get the business ready to attract a buyer?'

There's no avoiding her gaze, but how would I know?

'If the intention was to sell up, Thomas would have delivered the news himself, because that would mean he'd effectively have signed everything over to Elliot, to do the deed. Thomas has never, ever, walked away from a difficult conversation and the two of us have had a few even in my time here. It was the same with Robert. Elliot's methods are just different, that's all. It's too soon to judge our new boss, Sienna. But when he gets back, I hope he realises that communication is key. Rumours and speculation put a dent in staff morale.'

She sits back, her shoulders slumped. 'Ignore me. Everything seems like the final straw right now. We're one short in the office this week, so the timing wasn't exactly good. Right, I'd best get off. Cam is due back late tonight and I want to give the house a quick clean through. Hopefully we can sit down and clear the air – that'll be one thing less to worry about. It's tough having angry words over the phone.'

Being on my own and occasionally wishing I had someone to come home to, I tend to forget that it adds another layer of complexity to one's life. The minute I open the front door and step inside my cosy, contemporary little cottage I can relax, no matter how trying the day has been. And if I'm in a bad mood I don't have to make conversation for the sake of it. Being single has its advantages at times, I admit.

'Just tell Cam you've had a trying few days, and suggest you hold off on that discussion until the weekend. You two need some quality time together just to relax and take stock. It's lucky you're not working on Saturday. And as for this place . . . let's see what tomorrow brings. Who knows? There's still a chance that we'll end the week on a high note.'

Sienna flashes me a dubious smile. We stand, and I lean in to give her a comforting hug. I had hoped to suggest that the two of us do something together on Saturday as I have the whole weekend off, too. It's rare that our weekend-off schedules coincide.

'You always know what to say when I'm at the end of my tether, thanks, Linzi.'

As I see her out, I catch sight of Gwyn's back as he hurries off in the direction of the car park. His head is down, his walk purposeful even with his awkward gait. His body language is that of yet another colleague who's had enough for one day.

Oh dear. It takes a lot to upset Gwyn, and the fact that he isn't talking about it doesn't bode well.

The following morning's classroom session is a deep-dive on soil management, and I aim to finish by ten thirty. Friday is hand-suckering duty and I want to get the trainees out there pretty sharpish as we want the growth to go to the grapes, not the shoots we don't need.

Talking about contaminants and explaining why a change in farming practices over the years has depleted the soil of essential nutrients is one of my pet topics. The impact of pollutants, both airborne and from contaminated groundwater, leads me quite nicely to an overview of the holistic approach to plant-microbe remediation. It's heavy going, but I have their attention and it's why this course is so popular.

'Don't forget to pick up the handouts on your way out. Next week we'll—'

The door opens and, to my surprise, Elliot steps into the room. He puts up his hand, pointing to a seat at the back and indicating for me to continue.

'Next week we'll look in more detail at the microbiological life of the vineyard. The emphasis is on maintaining a balanced environment with a diverse agricultural ecosystem, in order to enhance vine production in the longer term. Right, um . . . if you want to grab a thirty-minute break then head to the compound, I'll meet you there.'

Elliot immediately stands and walks towards me, acknowledging the trainees with a warm smile as they filter past him.

'It sounds like next week's sessions will be quite intense,' he remarks. 'What's the plan for the rest of their day?'

'Cutting out unwanted new growth and inspecting.'

'Inspecting?' he queries.

'You should join us for a session to see what it involves. It's important we have eyes everywhere at this time of the year. Ladybirds and wasps will feed on insect pests, but caterpillars and beetles are bad news. Anyway, was there something in particular that made you seek me out, or did you just want to sit in and listen? Monday's session starts at nine if you have time to join us.'

'I wish I did, but I'm also conscious that you have a work schedule to stick to, although I would appreciate a quiet chat. It's a fact-finding mission really, because I can't get hold of my grandfather.'

'Oh. Well . . . of course. I can arrange for someone to cover for me if you specify a time.' Is Thomas purposely avoiding Elliot? I thought he said he was going to be in the background keeping an eye on things, and if that's the case, why is Elliot so concerned about the lack of contact?

He frowns, deep in thought. 'Uh . . . can you check with Sienna and ask her to schedule something? It'll take about half an hour at most, but I'm unlikely to be free until mid-afternoon if my memory serves me correctly. I'm just on my way to do a tour of the grounds with Gwyn and I need to change first.'

At least today he isn't wearing a jacket, although a pristine white shirt and black suit trousers aren't ideal when it comes to riding a quad bike.

'Sure. I'll pop in to see her now.'

'Great. Thanks. I'll catch up with you later.'

Thomas rarely wore a suit, although he always looked smart. He was usually sporting a Green Valley Vineyard fleece and it made him more approachable. I noticed that even the trainees were a little nervous when Elliot walked in.

After packing up my things, I hurry along to the office and all three of the staff are head down working. Sienna looks up and, when she sees it's me, she picks up a sheaf of papers and walks towards me.

'I won't be long,' she calls over her shoulder. 'I have that information you requested, Linzi. I just need to photocopy it for you.'

She thinks I'm here to ask how it went last night with Cam and as soon as we're in the corridor she blurts out, 'He's been delayed by a day! Can you believe it? Still, the house is gleaming as I was so angry that I literally cleaned until I couldn't keep my eyes open any longer.'

Goodness, that's obsessive because she's very particular and I've never seen a single thing out of place whenever I've called in.

'Try not to get wound up about it, Sienna. He won't have done it on purpose, you do know that?'

She hangs her head a little as I push open the door to the photocopying room.

'I know. But I was all psyched up.'

'I'm no expert on relationships, obviously, but I've had a few rows in my time and all but one ended badly because I lost control.'

'What was different that one time?'

'I was . . . I was in love with him.'

Sienna stares at me, her eyes searching mine.

'You were? And you've never mentioned it to me before? I thought I knew everything about you, lady.'

This isn't easy because there are things I studiously avoid talking about. 'It's painful, that's all. But the point is that instead of blurting out a whole host of things in the heat of the moment that I would have come to regret, I simply listened.'

Her eyes search mine. 'And?' she demands, impatiently.

'And then I cried when I realised that we didn't have a future together. We probably never did. But . . . none of that matters right now. What I'm trying to say is that you know Cam is the love of your life, and it's mutual. Be calm, explain how you feel and tell him what's important to you, then listen to what he has to say.'

Sienna takes a sharp breath in and raises a lukewarm smile. 'I know that's good advice but I'm feeling so het up. I don't know why, it's not like me at all.'

'Hopefully it will pass, you just have a lot going on. Oh, and Elliot said he needs half an hour with me sometime later today. It sounds like he's swamped.'

'Yes. He arrived back to a whole stack of messages he's been ignoring and they all need dealing with asap. He's with Gwyn now for the next couple of hours, then he has a conference call. Will four o'clock work for you?'

'Perfect, thanks. He seems upbeat,' I venture.

'I noticed that too.'

'He mentioned that he couldn't get hold of Thomas. You still haven't heard anything, have you?'

Sienna places a sheet of paper on the photocopier and presses the button. 'It's nothing to worry about. Apparently, Thomas and Katherine have gone off on a road trip in his brother's camper van, something about a leisurely drive around the Scottish coastline. The signal will be intermittent in the more remote places.'

'That's a surprise!'

She shrugs her shoulders. 'I think it was a spur of the moment thing.'

'This is Katherine making sure Thomas can finally relax, isn't it? I mean, what sort of signal will they get in some of the most isolated places in Scotland? That woman has a heart of gold because it's just what he needs, but a lot can happen in the meantime.'

Sienna passes me a piece of paper and I glance at it, slightly confused. It's the draft Christmas menu.

'You can't walk back empty-handed. Everyone is looking for signs about what's coming and I don't want to make it any worse. Elliot was impressed by this and I think he wanted to give Thomas an update. They're planning a big festive advertising campaign in some of the glossy country living magazines to fill the hotel at Christmas. It'll be the first time since the build was completed that we'll – fingers crossed – operate at full capacity.'

'Well, Elliot is fully invested in the future of the business, so maybe we're all worrying about nothing.'

Glancing at my watch, I realise I'll have to grab a coffee to go, as my trainees will be making their way to the compound in about ten minutes' time.

'I do like a little inside information,' I reply, jiggling the paper in my hand. 'My lips are sealed, though. And if you ever need space, my spare bedroom is always made up. Just a thought. Catch you later, Sienna!'

5.

The Plan Unfolds

What a day it's been, one that was full of surprises. My meeting with Elliot didn't happen as after his tour with Gwyn they disappeared into Elliot's office. When I popped in to wish Sienna luck for this evening they were still deep in conversation, but I noticed that she had a huge smile on her face. On the desk in front of her was an expensive bouquet stuffed into a vase. It was a touching and romantic gesture from Cam, and there's no likelihood now of her turning up on my door at midnight with a few things thrown into a bag. But it was a close thing and I'm relieved he realised that.

However, just as I'm pouring myself a glass of wine, there's a loud tap on the door. I open it, expecting to see Gwyn.

'Oh, hi, Elliot.'

'I want to apologise about earlier on. I'm really sorry I left you hanging around. I had a long session with Gwyn and it would have been awkward to break off.'

'Would you like to come in?' Elliot looks stressed and it's obvious he wants to talk to me about something.

'Am I interrupting . . . I mean, I don't want to take advantage just because you live here.'

The way he said 'live here' sounded a bit weird, but I swing the door open wide and leave him to shut it as I make my way into the kitchen-diner.

'I've just poured myself a glass of wine. Can I get one for you?' I call out.

He appears, having slipped off his shoes after noticing that I'm barefoot. Good manners I appreciate, it's respectful.

'This is nicely done. They should have asked you to oversee the furnishing of all the holiday cottages because you have a good eye for things. What a difference it makes.'

'Thanks. I love it here. Oops . . . have I poured a little too much? It's not restaurant measures I'm afraid,' I apologise as I hand the glass to him.

'Not at all, thanks. I need this. Have you eaten?'

I shake my head. 'Not yet. Have you?'

'No and I skipped lunch, too.'

'I could make us an omelette?' I offer, awkwardly.

He raises his glass to me and then takes a hefty gulp. That's not a good sign, given that he prefers beer.

'That won't be necessary. It's not what you know, but who you know.' With that he pulls the phone from his pocket and seconds later he's talking to Michael on speakerphone.

'Can I ask a huge favour? I'm with Linzi in Red Robin Cottage. We're having a bit of a work chat and neither of us has eaten. Is there any way you could magic up something and get a waiter to deliver it?'

'Of course! Leave it with me.'

'That's really appreciated, Michael, thank you.'

When Elliot clicks end call, I look at him, highly amused. 'What?'

'You're the boss and you call the shots. It's not exactly a favour. Anyway, please take a seat.'

'Thanks. And the customers come first, so I'd expect Michael to say if the kitchen was under pressure. In which case I would have offered to cook that omelette myself to make up for barging in. But, in all honesty, there's a lot I'd like to discuss with you and I'd rather it wasn't in the office. Closed doors worry people.'

'Should I be concerned?' I hold my glass up, temporarily distracted by the gloriously pink hue of last year's award-winning Green Valley Vineyard Sparkling Blush. It was a good summer with enough sunshine interspersed with showers to make the grapes sweet and plump.

'I'm aware that everyone is waiting with bated breath to hear my plans going forward.' He sidesteps the question, glancing at me across the table.

'It's good to know that hasn't gone over your head. You've been here for what . . . nine days now? Your style is different to what everyone is used to. With Thomas in charge and Robert running things, it has always felt like a family business. The only person working here who can even vaguely remember you visiting is Gwyn, and the staff don't quite know what to expect. Can I be honest with you?'

'I'm banking on it. Thomas said you're my greatest ally when it comes to influencing the others and yet you're no one's boss, which I find incredible. You're also the only person who lives on site. I'm just curious to know your history, I suppose, because my grandfather told me straight that if you're happy, he's happy. And now he's suddenly driving around in the wilds of Scotland and unobtainable. I've walked into a little community and there are questions I need answered, because I'm not here to step on toes.'

'Well, disappearing like that for a few days is cause for speculation. And visiting our suppliers without mentioning it to your managers, the people who deal with them on a regular basis, makes it look like you don't trust anyone here.'

Placing the wine glass in my hand down on the table, my gaze wanders over to the courtyard. The dark red climbing rose is now flowering, and the bees are loving it. I'm not sure what exactly Elliot wants to hear. People hate silences and when it's obvious I'm not going to continue, he clears his throat nervously.

'I'm asking because if I don't understand the internal politics, I can't firm up my plans. I've already upset Gwyn, and I'm hoping you can intervene and set his mind at rest.'

Either Elliot's style is subtly manipulative – because he could just snap his fingers and make things happen – or he's genuinely concerned about getting it wrong as he ploughs forward. But he hasn't made the best start. Do I play the dutiful employee and give him the benefit of the doubt? Or do I try and catch him out? He's acting more like a troubleshooter and that is a cause for concern. The lack of team meetings and any sort of initial feedback from his fact-finding sessions is odd, to say the least. Keeping everything so close to his chest is giving off the wrong signal and it's only natural that people will assume it's because bad news is coming.

'You won't find anyone as loyal to this place as Gwyn. He's spent his entire working life here.'

Elliot pushes his shoulders back, defensively. 'Please rest assured that I wasn't implying any criticism. But, as we expand, Gwyn will require some assistance.'

'Expand?' Is it my imagination, or did Elliot squirm a little in his seat as he uttered that word?

'Let's just say that I'm looking at various opportunities. Before I came here, on paper the sensible thing to do was to have the bulk of the forestry team reporting directly to you.'

It's hard to sit here quietly listening and not react, but now is not the time to interrupt his flow.

'Gwyn's role would then focus on site security and managing two groundsmen to deal with felling and boundary repairs.'

This is crazy. 'Two? But currently we have three.'

'Yes, the third person would then be a part of the team assigned specifically to the maintenance of the grounds and the vineyard itself.'

'You had a plan all worked up before you'd even familiarised yourself with how things are run here?' I can tell from his expression he wasn't expecting me to come back at him in such a forthright way.

'That's precisely what I've been doing since the day I arrived, Linzi. The organisation chart needs rejigging,' he explains. 'But it's a case of moving staff around, not reducing our numbers. However, you're right, because some of the assumptions I made didn't take into account unknown factors I've since identified. For the sake of staff morale, I'm keen to roll out the new set-up and quickly.'

'Which is?'

'It's obvious that you don't have spare capacity, so I'll be appointing a forestry team manager who will report to Gwyn. It will cut Gwyn's workload in half.'

'You're sidelining him?'

'No, but he's struggling and it's obvious. If he goes off sick, we have a major problem.'

Two years ago, a consultant told Gwyn that he requires knee replacement surgery, but he simply won't take the time off work. Like me, this is his life and without it . . . well, it gives us a sense of purpose and belonging.

'No wonder he's walking around with a face like thunder,' I mutter. 'He'll feel you're undermining his position, Elliot.'

It's obvious that Elliot isn't finding this easy. 'I can see that, and it's why I need your input. My grandfather will also have something to say about it when I finally get to talk to him, but I can't wait around out of politeness.'

'Politeness?'

The look he gives me is an honest one. 'This is just between us, Linzi. Joining a family business comes with its own set of unique challenges. I'm taking over on the proviso that while I will keep my grandfather informed, he can't veto any of my decisions. However, there is a caveat: I only have full autonomy over the restaurant and hotel side of the business. Decisions with regard to the vines are in your capable hands until I . . . as he termed it, "get my bearings".'

That's why Thomas said he'd be keeping an eye. But what if he's made himself absent to let Elliot cause an uproar just so he'll end up turning to his grandfather for help? It would be a clever way of Thomas subtly being able to exert a little control over Elliot's future plans. My frown deepens as Elliot's eyes scan my face.

'As one of the key personnel here,' he continues, 'I need

to tap into your insider knowledge to help me effect the changes in the most diplomatic way. What I'm finding is that writing a report and making recommendations is one thing, being in the hot seat and putting those changes into practice is quite another.'

I sit quietly sipping my wine as I mull this over. I will admit, albeit begrudgingly, that he's right about Gwyn needing help, and it's a good sign that he hasn't queried whether Gwyn is actually fit for work.

'Are you saying that you want me to have a word with Gwyn?'

Elliot's face relaxes; he can see he's winning me over. 'The truth is that I need you, Gwyn, and Michael on board to effect a smooth transition.'

'Michael? You're going to make changes there, too?'

'As the hotel and restaurant manager, he's getting far too involved in the daily operation of the hotel when we have a head of housekeeping. I'll be looking at that part of the structure next.'

I wonder how Michael feels about that, or Quinn Houghton who recently took over that role and reports to Michael. Elliot sits forward in his chair, just as there's a sharp rap on the door. I hurry to open it, and my favourite waiter greets me with a bold smile.

'Hi, Allan. Let me give you a hand.'

We lift the trolley over the threshold, and he wheels it through to the kitchen.

'Would you like me to serve?' he asks Elliot.

'No, that's fine. Thank you so much, Allan.'

'Well, enjoy your meal.' He turns on his heels and I see him out.

'Please thank Michael and Chef. Sorry to have pulled you away.'

'Oh, it's no problem at all,' he replies. But just as I open the door and he's about to step outside he leans closer, lowering his voice. 'Everything is OK, isn't it, Linzi?'

'It's all good, Allan.'

'Great. We've just had three big parties arrive so it's going to be another busy one. Don't work too late.' He grins at me, rolling his eyes, and I flash him a smile.

When I rejoin Elliot, he's already uncovered the dishes on the trolley. His phone kicks into life and he utters a low groan, pulling it out of his shirt pocket and glancing at the screen.

'Sorry, Linzi, I really need to take this. Do you mind if I . . .' He indicates in the direction of the patio doors and I nod my approval for him to go ahead and open them.

As he steps outside, I place the metal domes back over the two plates of aged Welsh fillet steak, confit butter garlic and triple-cooked chips, but not before I pinch one. I'm so hungry I feel a little light-headed, and I hope his call won't take long. Unfortunately, he left the sliding doors ajar, and as he walks around my colourful courtyard, I can hear his voice quite clearly. It's wrong to listen to someone else's conversation but it's not my fault he's so loud.

'. . . and no, I'm not avoiding you. We've been through this; I've got a lot to do in a short space of time, that's all. When I get a breather I'll be in touch – I promise – and then you'll have my full and undivided attention again. Are you happy now?'

The way his voice softens at the end makes me wonder whether this is the mysterious Isobel that Sienna mentioned.

There are a few seconds of silence and then he bursts out laughing. 'I'll hold you to that!' he declares. 'Anyway, I must go. Work calls. And no more phoning here and leaving messages with my assistant. If it's important, email me and be prepared to wait until I have time to respond.'

He's obviously keen to get off the phone so I busy myself grabbing napkins and cutlery from the trolley.

'My apologies, you must be hungry by now,' he says, as he steps back inside. 'Shall I leave the door open? It's very pleasant and sheltered here. That's quite a little suntrap.'

'Yes. I'm very lucky,' I reply as we reach out to grab a plate before the food gets cold.

He looks up and grins at me as we're both going for the chips first, and it breaks the ice. 'Who can resist?' I observe.

'Not me. Good food on tap is a big temptation. Do you eat in the restaurant very often?'

'No, rarely in fact.'

'I guess once you shut the front door you want to switch off from work, except for this evening. Which I appreciate. Do you live here for convenience? It's a little unusual.'

I'm so hungry that I've just popped a large sliver of medium rare fillet into my mouth. The garlic butter is making my taste buds very happy indeed. Elliot waits patiently, as he too savours his perfectly cooked steak.

I thought I'd successfully dodged his earlier question, but obviously he didn't take the hint. I take a sip of wine before answering, sitting back to consider whether it's information he wants, or if he's simply making conversation to relax me.

'It was a part of the package Thomas offered at the time. It was supposed to be temporary as I'd just returned to the UK, but it's now a part of my contract. I've no objection to paying rent, it's just not something Thomas has ever mentioned.'

Elliot is embarrassed. 'Oh, I wasn't intimating that . . . I mean, it makes total sense to me, but it's rather restricting for you, isn't it?'

He picks up his wine glass and I can see that a sparkling blush isn't his thing. Getting to my feet, I open the fridge and pull out one of the beers I keep for Gwyn. I pop the top and grab a glass, before handing it to Elliot.

'Try this. It's made by Mumbles Brewery – a traditional pale ale with a distinctive taste.'

'Thanks. I'm afraid I don't really do fizzy anything when it comes to wine – even champagne does nothing for me.'

'Well, the bottle you're passing over is one of our biggest sellers.'

He gives me an apologetic look. 'All I can say is thank goodness for our discerning customers.' He takes a hefty gulp of beer. 'Hmm . . . this is . . .' He struggles to find the right words as he holds his glass up to inspect the amber liquid.

I come to his rescue, although I can see he's winding me up. 'Full-bodied and well-rounded without being too heavy, would be appropriate.'

He starts to laugh as I recommence eating.

'So, you're on board and you'll help me smooth things over with Gwyn?'

I nod my head. It's going to benefit everyone if I cooperate to fill in the gaps and hopefully avoid any head-to-head situations that arise. Assuming Elliot is being straight with me, I'm guessing that he's well aware it's in his best interests to accommodate Gwyn. What that man doesn't know about this place isn't worth knowing. Anyway, it's been a long week and I'm done talking about work. Besides, I don't intend to let this food go cold and, by the look of it, we have dessert too.

After last night's chat with Elliot, I figure a little trip to Gwyn's house might be a nice touch on a sunny Saturday morning. Especially given that he's been avoiding me at work.

I pull up outside his semi-detached house in the village of Arlingham and suddenly I'm wondering whether I should have called first. But I'm here now and I ring the bell, standing back and trying to look relaxed.

'This is a surprise. What's up?' It's not quite the reaction I was hoping for when Gwyn opens the door. 'Come on in. I'll put the kettle on.'

A lump rises up in my throat as I follow him inside. Everything looks exactly the same as when his wife, Wendy, was alive. The kitchen is pristine. She wasn't one for ornaments and the worktops are clear, save for a few essential items. A toaster, the kettle and a little vase full of bright pink roses. Wendy always had fresh flowers, no matter what time of the year, but these are most definitely from the garden.

'What a beautiful scent,' I remark, trying to hide the

sadness that is flooding through me for his loss. How do you go on when the love of your life is no longer there beside you? Now that takes courage and strength.

'Wendy's favourites, Linzi. This year they've done us both proud. The fragrance is comfortin' and I know she'd be happy I'm continuin' on as normal.'

Gwyn adds tea leaves to an old brown teapot, then collects two of Wendy's best bone china cups as he sorts out the tray. I watch, transfixed, because it's like he's on autopilot. He gathers everything together and lifts the tray, indicating for us to make our way into the sitting room.

This is hard to witness as it's Wendy's little routine to a tee. I did think it was strange that he hasn't invited me over since she passed, almost eighteen months ago. I'm troubled to see that it's like a shrine to her. Is that the only way he can get through the time he spends here, as if she's just popped to the shops and could walk back in at any moment? I wonder. My heart breaks for him all over again. But I'm here for good reason and that's to support him, so I put on a cheery expression.

Gwyn limps to a halt in front of the coffee table, indicating for me to take a seat on the sofa. He begins pouring the tea as if it's somewhat of a ritual. I try to remember the last time I saw a tea strainer and realise that it was here, the Christmas before Wendy died.

'Help yourself to sugar and milk,' he mutters, placing a cup and saucer in front of me. 'You've somethin' to say. Best get it off your chest, Linzi. I can tell when somethin' is up.'

I shouldn't have come. Why didn't I just wait until Monday and bump into him at work? Now's he wary and he thinks I've come bearing bad news.

'You know that there are only a handful of people who mean a lot to me, Gwyn, and you are one of them. I say this with the greatest respect, but it's time to stop ignoring the obvious.'

'That Elliot is lookin' to replace me?'

He's lost the woman he loves and now he thinks Elliot doesn't want him to be a part of the vineyard going forward.

'No. We both know what's really going on, Gwyn. Let's not pretend otherwise. You've been more of a father to me than my own dad. All I'm concerned about here is you.'

He grimaces. 'I'm fine.'

'No. You're not fine and I should have said something long before now. You need to get that knee fixed and Wendy would agree with me.'

His face pales and I wonder if I've gone too far. Moments pass and it's a silence that's almost too much to bear, but it's time to sit back and listen.

'She's with me still, Linzi. Every evenin' I glance over at her chair and she's there, smilin' back at me. And now you think I'm crazy and maybe I am, because I don't believe in any of this afterlife stuff. But she still tells me what to do.'

How do I respond to something like that? It sounds as if he's lost his grip on reality, but strangely enough I believe him.

'That's amazing, Gwyn. They do say that true love never dies, and I like the idea of that.'

'Me, too, Linzi. I started usin' microwave meals for a while and the missus wasn't happy. She said I was bein' lazy, and I should know better. Imagine that, eh?'

My heart says it's true, but my head is struggling to believe it.

'You can't ignore the problem with your knee forever, Gwyn. Elliot doesn't want to lose you – that's why he's trying to ease your workload.'

'You don't think he's goin' to try and push me out?'

I look Gwyn straight in the eye. 'No, not for one moment. Like it or not, he's the boss now and it's his job to make sure the business is in the best possible shape. Which means identifying potential problems and finding solutions.'

'Where does that leave us? We'd be lettin' Thomas down if we didn't rise to the challenge.'

'Elliot wants to please Thomas, although he's the one

in charge now and we must never forget that. He's astute enough to understand that his grandfather has an allegiance to the people who've supported him over the years. Common sense tells me that the last thing Elliot wants is to lose our combined experience.'

'Our?' he questions.

'We're in this together and I'm going to talk to Michael next. I know the timing of this is awful, Gwyn, but you need to get yourself back to fighting fit again. For your own sake, because some days you literally hobble around. I don't know how you manage to cope with it now that it's affecting your back and your hip.'

He lowers his eyes, letting out a troubling sigh. 'The pain is almost constant, Linzi. I can't even rest properly at night. And I'm strugglin' to help Wendy's brother, Fred. He's ten years older than me and has emphysema. I pop in for a couple of hours after work each night to make his evenin' meal. He does have someone from one of these agencies who calls in every day. Like me, he's on his own now, and it's tough at times.'

Gwyn rarely talks about his life outside of work, or Wendy, and this is a real surprise.

'It's too much for you at the moment, Gwyn. Isn't there another family member who can step in and take over?'

He shakes his head. 'He has a daughter, but they haven't spoken for a while. He's a stubborn man and they had a fallin' out. I do have her number, for emergencies. Wendy's younger brother lives up north and both of his sons have young 'uns of their own. Him and his wife help out with the school runs, so they don't visit that often.'

'And how about you?'

Gwyn looks at me, frowning. 'What do you mean?'

'If you get that knee sorted, is there someone close by you can call on?'

His expression instantly changes. 'I've never been one to put on other people,' he replies, sharply.

Reading between the lines I think I've discovered why he's soldiering on regardless. Maybe there isn't anyone he can ask to come and look after him post-surgery.

'Look, you're a key member of the team and Elliot knows that. He'll do whatever he can to help, not least because if you had an accident on the job he could be held liable if he ignores something so obvious.'

Gwyn lets out a deep and troubled sigh. 'Looks like I might have no choice in the matter.'

It's not a good note on which to leave, but there's no avoiding the truth of the situation. Something has to change, and soon.

After a relaxing Sunday, I'm up with the lark and eager to begin my working week. As I'm about to leave the cottage, my phone lights up and my eyes widen when I see the caller's name.

'Thomas, what a lovely surprise! I thought you were touring the wilds of Scotland,' I exclaim.

'We are and the signal is a bit hit and miss. Of course, it would help if I was allowed to turn my phone on occasionally.' He roars with laughter. 'It was nice catching up with family and friends and now, after ten days on the road, I'm adjusting to the slower pace of life. Katherine says she's waited years to take a trip like this and it's time for us both to unwind.'

The sound of his voice puts a smile on my face and I'm glad to hear that being unobtainable is a part of the plan to get his retirement back on track. I'm intrigued as to why he's calling me, though. 'I did wonder whether you'd get in touch at some point.'

'I told you. I intend to smooth the way. I'm putting my trust in Elliot but there will be a few bumps, I'm sure. He emailed me late yesterday about a few changes he's about to make. I was wondering how Gwyn took the news.'

My mouth goes dry, and I hesitate before replying.

'Linzi, you're a loyal person,' he continues. 'I don't expect you to share confidences, either work, or personal, but Gwyn has a problem. It would be wrong of Elliot to ignore it. Not least from a due diligence point of view, let alone the health and safety aspect.'

Thomas is merely pointing out the obvious.

'Gwyn knows he can't continue to ignore the issue but dealing with it is another matter entirely.'

'Hmm. As long as Gwyn doesn't feel he's being backed into a corner for the wrong reason. Can you do me a favour, Linzi?'

'I'm listening.'

Thomas isn't a fool. He can't interfere directly, but he is concerned on Gwyn's behalf.

'If it looks like there's going to be a bust-up between Gwyn and Elliot, can you give me the heads-up? I don't want Gwyn doing anything daft like handing in his notice.'

'I'll try my best, but Gwyn isn't very approachable at the moment.'

'I said I wouldn't interfere, but this is a little different. Anyway, hopefully it won't come to that. Take care, Linzi, and thanks.'

Elliot

6.

The Grass Isn't Always Greener . . .

'Morning, Elliot. Thought I'd catch you bright and early on a Monday before you get snowed under. Just wanted to say thanks for sorting out my little dilemma so promptly. It's good to know you're only a phone call away.'

'It's not a problem, Nate. You've put a lot of business my way over the years.'

'How is it going deep in the heart of the Welsh valleys? I could do with a little of that tranquillity right now. This new acquisition of mine has been a big headache from day one and I'm grateful to you for making that call to save me a lot of hassle.'

'Wales is very green and fertile, thank goodness. It was a bit of a shock coming back and seeing the changes. It's going to take me a little longer than expected to update the business plan, but I'm getting there.'

A loud 'Hmm' echoes down the line. 'Not quite as easy to lick it into shape as you thought, eh? Still, knowing you I bet you're on it 24/7.'

I lean my head back against the chair and laugh. 'Something like that. Anyway, you must come down and sample what we have on offer. The new wing has some executive suites with views over the vineyard and relaxation is guaranteed. If you can give me a little notice, I'd love to entertain you and Penny for the weekend.'

Getting someone like Nate, a heavyweight investor, and

his gorgeous young wife here, posting selfies on social media, could have a huge impact on bookings. She's an influencer in her own right and together they are quite a power couple.

'That's a generous offer and we'd love to take you up on it, just as soon as this latest hiccough is resolved. Money doesn't make itself; you have to keep playing the cards until you get the right combination and then be ready to sell when the pot is looking healthy.'

Sometimes Nate sounds more like a gambler than a multimillionaire renowned for his ability to know when to buy and when to bail.

'Too right.'

'Remember, I owe you one, my friend!' he replies, adamantly.

I much prefer it when I'm the one who is owed favours and Nate knows a lot of other investors who pump him for leads. It's not an option I'm considering right now, but that's not to say I might not be forced to rethink that decision further down the road. As the line disconnects there's a ping and it's a text from Isobel. She's starting early today.

Talk to me, damn you!

Now I'm in trouble.

I thought we agreed you were going to give me a few days' peace and quiet? Wasn't the weekend enough?

Nothing is ever enough when it comes to Isobel.

Hardly, I'm used to monopolising your time and now I'm the last person on your mind. It's not fair! 😔😢

When Isobel is in a mood, it's impossible to deal with her and now she's intimating that I'm neglecting her and our shared interests.

Well, I'm afraid you're going to have to get used to it.

There's a tap on the door and Sienna appears. 'Oh, sorry! I didn't realise you were on the phone, Elliot.'

'Just texting. What's up?' With that, my phone rings and it's Isobel. If I don't pick up she's going to spend the day bugging me. I answer. 'Hang on a moment, Isobel. Sorry, Sienna. Is it something that can wait?' It's obvious now is not a good time.

Sienna shrugs her shoulders. 'Linzi's in the office. She asked if you could spare her five minutes before her morning tutorial session begins. Shall I suggest she catches up with you at lunchtime?'

'No, ask her to come in,' I reply, putting the phone back up to my ear.

'Isobel, something has come up. I must go.'

Just as Linzi steps through the door, Isobel launches into full-on rant mode and I can't just end the call. I indicate for Linzi to take a seat, but she looks uncomfortable. I watch as she pulls something from her pocket, scooping that long, wavy hair back into a ponytail and fiddling with it as a few strands fall down. I'm temporarily distracted, and immediately look away.

'I know,' I interrupt Isobel's flow, 'and I agree, but the first couple of weeks are intensive, you know that. Next time I'll try to stay two nights. I'll call you later.' I disconnect before Isobel has a chance to reply.

'I didn't mean to interrupt,' Linzi immediately apologises.

'Oh, it's not a problem. Just loose ends that need tying up in London and, unfortunately, I didn't manage to get everything sorted over the weekend. Anyway, I hope you had a relaxing one and enjoyed the sunshine.'

'Yes, I did, thanks. I also popped in to see Gwyn on Saturday.'

Now Linzi has my full attention. My grandfather finally answered my email at seven this morning. True to form, he didn't have a lot to say, only that there's an excellent candidate on the forestry team who's more than ready to take on more responsibility. He didn't even give me a name.

'Has he calmed down? I tried to be as diplomatic as possible when we were talking on Friday.' Linzi stares back at me rather intensely. I thought I was getting somewhere with her, but if she doesn't trust me then I'm sunk, because the others will pick up on that. 'Look, this isn't an attempt to push Gwyn out, but I can't pretend that as things stand there isn't an issue. I'm trying to address it in the best possible way. I want to make friends, not enemies.'

'It's not just anger about the proposed changes. Gwyn's in a lot of pain at times and you probably caught him on a bad day.'

She sits back in her chair, and I think the tide is finally turning. 'Then why doesn't he just get his knee fixed?'

Linzi looks at me, clearly exasperated. 'He's a widower. Surgery means putting his life on hold for a while. And given the circumstances here, if you bring in someone new while he's off recuperating, he'll no doubt be wondering whether his job will still be waiting for him when he returns.'

I hope that's not what she's thinking too. As I lean back in my chair, studying Linzi's face, I'm aware that she's an attractive woman, but she makes me nervous. It's like there's this invisible line she's drawn, and you have to be invited to step over it. And yet, Linzi doesn't hold back if you ask her opinion on something. She looks away nervously and I watch as her ponytail flicks around and touches her cheek. She's one hundred per cent business but doesn't seem to have any aspiration to increase her role. Managing people adds weight to a post and most people would be eager to boost their position.

'What's the answer?' I pose, putting the ball firmly in her court.

'It rather depends on your agenda.' Linzi's response is to the point.

'Would it make it easier if we chose an internal candidate as Gwyn's assistant manager?' I'm a good judge of people, but for some reason I'm never sure what's coming next with Linzi, and I don't like being on the back foot. If, as I hope, she has a solution, then this could be a win-win situation for me. It would keep my grandfather happy if I don't bring in someone new and now I can understand why. This sort of juggling act is precisely why I didn't want to get involved with the vineyard and I can't believe I let myself get talked into it. However, Grandma can be very persuasive and I wouldn't upset her for the world.

'Yes, obviously, but bear in mind that Gwyn makes the job look much easier than it is. Given the compact size of our team, there's a lot to juggle with the daily schedules and he makes the call when it comes to prioritisation. That's easy with his level of experience, for two reasons. One because he's proactive and tries to address potential issues ahead of time, and two because he's earned the respect of the team.'

Linzi is easing me into what she really wants to say and I find it amusing. It's not often people play me, it's usually the other way around.

'And the solution is?'

'If Gwyn were to come here after his operation and stay in one of the new ground floor suites, it would make his life a whole lot easier while he recovers. He wouldn't need to cook for himself, or clean, and it's a level walk to the car park when it comes to transport for check-ups and physiotherapy. The bonus is that whoever you deem suitable to promote on a temporary basis would also have his boss on hand. Gwyn would have plenty of time to rest, while still being involved, which would alleviate any anxiety he might have about his future.'

'What a brilliant idea, Linzi. But we need to get it sorted quickly. I'll get Sienna started on making a few discreet enquiries, there's bound to be a private hospital somewhere reasonably close by.'

'That's something you'll need to talk to Gwyn about first, though, as I'm not sure he can afford—'

'We'll foot the bill, or our health insurers will. Are you happy to put this to him?' I don't want to make her feel I'm stealing the glory here when she's come up with the perfect solution.

Linzi looks relieved. 'I don't feel comfortable talking about the personal lives of my colleagues, Elliot. This is an exception to the rule, and I want to make that very clear. My friendship with Gwyn is dear to me and my involvement in this matter ends now. I'm afraid it's over to you to put it to him.'

Fair enough. 'I think he'll see it makes sense and I can't thank you enough. Gwyn's a key member of staff and I want him to understand that.' The bonus is that in mentoring his assistant, we'd have someone skilled-up if, and when, Gwyn decides to retire.

'It would help your case considerably if you point that out to him,' Linzi adds.

'Understood. I can assure you that I only want the best outcome for everyone involved. I'd be failing you all if I don't address the issues that could pose a threat in the not-too-distant future.' Damn it, I have no idea why I constantly feel the need to explain myself to her, but I do. 'Obviously, Gwyn's situation is a major headache as it's such a sensitive issue. This conversation remains just between us, and I'll talk to Gwyn this morning.'

Linzi glances at her watch. 'Good. On that note, I'd better head off to class – I'm already a few minutes late.'

I stand and lean across the desk, extending my hand. 'I really appreciate your cooperation, Linzi.'

Her expression is often difficult to read, but her handshake is firm and purposeful. I think I can safely say that I've succeeded in getting her on my side. That's quite an achievement because she can be very reticent at times. I hope that's not because she doubts my intentions.

'Robert relied heavily upon Gwyn, as did Thomas, Elliot,'

Linzi states as I look directly into her eyes. 'And if it weren't for Gwyn I probably would have upped and left after a few months. He has a way of resolving problems without drama and people trust him because he's a man who believes in treating people fairly.'

With that, she turns and is gone, leaving me a little breathless. It's disconcerting, but she's just solved a huge problem and it's going to put a big smile on my grandfather's face once I get it sorted. Grandma said I can only deliver good news for the time being. But she doesn't know the half of it, yet.

Anyway, that's one problem less on my mental tick list, but I'm a long way away from heading back to my life in London. With Isobel simmering and about to reach boiling point, I don't think I'll break the news just yet. It's not going to be easy to sort out the problems here and I can't allow myself to get distracted.

Now it's time for me to tackle the finances. You spend to accumulate, as they say, but someone took their eye off the ball and the bottom line on the balance sheet isn't where it should be. Hopefully, I've arrived in the nick of time to rescue the family business, but I'm afraid none of the viable options are likely to be well received. Most people hate change and that's a fact.

Linzi

7.

Oh, Deer . . .

Monday morning's classroom session overran; we got into the importance of ecological infrastructures, and it sparked a lot of interest. Hedgerows planted with native vegetation and trees aren't solely there to act as a windbreaker for the vines, but to offer a habitat for local wildlife. Balance is everything and, while birds do help keep down some pests, there's also a need to encourage birds of prey. Today's project is to pick suitable sites to increase the number of nesting boxes and facilities for a variety of local birds – including kestrels, owls, tits and sparrows.

During the lunch break, I'm sitting in the cottage and eating a sandwich, when Gwyn calls me.

'I'm down in the south corner. I think you'd better come and take a look at this, Linzi. It's not good news.'

Conscious that I only have twenty minutes before the afternoon session begins, I don't hang around. Making my way to the car park, I mount the stile and break into a half-jog. It's more or less inevitable that whenever there's a problem it's always one of the furthest points away, and by the time I get there, I'm a little breathless. But even so, my jaw drops as I survey the damage.

'What happened?' I gasp, more from shock than lack of breath.

'A deer somehow got into the vineyard, no doubt expectin'

it to be a fallow field when it hopped over the hedge. It must've panicked when it saw the vines and heard the noises comin' from the restaurant terrace. The brave thing leapt straight over into the adjacent field, not knowin' that Pryce was the other side of it, sittin' on the mower.'

The sit-and-ride machine has ploughed through the hedge and demolished the ends of two rows of vines. It's caused a partial collapse of both structures and my heart sinks.

Pryce is standing a few feet away, still in shock.

'You could do with a cup of tea, Pryce,' I state, looking around. 'It's a miracle the deer got away.'

'It's a bigger miracle the unfortunate animal didn't land on my head!' he blurts out.

Gwyn is equally as aware that this isn't a bad result considering what might have happened. 'Go on, Pryce, get yerself up to the rest room and have a bit of a break.'

'Thanks, Gwyn, and sorry, Linzi. If I'd had me brain in gear, I'd have swerved the other way.'

He looks forlorn.

'No, you did great. It's a freak accident that could happen to anyone and at least no one was hurt, man or animal,' I reply heaving a sigh of relief.

Pryce gives an acknowledging tilt of his head before heading off, leaving Gwyn and me to appraise the full extent of the damage.

'I took some photos with me phone but I'm not sure it's worth gettin' the insurers involved. There's a dent in the front of the mower but it's had its fair share of knocks anyway. It's just a shame that we've lost a few good plants,' Gwyn acknowledges. 'I'll get two of the guys on this in the next hour. It's a fair bit of work, though. Probably best if we disguise the hole in the hedge with a gate.'

'I agree. Lunchtime is almost over, so I'll gather up the trainees and we can start clearing up. If one of your guys can bring a couple of new end poles, my lot will get to work clearing the debris and strengthening the structure.

It's all in a day's work and a great example of never really knowing what might crop up.'

'At least the deer didn't run rampant, tramplin' everythin' in sight. The poor thing must have been scared witless. Anyway, let's get this underway.'

As we start walking back, Gwyn gives me a grimace. 'If I'm too slow for you, don't feel you have to hang back, Linzi.'

'It's fine. Officially, I'm still on my break.'

'It's a shame this happened to Pryce. He's a hard worker and he'll turn his hand to anythin'. The poor guy was mortified when he called me.'

'I bet, but these things happen.'

'If I were lookin' for a deputy, he's the man I'd pick. Admittedly, he's got a lot to learn still, but he's done every job on the forestry team in the six years he's been here. What do you think?'

It doesn't sound like Elliot has had a word with Gwyn yet about his knee. This obviously harks back to their chat on Friday. Clearly, Gwyn has been thinking about it over the weekend.

'I agree that he's the best candidate.'

'Then I'll put it to Elliot,' Gwyn replies resolutely, but there's a hint of reluctance in his tone.

'To be honest, Gwyn, when you're on holiday and I'm pulling my schedule together to pass to him, I always have a word with Pryce before I finalise it. He's willing to point out things I've missed and, while he'll need some guidance, I think it would take a lot of pressure off you.'

'What, takin' a step back?'

'No. It's called delegation, Gwyn. It will free up some of your time if you only sign off the schedules. That way you still have control, but you know that you're overloaded at the moment.'

Gwyn grunts. 'There's no foolin' you, Linzi. That deer got in through a broken fence. Somethin' I'd normally have picked up immediately. A lot of accidents can be avoided if you keep on the lookout and I slipped up because I'm not as mobile as I used to be.'

'It's not a criticism, Gwyn, you know that. No one works harder, or is more loyal, than you. But I have a feeling that changes are coming. Elliot is going to need our support, so make it as easy for yourself as you can because you'll want to be a big part of it.'

We continue walking in silence. Gwyn is a proud man and he'll only take Elliot's offer if he truly believes he's needed. He is, but I don't think he realises quite how much. We are a family here. People come and go, although the vast majority stay because, even though we work in our separate teams, whenever there's a problem we pull together. Everyone feels a part of this success story and that means something. I genuinely believe that Elliot is beginning to understand – and value – that. It doesn't mean that I trust him implicitly. Or that if I feel something is off then I won't contact Thomas for a quick chat: there's too much at stake. But the way Elliot reacted to my suggestion regarding Gwyn was heartening. It's a good start.

'The boss is tied up with Michael for the rest of the mornin'. Do you have any idea what that's all about?'

I shake my head, a frown forming on my face. 'I'd be more concerned if he wasn't, to be honest. Michael is another one who is overloaded.'

'Well, at least Elliot's pickin' up on the right things and not lookin' at makin' changes for the sake of it,' Gwyn observes, pragmatically.

It's reassuring to see Gwyn much calmer today but it's hard to ignore the way he keeps wincing as the exertion begins to take a toll. I just hope that Elliot is able to speak to him this afternoon.

'Right, everyone. First off, we're clearing the debris from the hedge. Pryce is on his way with a trailer and will take it away to be chipped. Adam, grab those pruners and we'll see what we can salvage on the damaged vines.'

It's a sorry sight, for sure.

'This first one took the brunt and isn't salvageable. It'll need digging out. If you can snip off the broken pieces on the next two, I'll do the same with the second row.'

'No problem, Linzi.' He's keen to get hands-on and appreciates the trust I'm putting in him.

I leave Adam to it and turn my attention to the debris. If the hedge hadn't slowed down the mower it could have taken out a heck of a lot more plants. It's good to see my little group working together as a team. It'll be the first time they've been involved in repairing the core structure supporting the vines.

The sound of the small tractor means the trailer has arrived and a few minutes later Pryce appears at my side.

'How are you feeling?' I ask, gazing up at him.

'Mad at meself still, but after a mug of strong tea I'm ready for action.' He gives me an apologetic look as I stand, throwing a handful of broken stems onto a pile next to me.

'It's not as bad as it looks. I reckon half an hour and most of the damage will be cleared away. Is someone going to bring some replacement posts and wire?'

'It's already on the trailer. I'm just about to offload it. Once your guys have loaded this lot up, I'll take it back to the compound and find someone to give me a hand putting in a gate.' He leans closer, lowering his voice. 'The boss just called Gwyn into his office. This was down to me and it's not fair he should take the flack.'

'Listen, it was no one's fault, Pryce. I seriously doubt Elliot even knows about the incident, so don't worry.'

A look of relief flashes over his face, but he's embarrassed.

'There's not as much damage as I thought, and we'll get this all sorted by the end of the day.'

My comment seems to lift his spirits and he gives me a cheeky grin. 'You don't hang around, Linzi, and I'm grateful to everyone for giving a hand. Right, I'll offload those materials and then I'll muck in alongside your crew.'

As I return to the task in hand, I glance over at Adam, who is doing a great job. While I don't have favourites, he's not overconfident and he listens. While a couple of the others lark about at times when they're doing routine tasks, which is a natural part of the team-building thing, Adam is one of the quieter ones, but he shows a lot of promise.

Just as I'm about to sit down at the end of the day with a well-earned cup of tea, someone knocks on the door of the cottage.

'Sienna! I thought you'd already left for the day. I've just boiled the kettle; is this a flying visit, or do you have time to join me?'

'Yes please,' she replies, slipping off her shoes and shutting the door behind her. 'I have exciting news and a bit of info you need to be aware of.'

'Judging by that smile on your face, you'd better give me your exciting news first.'

Sienna takes a seat at the table as I pass her a mug.

'Cam is working from home all week. He rang me at lunchtime to say that we're viewing two properties straight from work on Thursday.' I haven't seen her as animated as this in a long time.

'That's brilliant, Sienna! I'm so pleased for you both.'

'I've been dying to share this with you all afternoon. I really was at the end of my tether, worried sick that after our heart-to-heart at the weekend he might have second thoughts.'

'Why would you think that?'

She scoops a spoonful of sugar into her mug, avoiding my gaze. 'He works away a lot, Linzi. How do I know what goes on when we're apart?'

My jaw drops. 'You think—'

'No . . . of course not . . . but he's a good-looking guy and I guess I was letting my imagination run wild.'

'And some. He could say the same thing about you.'

She stares at me blankly, then blinks. 'Oh.'

'You obviously got your point across and clearly it spurred him into action.'

She flicks the hair back from her face with her hand, sporting an artful grin. 'Poor Cam, but it needed saying.'

That makes me chuckle. 'Anyway, I'm excited for you!'

'The other thing is that Elliot had another lengthy meeting with Gwyn this afternoon.'

I glance at her, trying not to appear anxious, but she's here because she knows I'm worried about him.

'What was Gwyn's expression when he left?' Sienna can't divulge specifics, but his demeanour will have reflected what went on.

'If it weren't for his knee, I think he'd have a bit of a skip back in his step! Whatever Elliot said went down well. Curiously, the boss sent me an email shortly afterwards and he wants to talk to me first thing tomorrow morning on an HR matter.'

It would be wrong of me to press her, but if Gwyn was smiling that's all I need to know. 'I'm glad it went well.'

Sienna looks at me, rolling her eyes. 'Something tells me that doesn't come as a surprise to you, Linzi. I just thought a little feedback was in order on this particular matter.'

I give her a wink. 'Enough said but I really, really appreciate it.'

'He has a bit of a way with him, doesn't he?' she replies.

'You mean Elliot?'

'Yes. Most people are a little wary of his direct approach. I've noticed that he's different with you, though.'

'Probably because we've spoken enough for him to know that I have no problem saying what I think.' Sienna narrows her eyes as I shrug my shoulders.

'No. It's not that. He's curious about you. Don't panic, he hasn't been asking questions, but he pulled a few staff files and the only one he hasn't returned yet is yours. It's still in his drawer.'

'It is?' It's hard to keep the surprise out of my voice. 'I guess everyone's position is under review.'

It would be wrong of me to break a confidence and tell her about the conversation I had with Thomas asking to keep him updated. I am, unwittingly, beginning to feel a bit like a spy in the camp, it's true. However, this affects us all, albeit some more than others. The phrase 'together we stand, divided we fall' comes to mind.

'Unless his interest isn't just work-based . . .' She throws that out there, waiting for my reaction.

That deserves a dismissive look. 'I seriously doubt I'm his type and he's definitely not mine. Besides, his girlfriend might have something to say if that were the case.'

'Do you know something I don't?' Sienna asks, pointedly. 'She's stopped bombarding me with messages for him, thank goodness. Isobel Weatherford is the sort of woman who doesn't expect to be kept waiting around. I still get the feeling that he's not returning her calls, so perhaps they've had a tiff.'

'That's a little unfair when the poor guy is being pulled in all directions.' I remember sitting in Elliot's office while he finished his phone call with Isobel. I heard him promising her that the next time he was in London he'd stay two nights. After that, he literally cut her short and I bet she didn't take that too well either.

'Whatever, I just thought I'd mention my casual observation, that's all. Sometimes opposites attract.'

'Enough! I'm going to pop something in the oven because I'm starving and you need to get off as your man is waiting.'

But as Sienna is about to walk out the door she stops, looking at me pensively. 'Whatever happened in the past . . . in Italy, being on your own is fine until it suddenly isn't. Trust me, I know that for a fact. What if one day you wake up and regret not putting yourself out there to see whether it's worth another shot?'

I walk over to give her a parting hug, smiling as I pull away. 'I know you're only looking out for me, but I'm better off on my own. My vines come first and they're a lot less trouble than a significant other.'

It's a good enough answer to satisfy Sienna, but as the door clicks shut the truth that I've been holding back for a long time is on the tip of my tongue. If I talk about it, it makes the longing return and I never want to put myself back in that position. Anyway, having had my heart stolen, it may never be my own to give again. As for Elliot, he's astute enough to know he needs his managers on board to push the changes through. He more or less admitted exactly that to me. His interest is in getting things set up so that he doesn't have to spend all of his time here. I can understand that, as it's tough to maintain a relationship at arm's length. As for me, well – trust must be earned and, it's sad to say, I don't trust easily anymore; that includes Elliot Montgomery until I know a lot more about him.

8.

How Much Does What You Don't Say Matter?

As a pleasant mid-week treat for my crew, I've persuaded my buddy and wine-tasting expert, Raffaele, to come along and do a talk. Sadly, they won't be actually sampling wine today, but he's in demand because of his passion and knowledge, so they're in for a captivating morning.

I'm spending the time at my computer in the Forestry Outpost. It's peaceful up here and it isn't long before Gwyn arrives. His desk might be covered in piles of paperwork, but if you ask for something he can always put his hand on it immediately.

'Early start for you today, Linzi. I saw you out patrollin' at six this mornin'. Great job you all did repairin' the damage on Monday, too.'

'Did you inform Elliot?' I check.

'Yep. I went straight up to tell him as I didn't want him to hear it from someone else. I commended Pryce for his quick thinkin'. Elliot will probably take a look for himself when he has a moment, I shouldn't wonder.'

Gwyn certainly sounds cheerful as I put my head back down, drafting out the schedule for next week. He noisily shuffles some papers and clears his throat, making me look up.

'Elliot made me a generous offer yesterday and I need to ask you a favour before I give him my answer.'

As Gwyn explains what Elliot and I discussed, a little wave of guilt courses through me. Will it change anything if I don't make Gwyn aware of my involvement? As it stands, he sounds like he's already made up his mind anyway. Which is a huge relief, as I really don't want to be put in a position of giving my opinion. That wouldn't be right.

'Elliot said the company's health plan will pay for the operation and afterwards I can come and stay at the vineyard until I'm back on me feet. The thing is, the few days that I'm not around, Pryce will need someone to keep an eye out for him. Watch his back like, so he can't get himself into any trouble. Would you do that for me?'

'Naturally, I will. If he gets stuck he can ring me at any time at all. Even if I'm teaching, I'll drop everything to give him a hand.'

'That means a lot to me, Linzi. This temporary promotion will come as a bit of a shock to Pryce, but we both know he deserves it.'

I could punch the air, knowing that with a bit of luck by the end of the summer Gwyn could be back to his old self.

'I'll be able to pop in to see you every lunchtime when you're convalescing.' I grin at him. 'Thomas will be utterly delighted when he finds out about it.'

Gwyn's smile fades a little. 'Now that's sorted, I still need to get someone to cover for me with Wendy's brother, but I'm thinkin' that's not a bad thing. He needs to consider whether it's time to go into a place with assisted care. Maybe this will make him reach out to his daughter because sellin' his home and movin' is a big deal at his time of life. I do my best to keep his house tickin' over, but it's gettin' harder with each passin' year.'

Gwyn sounds disappointed in himself, when he should be elated at the thought of being fully functional again.

'Don't feel guilty, Gwyn. You've done your best. If someone is seriously incapacitated it's a risk spending long periods of time on their own.'

'And he's a law unto himself. I found him up a ladder once, a shattered light bulb in his hand! He'd tried to unscrew it, but it was a bayonet type he'd had in there for years. To be honest, I don't know how much longer I could go on like this anyway.'

The look we exchange is one of acceptance.

'I'd be a fool to turn this down, Linzi, and I know it. If that's settled, I'm off to have a word with young Pryce and then, fingers crossed, it won't be too long before the old me is back and rarin' to go.'

Without thinking, I jump up and go over to Gwyn, throwing my arms around him. 'Good man!'

He pulls back, looking at me with a dour face. 'I don't do flowers. Just sayin'. . . '

To which I burst out laughing.

Three hours later, I'm making my way back to the cottage to have lunch, when my phone rings. I answer without looking, deep in thought about Sienna and Cam, who must be so excited about their viewings this evening.

'Hello?' I reply, sounding as jolly as I feel.

'Linzi, it's Mum.'

Like a balloon coming into contact with a sharp pin, immediately I feel deflated.

'What do you want, Mum?' I don't blame her for the falling-out, but for automatically taking Dad's side every time we butted heads. Even when I sensed at times she didn't necessarily agree with him.

'Your sister is getting engaged. We can't leave you out of the celebrations, Linzi, as if you don't exist. Juliette's partner, Ollie Richardson, is a lovely man and it's rather awkward because, naturally, he's expecting to meet you at the engagement party.'

'Is he, now?'

Mum heaves a sigh. 'I'm sorry for the way things have worked out. It broke my heart.'

And mine, too. But during my time in Italy there was hardly any communication between us and it more or less severed our ties. We were well over a thousand miles apart and our lives couldn't have been more different.

'Send me the details and I'll do my best.' My anger level is at a seven and I'm trying to keep a lid on it.

'Juliette is awaiting confirmation of the booking, but she said she'll send you an email with the details once it's settled, so you can put it on your calendar. If you don't turn up she'll be so upset.'

I bet she will. The sister who didn't respond to my last text, or email, and that was nearly a year ago.

'I've got to go, Mum, I'm at work.'

'We've all made mistakes, Linzi,' she blurts out. 'We're ticking over, but it's not the same without you in our lives, my darling. If you can find it in your heart to put that to one side to celebrate your sister's engagement, I'd really appreciate it.'

She said 'I', which probably means she hasn't told Dad that she's contacting me. That won't go down well when he finds out. Even so, it's too little, too late.

'I'll think about it.'

What should I be upset about first? Having been labelled irresponsible, or being cast aside as a failure? I can now see quite clearly that my father is a bully and always has been. The scorn he heaped upon me when I was at an all-time low was no less than I expected, because he made me feel worthless. Having learnt I'd had an affair with a much older man, he didn't know the circumstances. Sometimes things aren't quite what they appear to be. Heartbroken, suddenly uprooted and having to start all over again, being told I wasn't welcome at the home I was brought up in hurt. It was obvious that neither my mum, nor my sister, had forgiven me either. The truth is that I hadn't turned my back on them; I was on a personal journey of discovery.

My appetite has disappeared without a trace and instead

I wander outside to sit in the courtyard with a bottle of chilled water next to me. There's something so healing about the warmth of the sunshine and the sounds of nature all around me. It doesn't take long to shake off the anguish that hearing Mum's voice enveloped me with. It's usually me reaching out and suffering the indignity of rejection because Mum and Juliette don't want Dad to feel they're betraying him. In the end, that means they all betrayed me and that's not easy to forgive. But it's an embarrassment for them having a daughter they've cut off, and it won't be easy to explain away my absence from a big family celebration. I can't help feeling they don't want to lose face with our wider family and friends. So much for integrity, or honesty for that matter.

After spending most of yesterday working indoors, today we're working outside and, Sod's Law, it's raining. My crew and I will be putting up bird boxes and creating habitats for the local wildlife. One thing every gardener can't abide is the little rivulets of water that somehow find their way inside the waterproofs. And when you're working it can be hot and sweaty, too, so it's like being in a sauna until you ease up. Then it's plain old damp and miserable. But that comes with the job and I'm surprised we don't have any moaners among this year's trainees. In fact, there's a fair bit of banter as we spend the morning in the semi-shelter of the wood-cutting shed, with varying degrees of success.

'Remember, guys, if you drop a piece of wood down on the ground and come back a week later, when you turn it over all sorts of things will have made it their home – woodlice, earthworms, beetles, centipedes. Think simple,' I remind them.

Making my way back to the training room after lunch, I was hoping to cross paths with Sienna, but as I peer through the small window in the general office door I see that she's on the phone and has a stack of paperwork in front of her. The pressure is beginning to show. It's probably not a great time to fill her head with my family woes anyway, although now I fear I might have overreacted. Why is it that I always end up feeling I'm in the wrong?

After what turned out to be a productive and fun day, with the sun coming out just as we started our afternoon session, tonight sleep eludes me. Sitting out under the stars, surfing the internet, I'm conscious that everyone else is tucked up in bed when my phone pings, and I immediately turn down the volume. I'm shocked to see that it's a message from Sienna and I wonder why she's still awake, because it's almost one in the morning.

I can't sleep because I'm so excited and I noticed you were online. We're a right pair of night owls ha ha!

My fingers get clicking. I've been on edge all evening expecting her to call me and was a little disappointed that she didn't.

We'll regret it in the morning. I'm assuming the house viewings went well? Wanna give me a call? ☺

I wait anxiously, as she's typing.

Give me two minutes while I head downstairs. Cam and I were up until midnight talking and he's only just fallen asleep!

While I'm waiting I go back inside to make a quick cup of coffee. So many things are whirling around inside my head and it's not just the dilemma I'm in over what excuse to make to skip Juliette's engagement party. It feels like the world is shifting around me. I wasn't expecting to feel this unsettled but even small changes ripple outwards, shaking the foundations of my little world.

When my phone springs into life, I pop it straight on speakerphone.

'I'm just making a coffee as I've given up on contemplating sleep,' I moan.

'Me, too! What's keeping you up?' She sounds happy and wide awake.

'Realising I've become set in my ways. The thought of the changes that are coming is making me edgy.'

'You won't leave, will you?' Sienna's voice suddenly loses its sparkle.

'No, of course not.'

'Has Raffaele given up trying to entice you to join him at The Black Ridge Vineyard, then? You know his boss is hoping that one day he'll succeed in poaching you. Why do you think he jumped at the chance of coming in to talk to your trainees, if not to see for himself whether now is a good time to swoop? I half wondered whether that's why you called him in.'

The thought of Raffaele puts a smile on my face. 'All right, I admit that Raffaele's boss has made me another offer, but he knows I have no intention of moving on.'

'Phew . . . thank goodness for that, although I might be dropping a bit of a bombshell of my own on Elliot tomorrow. If you were going to leave I'd need to rethink the plan.'

I gulp. 'The plan?'

'Cam thought I'd fall in love with the first house we viewed. It was a new-build, three-storey townhouse. The entire top floor was taken up with the master bedroom, an en suite and the walk-in wardrobe of my dreams. And then there was the wild card.' Her voice immediately brightens.

'I assumed that both of the properties you were viewing were similar.'

'Cam was playing it crafty. The second one was a fixer-upper and the irony of the situation is that it blew us both away.'

'It did? But you aren't exactly DIYers, are you?'

'No, and to afford to gut it and turn it into our perfect

forever home means Cam will be spending more time working away to boost our savings. But we reckon six to nine months tops, and then he'll be able to ease back.'

'The wedding is on hold?' I'm shocked because that's a total turnaround for Cam.

'Yep and he's fully on board with that decision. He agrees that it's worth waiting because houses like this one don't come on the market very often. The owner went into hospital and sadly died a few months ago. It hasn't been updated since the eighties, can you believe? The bathroom suite is a lovely shade of avocado!' She laughs.

'Nice. They do say if you wait long enough everything comes back into fashion eventually, but you might have to wait a while for that particular trend to return. You said you'd be dropping a bombshell?'

I hold my breath in anticipation. She hasn't mentioned the location and the thought of her moving even further away is daunting. Sienna leaving on top of everything else is a scary thought.

'Cam wants me to go part-time. Not permanently, but one of us will need to be around to keep an eye on the work as it progresses. He says that even experienced builders will need constant input from us and if Cam is going to be away much of the time as he takes on jobs further afield to make more money, that responsibility falls to me.'

'How do you feel about it?'

She utters a little sigh. 'It's a big step for me to take but I'm rather excited. You know that I love my job and I'm also conscious that the timing isn't good from Elliot's point of view. I'm not sure whether it would be best to hand in my notice and find a part-time position somewhere else. That would suck, but Cam's making a huge sacrifice and I have to do the same because that's what couples do. If we succeed in getting the house, how do you think Elliot will take the news?'

Sienna is right, this is the most inopportune time. 'Well,

regardless of how he takes it, this is your future you're talking about. You've got to do what's best for you and Cam.'

'It's a huge challenge, Linzi, but we both feel it's the right thing to do. Cam is going to put in an offer later this morning, so I'll be a wreck until we hear either way. He's going in slightly under asking price, as every penny will count. We can come up a teeny bit but that's all. With a bit of luck, we'll know by late morning if it's ours. The estate agent told us they haven't had any offers on it yet and it's been on the market ever since the owner went into hospital, which means we're in with a chance.'

'Well, I'll be keeping my fingers crossed for you, Sienna.'

'The great thing is that it's only a ten-minute drive away and no motorway travel involved, unlike now. How on earth Cam can sleep, I have no idea.'

I stifle a yawn and it's catching.

'Uhhh,' Sienna mirrors me. 'My body is tired, but my mind is buzzing. The coffee is a mistake, isn't it?'

That makes me chuckle. 'I think we should both at least try to get a little sleep. Tomorrow is going to be an exciting one!'

As we say goodnight, it's obvious Sienna has too much on her mind for me to distract her. I'm still mulling over what to do about my sister's engagement party, but it's a decision only I can make.

Ironically, the conversation has stirred up other thoughts. Home is a sanctuary from the world and Sienna is really unhappy in the property they're renting. The thought of putting down roots means they're prepared to give up a lot to get what they want. I, on the other hand, have everything I need here. I'm already living in my perfect home, but how secure is it? I wonder. And what if something happens and I end up hating it here? My life is in Elliot's hands and that's not a great position to find myself in. The thought of going elsewhere is depressing, even just to The Black Ridge Vineyard. It's a big commercial operation, run by a group who have several vineyards around the world. That's not my style and I could never be truly happy there. Raffaele knows that too, because after our time together in Italy he understands what makes me tick. Even if I were tempted by his boss's offer, I have a sneaking suspicion he'd talk me out of it.

9.

Out of Sight but Not Out of Mind

As part of Pryce's new job description, Gwyn hands over the Friday morning session with my trainees to him. It's important they understand the basics about managing the hedgerows and boundaries. After the recent accident, it's also a great springboard for discussion as they've now seen the potential damage at first hand. We live alongside nature and a lot of what we do is as much to protect the animals themselves as it is the crops we maintain. When a deer jumps a hedge it doesn't stop to think about what's on the other side. And if there's a broken fence, all sorts of animals can wriggle through. It's a part of the job about which Pryce is well informed and has enough experience to answer whatever questions are thrown at him. I hope that it will also go some way to reassuring him that he made the right decision stepping into the new role. It's easy to take what you know for granted and I'm hoping this morning will serve to bolster his confidence.

It's not often I have the Forestry Outpost office to myself, which is great as it means I can whip through a lot of outstanding paperwork and place a few orders. But when there's a sharp rap on the door and it opens to reveal Michael standing there, frowning, my stomach turns over.

'Are you too busy to talk?' he asks, his tone subdued.

'No. It's fine. Grab a seat. I've been meaning to seek you out for a chat – it's been a while.' And it was remiss of me not to make it a priority, reading between the lines of the little Elliot has already told me.

He slumps down into the chair, and I hope it's only from the exertion of trekking up here. Something about his posture tells me that's not the case.

'Elliot is looking to pare back the budgets across the board.'

'Is his request unreasonable?'

Michael's immediate response is a dismissive wave of his hand. 'If he expects us to continue to deliver a five-star service, then I'd say yes.'

'That doesn't bode well.'

'I know how it looks on paper. The hotel is running well below capacity, but we're operating with just a handful of permanent staff, anyway. That's why our agency budget looks excessive. It's the only way to cover staff holidays and sickness, and a sudden influx of guests. It's not the cheapest way to handle it, but that was the way Robert ran the operation.' He sounds miserable and at the end of his tether.

I'm playing devil's advocate here. 'It must feel like it's a stab in the back. Your staff went that extra mile to keep everything running smoothly for our regular customers during a hectic phase in the expansion plans. On the other hand, it's a fine balance between making a profit and a loss.'

'Finance is Elliot's thing, I get that. Managing this place? It's more complex than it looks, you and I both know that. Do you trust in his ability to turn things around without it coming crashing down around us?'

Oh, how I loathe the word *trust*. Having experienced betrayal first-hand it's a question I struggle to answer. I got it wrong once and I could get it wrong again.

'Elliot has a lot to lose, Michael. It's a responsibility he's inheriting, so failure is not an option. What better motivation is there for someone to succeed?'

Michael takes a moment to consider my response before answering. 'That's a valid point. It's easy to forget he's a part of the family because he's a stranger to us all. But even that's a little concerning. If he knew from the start this was his future, why didn't he take a bigger interest in the business long before now?'

Michael is simply asking for my take on it. 'I think that's a question only Elliot can really answer. For what it's worth, I'm surmising that he wanted to prove himself in a different environment first. Having been successful in his own right, it must have been a tough decision to walk away from that and come here to start over again. No one expects to lose their father at such a young age and Elliot probably thought he had plenty of time before he was presented with the inevitable.'

The point is that when Thomas approached him he didn't say no, when he could so easily have done.

'Don't get me wrong, I respect the guy's business acumen and I like the fact that he won't put up with any nonsense. He's prepared to listen to well-reasoned arguments before making his final decision. Unfortunately, it didn't quite go the way I'd hoped, which means he doesn't have a choice. So, it seems that I have some tough decisions to make.' Michael heaves a heavy sigh.

'Is it really that bad?'

'It means losing one housekeeper and two part-time cleaners. I'm about to sit down with Quinn and look at the individual housekeeping schedules to see if we can organise things a little more efficiently. It's a long shot, but we have to give it a try. Cover for the front desk stays as it is for now. In the restaurant, Elliot is looking to trim two of the waiting staff. It'll be on a last in, first out basis, which means we'll lose Allan and James.'

I shake my head, sadly. 'I'm so sorry to hear that, Michael.'

'It's all under wraps for the time being.'

'You never know, Elliot might find another way around the problem.'

Michael glances at his watch. 'Hmm. Let's hope so. I'm due on shift shortly, so I'd best get back before I'm missed. Thanks for listening, Linzi.'

'Any time, Michael.'

As I watch him leave I hate to see him looking so dispirited. I can't even begin to imagine how tough this is for Elliot, either.

An email alert makes me grab my phone and my heart sinks a little when I see it's from Juliette. I can't deal with that now and I get back to work with a heavy heart.

Sitting across the table from Elliot in The Red Dragon Inn on a Friday night feels strange to say the least, but especially so as it's been a rather eventful week. What doesn't help is that I'm flagging after a sleepless night, followed by a long day tending the vines and listening to Michael's concerns. Add to that a tense, nail-biting morning culminating in Sienna and Cam having their offer accepted on the house, and I'm ready to switch off. Or I was, until Elliot waylaid me.

'Thank you for agreeing to meet me here for a drink, Linzi. I'm sure you're wondering why I wanted to meet up off-site.'

There's a hint of amusement in his eyes, as naturally I'm curious – the tension is mounting back at work and the constant round of meetings doesn't help matters.

'What with Gwyn's upcoming operation, Pryce's promotion and now the change in Sienna's personal circumstances, there's a lot going on. I'm assuming you're in the know about that?' he checks, and I nod my head. 'Anyway, I feel the timing of these unrelated changes is unfortunate. I just don't want the staff reading more into a meeting than there is, if you get my drift. If we're spotted in here you could simply be showing me the local inn.'

It's obvious everything at the vineyard is under review, but people's imaginings and fears are often much worse than the eventual outcome. It's in Elliot's best interests to manage both Gwyn and Sienna's circumstances, rather than risk losing them. It's not like he's shaking things up, but from the outside looking in it could appear that way.

'You're right, I think a little caution is in order. Is there anything I can do to help?'

The look of relief that creeps over his face is reassuring. 'There's no one I can really bounce ideas off right now so we're talking theoretically, not factually, if you get my meaning.'

In other words, it's off the record. 'Understood.'

'Managing the office is a wide-ranging role and if someone wanted to do a job share for, say, nine months, I'm not sure it would work. It's a key position.' This is about Sienna. He leans back, sipping his non-alcoholic lager with relish. I bet he'd love to change that for a pint of real ale but that's the price he pays for getting behind the wheel and not walking.

'It certainly is.'

'And there's no guarantee after that period things would revert back to normal.'

'But you've plenty of time to find the right person, which helps,' I reply, encouragingly.

'That's the problem. I'm told that things will probably be happening very quickly indeed.'

Now that's something I didn't know. 'Ah, I see.'

'Which would mean three of the four members of my management team have changes in the pipeline that will add additional pressures to their normal workload. You're the only one who is unaffected.'

Three out of four? So, his intention is to progress with the cuts to Michael's budgets, he's simply delaying the formal announcement. Michael is going to be gutted.

He's watching closely for my reaction, but I refuse to be drawn. 'That's unfortunate, Elliot.'

'I hope that it's business as usual for you now that Pryce is shadowing Gwyn.'

Is that his way of reassuring me the changes won't affect what I do?

'The nature of my job is that the seasons are the driver. It takes a lot to disrupt nature's routine,' I reply, drolly.

Elliot shifts position, as he settles back into his seat. He's not sure what exactly I've heard. He's nervous, though, and I notice he keeps glancing around, as if expecting to see someone from the vineyard walk through the door.

'You can relax. This is aimed more at families and the handful of staff working at the vineyard who live close by tend to look for more of a buzz when they're socialising.' The majority of our waiting staff have an average age of around twenty-three, at a guess.

'Thanks. Actually, it's nice to get away for an hour. To be honest with you, I'm finding it really hard to switch off. With everything on hand, there's no incentive to jump in the car and explore, even if I had the time and the inclination.'

'My car doesn't clock up many miles either,' I agree.

'Your family live close by?' He's looking less tense now and I can appreciate how difficult things are for him. Some people might think he was taking advantage wanting to talk business outside of working hours. And off the record. But I want him to succeed, because we've seen the alternatives, and so far no one has measured up to Robert, let alone Thomas. Elliot is definitely the best option, so any help I can give him is there for the asking.

'About an hour, but we're not close.'

'That's a shame,' he says, with sincerity.

Making polite conversation before you ask for a favour, which I'm sure he is, only works if you pick the right topics. With me it isn't family.

'It's not in my case. I'm the proverbial black sheep of the family.'

I can tell from his reaction that he thinks I'm joking. 'I seriously doubt that. It is good to get to know a little about the person behind the job title though.'

Is this about building trust, or getting me on his side? It's a difficult request to refuse, just not one I'm comfortable with, but given the situation I don't really have a choice.

'Fair enough. That works two ways, obviously.'

'Agreed.' His response is instant with no sense of hesitation whatsoever.

'My family are high achievers. My parents are university lecturers, and my sister is the youngest head of department in the school where she teaches. Then there's me. The university dropout who shocked everyone, not least my father. When I decided, instead, to travel the world, he was livid and said I'd let both myself and the family down. What he really meant was that he was embarrassed when his peers expressed their surprise that someone with such huge potential, as they put it, threw everything away. I wasn't born to be an academic, I'm afraid. It turns out I was born to spend my life growing things. The added irony was that I only got as far as Italy.'

His eyes haven't left my face and as a distraction I peer down at my glass, swirling the straw to mix up the berries in the refreshing summer fruits spritz.

'It must have been something very enticing to divert your plans to travel extensively,' he concludes.

'I fell in love with the vines and the sunshine. What more can I say?' Well, that's my standard response and I'm sticking with it.

'And now you're the keeper of the vines here in Wales and you gained your knowledge from one of the best, my grandfather told me. He said other vineyards have sought you out and yet they haven't succeeded in enticing you away.'

Now this is getting awkward. 'We're a tight-knit group and that's why staff turnaround is minimal. It's mainly the part-time waiting and housekeeping staff who come and go, although we do have a core of people who've been here almost as long as I have. The Green Valley Vineyard has a reputation for being a good and fair employer, thanks to your grandfather and then your father. Given the location, that's imperative.' I mustn't lose sight of the fact that Elliot is coming into this without necessarily understanding the problems associated with what is an idyllic, albeit rather remote, setting. He might not even be aware of the issues we have when it comes to replacing staff if they leave, which is a big concern for Michael.

'Please believe me when I say that I want to cause minimal disruption while sorting out a few of the problems.'

It's all about eye contact, and the man I'm talking to now is very different to the man I see in work. He's making an effort to gain my trust and it's a promising start.

'That's not easy to handle, I should imagine. And the reason why you need a strong team around you.'

'Precisely.' He nods his head, seemingly happy with how our little chat is going.

'It must feel strange to you, living in the hotel and not having a commute to work. You mentioned you'd be splitting your time between here and London once you get things sorted. Do you have a timescale in mind?' I ask, feeling it's a fair enough question.

'Hopefully before the end of the summer, but there's no firm cut-off date. My plans depend upon a number of different factors all falling into place.'

For some reason I instinctively glance at his left hand and Elliot catches me checking it out.

'It's not family reasons, just business interests. It's hard to sustain a meaningful relationship when you work long hours and business is your main priority. I saw that up close and personal with the constant battles it caused between my parents. I'm not at the stage where I can work nine-to-five and expect things to tick over, so it wouldn't be fair to pretend otherwise.'

Poor Isobel, she must really think a lot of Elliot to accept that. Maybe she's more of a *convenient* friend, off and on, although the fact that she's chasing him probably means there's more to it. At least from her point of view. I've never understood people settling like that. Why waste time being with someone if you know they aren't the ultimate one for you?

'Honesty is the best policy, but it's hardly a good opener for a first date,' I joke, feeling a little awkward. Then I realise he might think I'm implying tonight's little meet-up is a date. 'Um . . . when you do have time to . . . socialise.'

'I'm more the sort of guy who opens with "what you see is what you get and, sadly, I'm a workaholic". Maybe that's what comes of following in the footsteps of successful parents. It's both a blessing and a curse.'

Elliot is the only person I've spoken to who actually understands that. 'Tell me about it,' I groan. 'My father thinks I was rebelling because he placed a lot of expectations on my younger sister, Juliette, and me. She won't forgive me for grabbing my chance of freedom and, from her point of view, leaving her behind. Juliette was only fifteen when I upped and left, whereas I was three years older and obviously much more worldly,' I brag, laughing at my youthful, inexperienced self. It's painful to think about the past, but I suppose everyone has baggage of some sort to carry around.

'Our stories have a similar vein running through them, Linzi. It was always expected that I'd be involved in the family business. It was a severe blow to both my father and my grandfather when I graduated and entered the world of finance and investment. I love figures and to me they read more easily than a page of text. They tell a story and it's usually the truth, although there are ways and means of doctoring everything.'

Gosh, that's quite a statement to make. I'm intrigued. Elliot might have had the business handed to him, but I can appreciate his hesitation if running a vineyard isn't something he feels particularly passionate about.

'I have a couple of problems, Linzi,' he admits. 'Sienna is too good to lose but splitting her job and working with someone who has no history here is going to hamper my progress. She doesn't just manage the office, she's also my eyes and ears. She takes the pulse of the vineyard and reports back to me. It won't work if she's only around half of the week. If I suggest she takes on a lesser role, so that I can appoint a temporary full-timer in her place, I'd be no better off and she'd probably end up leaving.'

'Sienna is a real asset and well regarded, so how you deal with her request will likely be scrutinised.'

'I'm glad you understand that I'm trying to look at it from all sides to come up with the best solution.'

His level of honesty is reassuring, and I am a little flattered that he's taking me into his confidence.

'Look, Elliot, if you succeed we all benefit. I can't pretend to understand the business side of things, but I know the staff and I'm a good listener. As long as you're prepared to be fair and honest in your dealings with everyone, I realise there will be issues to smooth over. Whatever we discuss will go no further.'

The sigh that escapes his lips makes me wonder if he's been sitting there for a few moments holding his breath. 'Thank you, Linzi. I know how loyal you are to your trainees and the staff here, but being a good manager means setting aside emotions and looking at the facts. And you're right about Sienna. What I'll lose when she's not here is being able to ask a delicate question and get an honest and . . .' he pauses for a moment '. . . *reasoned* answer in return. That can only come with experience and knowledge of the history of the vineyard and the people it employs. As I don't have the benefit of that, can you be my off-the-record, go-to person? Just until things are running on a more even keel?'

That last statement grounds me. If the vineyard is in trouble then it affects everyone.

'You can count on me, Elliot.'

'That's much appreciated, Linzi. Knowing that I have you on my side means a lot. I need someone to be a calming influence if the overall perception is that too many changes are happening at once. As it turns out that's likely to be the case but it's unavoidable, I'm afraid. And I'm fully aware that I'm asking a lot of you when I've only just arrived. But if you ever need a favour in return – anything at all, as I have contacts everywhere – you only have to ask and it's done.'

Elliot's honest appraisal of the situation has won me over. Robert was fixated on expansion and yes, it did worry me at the time. Then when Thomas came back to pick up the reins again, he was never his old smiley self. My gut tells me something isn't quite as it should be, but it seems that Elliot is going to sort it out once and for all.

He's not the only one who is going to miss Sienna when she isn't around, I reflect. Let's hope her job share is with someone who can hit the ground running, because they're going to have a big hole to fill.

10.

Feeling Frazzled

It's been another difficult week and still there's no official announcement from Elliot. The days have flown by and yet another weekend is looming. A few more days and it will be goodbye July, hello August and everyone is wondering why Elliot is dragging his feet.

For the first time since I started here we don't feel like one cohesive team anymore at the vineyard, and little fractures are beginning to form. There's a lot of muttering and nervous eye contact as staff huddle together to talk about the rumours of job cuts.

In the midst of this, Sienna is walking around with a huge smile on her face, because Elliot has agreed to interview some candidates for the job share. And Gwyn, having seen the consultant, now has a date for his operation, which is only just over four weeks away. The effect it's had on him is uplifting to see, but the contrast in people's moods around me is getting difficult to negotiate.

On the other hand, Michael's shoulders are slumped and he's going around wearing a permanent frown. But just as worrisome is the fact that Elliot has been impossible to get hold of since Monday. He's hardly stepped outside of his office. Whenever I've tried to have a quick chat with him, Sienna points to the printout on her desk and he's either in an online meeting or his diary is blocked out and he's uninterruptible. Whatever he's dealing with is serious and Sienna, as I would expect, is saying nothing.

To make matters worse, one of the trainees tripped over and sprained his ankle and, quite frankly, although I'm working tomorrow the thought of not having to teach is a bonus. The day after Elliot and I met up at the inn, he sent an email asking me to come up with a plan to use some of the landscaped areas at the entrance for vines. He's very forward thinking and visitors entering the site will be impressed if the first thing they see isn't some pretty shrub, but grape vines. He said we'd catch up soon, as it was something he was keen to action quickly, but until I can get his approval for the plan I submitted, my hands are tied.

As for me, I still haven't opened Juliette's email and it's troubling me. Sienna has so much going on right now that I couldn't bother her with it, so I turned to Raffaele. He's a good listener, and as Italy was where our friendship began, he understands why it's a tough decision to make. His advice was that I should think long and hard about it because this is the first time Juliette has ever reached out to me.

I'm at a bit of a low ebb if I'm being honest with myself. Who knows for sure where things are going here at the vineyard? At one point this week I found myself wondering whether Elliot is avoiding me, but several people have noticed he's keeping himself to himself.

We all expected a period of transition, but this feels dire. Like our future lies in the balance and it's what we're not being told that's important. Elliot needs to gather the staff together and give us all an update, because morale is dipping, big time.

As I'm walking back to the car park after our Friday afternoon wrap-up in the Forestry Outpost, Sienna waves to attract my attention as she hurries over to her car.

'You were deep in thought there,' she muses, as we breach the gap between us.

'Yes . . . I was in a world of my own.'

Sienna makes a sad face. 'I wish I could stop for a chat, but Cam is waiting for me. We're going out to celebrate finding Ty Gwyn, our forever home.'

Sienna looks so happy I make a concerted effort to shake off my bad mood. It's not like anything in particular has gone wrong, but nothing seems right.

'The *White House*,' I exclaim, 'how lovely!'

'It is, isn't it?' Sienna gushes. 'Why don't you join us? I'll drop by and pick you up so you and Cam can both have a drink. It's about time you let your hair down. It'll be fun.'

I don't think I'd be good company tonight and I'd hate to put a downer on their evening. Casting around for an excuse that doesn't sound totally pathetic, I say the first thing that comes into my head. 'I can't I'm afraid. I have plans.'

Sienna draws in a sharp breath. 'Please tell me it's a *date*!'

Damn it, now I've piqued her interest and that wasn't my intention. 'No. I was thinking about a nice bubble bath, a glass of wine and lazing around reading a book.'

She pouts. 'You had me going there for a minute, Linzi. Seriously, you do need to get out more. If you change your mind give me a call. We won't be leaving until about seven-thirty, OK?'

'All right, but it's unlikely. Enjoy yourselves – a lot has happened in a short space of time, and that takes a little getting used to.'

Sienna leans in to give me a hug. 'I can tell that something is bothering you, my lovely friend. When you're ready to talk I'm here for you. It's not necessary to make excuses, not with me.'

I give her a sheepish smile. 'Thanks for understanding, Sienna. Now get off home. Cam will be wondering where you are.'

But when I arrive back at the cottage I'm not in the mood to cook. Instead, I shower, change and decide to take a leisurely stroll through the leafy lanes to my favourite country inn. Often, on a Friday evening, I'll grab a drink and my folding chair and wander down to sit among the vines. It's restorative, but tonight I'm too wound up to relax.

The Red Dragon Inn is renowned for their home-made pies, which they present on a wooden platter with a small bowl of triple-cooked chips. After placing my order at the bar, I settle myself down with a large glass of wine and my phone as I open the dreaded email.

Hi Linzi

We've been like strangers for so long, I'm not even sure what to say to you. How sad is that? But I'm getting engaged to the most wonderful man and we're having a summer celebration on Saturday, 17th August at Wendlesbury Manor House. It's an afternoon party and the invites are going out very soon.

I know you're probably rolling your eyes as you read this and already thinking up a suitable reason not to come, but there are things you don't know. When you reached out last year you had no idea what was going on, how could you? But trust me, it wasn't a time to sit down for a cosy, family chat. Maybe we're all at fault in our different ways but I genuinely believe it's time to heal the rift.

Mum said I shouldn't mention any of that, just ask you nicely if you'd do me a favour and attend. I told her that you've always done your own thing and you probably won't listen to my request. But no one knows what the future holds, and Ollie and I want all of our family and friends to share in our day. For me, that includes you.

My party won't be the same without you, Linzi. Everyone will want to know where you are and how you're doing. Which means that people still care. If you can't do it for me, please do it for Mum. She's suffered more than the rest of us and it will break her heart if you're not there. As for Dad, he doesn't get to decide who I invite.

My phone number is still the same if you want to chat.
And Ollie said to say 'hi' and that he's looking forward to
meeting you as Mum told him you'd be there.
Juliette x

Just as I flop back in my seat, bewildered because that's not quite what I was expecting, Elliot appears in front of me. He can tell from my composure that whatever I was reading has thrown me into a state of confusion.

'Are you feeling OK, Linzi?'

I nod, still unable to speak.

'I was going to ask if I could join you, but you seem . . . preoccupied.'

He hesitates and starts to turn away, but I draw in a deep breath and indicate for him to take a seat.

'It's fine. Really. Just family stuff. Please, it's a bit sad eating alone, isn't it?'

Slipping the phone into my handbag, I try my best to pull myself together as Elliot places his beer glass on the table and takes the seat opposite me.

'Rather, but you can just tell me to go away, you know. I'm not exactly scintillating company given the week I've had. And judging by the look on your face, that's a message you wish you hadn't read.'

The moment he finishes speaking I can see that he could kick himself. 'Sorry, it's none of my business, but I recognise the fallout from bad news.'

We pick up our respective drinks, and as our eyes meet over the tops of the glasses, I can see he's feeling as fed up as I am.

'It was an email from my sister. She's getting engaged. We haven't spoken in a long time and suddenly she wants to play happy families.'

Elliot pulls a face. 'Oh. That can't be easy. If you don't go you'll look like the one harbouring the grudge. And if you do, then it's hardly the occasion for speaking your piece, is it?'

He's said exactly what was going through my head. 'You must be a mind-reader.'

A smile tweaks at his lips. 'My father always said, "make friends, not enemies, even when they're the ones in the wrong" and it was good advice. Unfortunately, that applies to family as well as friends. As one black sheep to another, I know the score.'

Taking a second swig of my wine, I smile back at him. Maybe a little company is just what I need. It's a shame he's the boss, but I could do worse. Elliot is good company when he relaxes. A laugh echoes around inside my head. I bet there are plenty of women who would give anything to be sitting where I am right now. 'It's the same old story every time, isn't it? Are you eating?'

'Yes, but I'm sitting over there.' He points to the opposite side of the sprawling bar. 'When I spotted you I wasn't going to interrupt, but as I was returning to my seat I noticed that you'd gone very pale. I wondered if you felt faint, or something.'

That makes me chuckle. 'I'm not the fainting sort. That's more my sister.' It's ironic that we both chose to sit in a corner, slightly hidden away. I wave to the waiter, pointing at Elliot and he puts a thumb up. 'There's no point taking up two tables when one will do.'

'Thanks. To be honest, I'm a bit sick of my own company.'

We stare at each other, two lonely people who got themselves into this situation with no one else to blame.

'Me too.'

As if on cue, the waiter appears bearing two platters. If one thing is guaranteed to cheer me up, it's a hearty meal with chips.

'Snap.' Elliot looks at me, raising an eyebrow. 'Beef and ale pie?'

I nod my head, daring to pick up a chip and pop it into my mouth, even though it's fresh out of the fryer. It takes me a few moments to be able to swallow it, but it hits the spot. 'Yep. Comfort food. I walked, so I figure that by the time I get back I will have worked half of this off.'

'Same here,' he says, rolling his eyes. 'Living on the job isn't easy; it's hard to switch off at times. Everyone is nervous around me and that's understandable. Some things are taking a lot longer to sort out than I'd initially hoped. I don't want to rush a decision and live to regret it.'

That kills the conversation and we eat in silence.

Eventually, I put down my knife and fork, sitting back and feeling pleasantly full. 'I really needed that. And maybe another one of these' – I point to my empty glass – 'but I think I'd better have that back at the cottage. Are you having dessert?'

Elliot wipes his mouth on a napkin. 'No, I'm done. I really should head back as I have work to do.'

The last thing I need is to be left alone with my thoughts. 'I'm going to pass, too. Maybe we can walk back together and I can pick your brains. What I need is the perfect excuse to absent myself from this family party, and whatever I come up with will sound lame.'

'What if I asked you to go to Italy to do a little research? They couldn't argue with that.' His eyes light up.

'Italy is out of the question for me. Why?'

'What if we brought the whole process in-house, rather than just focusing on the growing?'

'I don't mean to be disrespectful, Elliot, but the term "running before you can walk" springs to mind.'

As the waiter approaches to clear our table, we both give him a nod of acknowledgement and stand, making our way to the door. Once we're outside, we set a gentle pace, and Elliot picks up where we left off.

'A research trip is out of the question?'

'Anywhere else and I might be tempted *if* I felt it was a good idea. Italy seems like another lifetime ago to me now. Anyway, the vineyard isn't ready for that sort of upheaval and it's a bit dramatic just to avoid an engagement party.'

'Then you don't really have a choice, do you, if you want to mend fences. In my experience, sometimes you have to grin and bear it. Then escape as soon as you can. Hopefully, it won't be quite as bad as you think it will. After all, it's a celebration.'

'It's just the thought of bumping into people I haven't seen in a very long time. I'm not sure how I'll cope with an endless stream of questions about what I've been up to. When they haven't been a real part of my life for so long, it's not easy to make small talk.'

As we walk side by side, Elliot kicks out at a stone, sending it skittering into a narrow strip of unkempt grass below the hedgerow and startling a rabbit. It streaks off down the road, its white tail bobbing around before it disappears out of sight.

'Poor thing, he's probably heading straight for the vineyard to get his own back,' Elliot remarks, drolly. 'Serves me right for being thoughtless.'

'The longer you're here, the more it'll open your eyes to what's all around you. The insects that are everywhere and not always seen, the bird nests you stumble upon where you least expect them. The snails who appear from nowhere overnight and munch their way through the juiciest of leaves. Moles, pheasants, badgers . . . you're never alone in the countryside.'

'I guess my training is only just beginning.' He gives me a rueful grin.

We continue walking and after a few minutes Elliot breaks the silence.

'Do you ever grab a drink in the bar at the vineyard?'

'Occasionally, but usually only on my days off and rarely during the summer months when I'm teaching.'

'The course is a nice little earner for the vineyard and kudos to you, as I hear it's always oversubscribed.'

Nothing relaxes me more than a walk and I'm sensing that it's having the same effect on Elliot.

'I was reluctant at first, but it saves recruiting casual staff during our busiest time of the year. As trainees, they're rarely out of my sight because they're eager to learn.'

Elliot looks impressed. 'I hadn't considered that angle. We save on the salary budget and at the same time you don't unleash them until you're happy they know what they're doing. Whose idea was it?'

'Thomas's. I'll be honest and say that I took some convincing, but I'm picky who I take on and I interview each candidate before offering them a place.'

'Did you get time to give any thought to my email? The entrance is attractive, but it's not the flowers our visitors come to see.'

'I did, and I sent you a detailed plan. Didn't you get my reply? It will take about a fortnight if I get my crew on it for a couple of hours each day. That won't be too disruptive to the rest of our schedule, and we have pretty much everything we need to get it done, which is handy.'

'Sorry, my inbox is overflowing. I know you'll do a great job so start it whenever you want.'

'But you haven't actually looked at my proposal yet?'

Elliot's gaze meets mine as I glance at him quizzically. 'If you're happy with it, then so am I.'

My eyes widen in surprise.

'Is there any reason why I shouldn't trust your judgement, Linzi?'

'Oh, none at all, but Thomas was always very particular about the planting. Your father . . . not so much, but he never signed anything off without a walk-around.'

'No,' Elliot replies, his voice suddenly changing and becoming more serious. 'My father was obsessed with a different sort of vision and it is amazing, but at what cost?'

I don't think he's actually talking to me, but to himself. The truth is that Robert put himself under pressure because of his obsession with transforming the vineyard into a hotel complex. It's not my place to point that out, or that it was at odds with Thomas's dream when he was in charge. Thomas wanted to focus on increasing production, and it saddened me that Robert didn't run with that idea.

As we walk through the gates and make our way along the path to the reception, we slow our pace and come to a stop where we are about to go our separate ways. It's an awkward moment and he seems reluctant to say goodbye. We end up standing back as a large party of diners arrive, laughing and chattering away noisily.

'Do you fancy a cup of coffee?' I ask, feeling obliged to do so.

'That would be great. Getting back to my desk isn't that appealing, and it was a mistake having such a heavy meal.'

I dig into my bag to find my key and he follows me inside. I automatically slip off my shoes; he goes to do the same.

'You might want to keep them on if we're going to have coffee outside,' I remark.

'No, it's fine by me if you don't mind bare feet.'

I glance down, smiling as he slips off his deck shoes and wriggles his toes. It's strange seeing him in blue jeans and a T-shirt, and as I raise my eyes, he's smiling at me.

'We seem to be colour-coordinated.'

We are. Denim and pale blue, although my T-shirt isn't a designer one. The decal says 'Weeds are plants, too'.

It breaks the ice quite nicely as we pad through to the kitchen and, as I pop on the kettle, I encourage Elliot to make himself at home in the garden.

When I join him, he looks comfortable lazing back in one of the rattan chairs, a leg resting on his knee. 'This really is a nice little spot. Very private and colourful,' he remarks, as he gazes around. 'Were these pots your idea?'

'Yes. Here you go, help yourself to sugar.'

'I feel bad encroaching on your time yet again.'

'It's not a problem. I'm just surprised you're not on your way to London for the weekend.'

He furrows his brow. 'My focus is on this place right now and I need to knuckle down. Everything else can wait.'

It's a fair enough answer, but I'm sure that news didn't go down well.

'It's a pity you can't find the odd hour here and there to tag along on some of the training sessions. I think it would be insightful,' I offer, constructively.

'I know, and I am defaulting on my promise to Thomas on that score, but it's a luxury I can't afford quite yet, I'm afraid.'

'I'm working tomorrow and I'm around on Sunday if you get any spare time.'

He inclines his head, obviously interested by my offer. 'What, and feel guilty for taking up even more of your time?'

I've been dreading Thomas getting in touch to ask how Elliot's training is going. I can't lie and say Elliot is making time for it when he isn't. It's not a criticism, as the poor guy has been working solidly.

'No pressure, but you might be glad of a little break as an excuse to get out and about,' I dare to suggest.

'Then I might just take you up on that offer, Linzi.'

'It wouldn't do any harm for the staff to see you out in the vineyard getting hands on.'

His brow lifts. 'Good point! And it is overdue. I am interested, you know. Please don't think that I'm not and, hopefully, before too long I'll have time to tag along. Even the trainees will be able to teach me something, I'm sure.'

He's a man with a lot of pressure on his shoulders and it shows. Is it just what he's inherited, or do some of his problems lead back to his affairs in London? I can't help wondering whether it's personal, or professional. I guess he has a ready-made excuse if he wants to avoid someone.

In one way I'm grateful to Elliot for a little distraction this evening, and already I've decided that I don't have to answer that email straight away. Left to my own devices, I might have dashed off a reply when I was fired up and feeling not in the least forgiving. Reading between the lines, it's more about Juliette wanting the attention to be on her and Ollie, rather than answering awkward questions because of my absence. Fair enough, it's her party, but if I attend does she really expect me to pretend everything is sweetness and light? After all, we're such a successful and caring family. Ha! That's only true if you fit the mould and, clearly, I still don't.

As Elliot puts down his empty coffee mug, he shifts uneasily in his seat.

I stand. 'Can I interest you in a beer? I'm going for my second glass of wine this evening. And it's going to be a large one this time.'

'Hmm . . . work . . . or a beer. Tough choice. It would be rude of me to refuse, wouldn't it?' Elliot's smile lights up his entire face, as if he was sitting there thinking that if I didn't make the offer he ought to make a move.

They do say it's lonely at the top, and that was very evident with Thomas. At least he found a little peace and contentment wandering among the vines, but I often wondered whether in hindsight his dream didn't turn out quite the way he'd expected. Personally, I think it's a mistake for Elliot not to head back to London, and Isobel, for a wonderful weekend so that he could return refreshed on Monday morning.

Anyway, the least I can do is be hospitable as there's a split in the camp. Those who think Elliot is being proactive, like Sienna and Gwyn, and those who are waiting for the axe to fall, like Michael. Me, I'm definitely in the middle.

11.

Keep Calm, Stay Focused and Everything Will Be Just Fine

I love working on a Saturday because it reminds me of when I first arrived here. Naturally, it was a much smaller set-up way back then. Nowadays, I rarely get to spend the entire day outdoors, which is a real shame. But on occasions like this, even quite strenuous activities feel more like pottering as I'm working to my own agenda, with no one else to consider, and that's bliss. No constant stream of questions, no sudden panics, and my phone is silent.

After my conversation with Elliot last night, this morning I'm making a start on pegging out areas around the entrance to the vineyard complex where the vines will be planted. There's a lot of cutting back to be done first, but some of the smaller shrubs can be transplanted to add a little extra interest to part of the forest trail.

I wave as Michael's car approaches. He pulls to a halt alongside, lowering the window.

'Morning, Linzi. There's a bit of drizzle in the air, do you think it will come to anything?'

'Hi, Michael. No, it won't last long. It's just enough to freshen everything up. We had the worst of it in the early hours, I think. My fleece is hardly damp.'

He shakes his head, smiling. 'All winds and weathers, eh? What's the plan here? It looks serious.'

'It's Elliot's idea. He thinks our customers should be greeted with a show of healthy, burgeoning vines intermingled with a few flowers. I have to agree with him, as that's precisely why they come here, isn't it?'

'It's a good idea. That's quite a bit of work though.'

'My crew is going to love getting stuck into this on Monday, but we'll spread it out over a couple of weeks. I'm conscious that this is peak holiday season and if we tackle a small area at a time we can still keep it looking presentable. It's early for you – I didn't think you were working today?'

'I'm not. Well, not officially, but I want to grab a couple of uninterrupted hours out of sight.' His eyes widen as he sighs. 'Just between us, Elliot has asked me to see if I can renegotiate better terms with the laundry company we use. He's expecting our occupancy to increase quite rapidly once the campaign is fully underway.'

I give him a sympathetic look. 'What sort of timescale are you talking about?'

'The first advertising feature hit the shelves last week and is being promoted on social media, so we're just seeing the impact of that. The agency is testing different publications over the next two months and will monitor the results. I only intend on staying for a couple of hours and then I'm off to the Gower coast with the family. We have a static caravan close to the beach and it's a great way to unwind. Are you doing anything special tomorrow?'

I shift my gaze, fidgeting with the tape measure in my hand. 'No.'

'Have you given up on the ramblers' club?'

'They're going further afield now and often stay somewhere overnight. It's not for me. I'm doing some repotting in the courtyard of my cottage. Well, that's the plan, but if it's hot I'll be lazing in the shade reading a book.'

Michael gives me a knowing look. 'Well, have fun and I'll see you on Monday.'

As he pulls away I wince, remembering the day my stalker, Karl, turned up here. Gwyn and Michael ended up escorting him off-site in full view of everyone. When he joined the rambling club Karl seemed quite normal, until he began focusing his attention on me. I'm friendly to everyone I meet, but he wouldn't take no for an answer.

It still gives me the chills, as it was obvious he was watching me. All those hours just waiting for me to take a trip into town and suddenly he'd appear, asking if I wanted a coffee. To his mind, a single woman on her own was fair game and his persistence ended up causing a huge ruckus. I most certainly wasn't playing hard to get, as he threw back at me rather caustically the day Gwyn banned him from the vineyard.

But what it has done is push me back into my shell, and even though I mentioned starting a new hobby to Sienna, I might let that slide for a bit. I thought I was safe with the ramblers, as it was a broad age range. However, there are a lot of thirty- and forty-something singletons out there who don't do dating agencies, but regard recreational pursuits as a great way to meet someone. That's fine if they don't assume that everyone else is in the same boat.

Right, it's time to chop up some of the logs on the wood pile to make a few stakes. And the drizzle has stopped on cue. I'm only a little damp, so I guess I won't need to head inside for a coffee and to dry off after all. It's time to clear my head and get wielding that axe.

What I love about my life is that I'm free as a bird. I might not want to spread my wings, but at least I'm not caged in by anyone, or anything. It's true that The Black Ridge Vineyard's offer doesn't tempt me at all, but it's not the only interest I've had recently. A small operation in France is hoping to expand its team, and they've reached out to me. I don't intend on going anywhere, but it's comforting to have a backup option. Just in case. There's a lot riding on Elliot's shoulders, and as the days pass, I'm beginning to wonder whether he can, in fact, handle it. And by the sound of it, Michael feels much the same way.

* * *

I force myself to stop for a quick lunch at the cottage, and as I'm on my way back out, my phone lights up.

'Good afternoon, hope all is well with you!'

'Thomas, it is, thank you. How's the road trip going?' As pleased as I am to hear his voice, my heart begins to sink as he's obviously calling for an update.

'We're looking out over Loch Lomond and marvelling at the fact that we can get a signal.'

Great, but I sincerely hope he called Elliot first to check in with him. 'It must be a bit of a relief and I suspect you'll be there a while making calls.'

'No, Katherine would throw a fit if she knew I was even talking to you. She's off ordering us a late lunch, so I'd best be brief. I'm assuming everything is ticking over at that end?'

The real question here is why is Thomas avoiding his grandson? 'Yes. There's a lot going on, naturally.'

'Ah . . . is there any news about Gwyn's operation?'

Well, at least he has now spoken to Elliot at some point.

'Yes, it's scheduled for Tuesday, the twenty-seventh of August, and Pryce rarely leaves his side these days. They'll both be ready when the time comes. Have you heard about Sienna?'

'No,' he asks, cagily. 'Problems?'

'Her circumstances have changed and she's going part-time. Probably for about nine months.'

Thomas's response is one of surprise. 'She's having a baby?'

'No. She and Cam are buying a house and doing major work to it. He'll be working away even more than usual and Sienna has to step up and manage the builders.'

'Good grief! Are there any other unexpected shocks I'm not aware of?'

Awkward. Elliot is obviously worried about finances, but I can't repeat that as Michael is sharing information with me because we're friends. And while Elliot is combing the figures, it would be wrong of me to assume it's the root of his problems. 'I doubt there's anything that Elliot hasn't already mentioned.'

Thomas grunts. 'He leaves messages but we've yet to have a proper conversation. Katherine doesn't want me influencing him unduly, whatever that means. My intention is only to guide him. What I want to know is whether he's asking you the right questions, then I can relax.'

Eek. Here we go. 'We've had a number of discussions and I'm making myself available whenever he can find the time. Obviously, he's holding a lot of meetings at the moment but that will hopefully begin to taper off very soon.'

'Good. But if you have any concerns get in touch. If I can't pick up immediately, I'll get back to you as soon as I can. Well, when my darling wife is out of earshot.'

'Are you enjoying yourself, Thomas?'

'It's lovely having so much time with Katherine, Linzi. When I retired the first time around I was constantly back and forth to the vineyard. It makes me feel guilty for all the years she wanted to do a trip like this one and I kept putting it off because of work. And now it's no longer my problem, I'm just grateful she stuck with me. Some wives wouldn't have put up with it.'

He's changed his attitude and some. This isn't delegation, it's abdication and that's a little worrying. Thomas must know that there are things going on in the background of which I'm totally unaware. What is puzzling is why Katherine can't understand he's going to be a little on edge suddenly being out of the loop.

'Well, enjoy every moment, Thomas, because you both deserve it.'

'And are *you* happy with the way things are going, Linzi?'

'The vines are doing well and we've had enough rain in between some gloriously sunny days to keep everything looking luscious. The restaurant is really busy, too.'

'And the hotel?' So, he is aware that Elliot has his work cut out for him.

'They've just kicked off a huge advertising campaign. Apparently, it's targeting the glossy country magazines with an aim of filling the hotel over the Christmas and New Year period. Hopefully it will be a bumper festive season.'

'It sounds like everything is in hand and I'm worrying over nothing. I'd love to chat but I'm pushing my luck staying on this long. If Katherine steps out the door of the café and catches me, I'll be in her bad books for the rest of the day. Thanks for talking to me, Linzi. I can tell you aren't totally comfortable, but for me it's the little bit of reassurance I need.'

I find myself biting my lip nervously because he's right. 'And Katherine is right to protect you, Thomas. A heart attack is a wake-up call, you know.'

He scoffs. 'It was only a mild one, but point taken. My darling wife is following the doctor's orders to a T and she said this holiday is just the start. Anyway, have a lovely weekend, my dear. I do so miss wandering around the vineyard with you. It was always the highlight of my day. Take care!'

If Elliot continues to take me into his confidence to help his agenda, this is going to get tricky with Thomas. It's not really fair on me and at some point I might have to address the issue. It's a pity the two of them can't talk openly and honestly to each other, but I can fully understand Katherine wanting to protect Thomas, given the scare he had about eight months ago. But her grandson, too, is in need of . . . not so much support or guidance, but explanations, I suppose. Having increased the size of the hotel accommodation so dramatically, why on earth didn't they start advertising as the build was coming to an end?

And then a cold sensation hits me square in the gut. Was Thomas's heart attack brought on by worry about what he found when he took back control after Robert's death? Is that the real reason he talked Elliot into getting involved?

I feel dazed and dispirited. I can only hope that I'm wrong, because if I'm not, then Thomas might have more than one reason to avoid a frank discussion with Elliot. Perhaps the news is so bad that he can't face it, or he knows his heart won't take it. That's a truly horrible thought, which I instantly dismiss.

Sleep comes in waves, interspersed with a troubled dream that won't seem to let me go. There's some sort of emergency that I can't get to the bottom of, but I know if I don't then all is lost. In the end, I awake in a cold sweat just before five o'clock, and pull on some leggings and a fleece. The vines are calling to me.

Despite the intermittent birdsong all around, there's a general sense of stillness in the air. I stroll down through the long row of vines, tuning in to what feels to me like a constant, low hum. It's like a pulse, the pulse of the earth. The scent in the air is fresh and sweet, it's the smell of luscious green leaves as the sugary sap rises up from the roots buried in the rich soil, to feed the new growth.

As I kick off my shoes, the grass is a little damp beneath my feet and suddenly I feel that connection move through my body. This is all that matters. People come and go; life's problems come and go, but nature is the one true constant.

I sit cross-legged beneath one of the vines, placing a hand over my heart. As I close my eyes and relax, my mind is flooded with bright colours. Vibrant greens turn to electric blues and it's a living tapestry. I see a curtain of raindrops that fade as quickly as they appear and then brilliant sunshine makes me squint. When I open my eyes, dawn is beginning to break. I watch as a rabbit skitters across in front of me and I smile to myself. I hold up my arms to the sky and then fold them across my body, saying a silent thank you for the start of a brand-new day. I feel renewed, but it's not enough to totally banish the little worries.

My Sunday mornings are indulgent. By now, I know the best time to sneak into the restaurant is before the guests, and I like to sit and read the papers after I've eaten.

To say that I'm pampered is an understatement. I have my favourite table overlooking the vineyard, which is an area that isn't usually open during the breakfast sitting. And our weekend staff know exactly how I like my coffee and that I enjoy a second cup once I'm done eating. Today, though, I'm sitting here wondering about the future, and niggling little doubts I would have instantly dismissed a week ago now seem to be growing.

When Thomas called me in for that talk before he left, he wasn't being totally honest with me and I'm gutted about that. He said that with Elliot coming in there would be no worries on the financial front and that was crucial at this stage in the development of the vineyard. How could he have been so wrong?

'Is there anything else I can get you, Linzi?' Bethan works on Reception Monday to Friday and does an early shift in the restaurant on Sundays because she's saving for her wedding.

'I'm fine thanks, Bethan. How are things with you?'

'Antonio and I have finally set a date. The twenty-first of December.' Her eyes are sparkling as she shares her news.

'How lovely – a winter wedding! Where are you holding it?'

'It's my dream destination. Sadly, it will be a small wedding party. Just grandparents, parents, my brother and his wife, Antonio's younger sister and six of our closest friends. You won't have heard of it, even though it's a big resort and spa. It's called Cristallo and it's in Bellini, only two hours from Venice. It's been a favourite destination for Italian high society for many, many years and Antonio's parents held their engagement party there.'

'It sounds idyllic and what a wonderful family connection,' I reply, as I glance at the clock on the wall and then push back on my chair. 'It's a lot later than I thought. Well, I'm thrilled for you both, Bethan. Now you have a date and a venue you're officially on countdown!'

She's already clearing the table, but the smile on her face tells me her fairy tale will be coming true. It takes a lot to hold in the emotions that are beginning to tear me apart and even before I reach the Forestry Outpost I'm battling to control random sobs. Is life being purposefully cruel to me? I question angrily, as I stare up at the sky. As soon as I unlock the door and step inside, the tears come thick and fast. I sink down into the chair, laying my head on the desk.

My mind wanders back in time to the day of the Leone family's big wedding. When the daughter of such a renowned vineyard owner gets married, everyone is invited. Vanna Leone became Vanna Valenti, and two esteemed families were joined together. No one worked that day, and we were all excited because Bethan is right, Cristallo is a very special place indeed. Little did I know that it would be a day I would never, ever forget for reasons of my own. It was the day I learnt the shocking reason why Umberto's wife – his daughter Vanna's mother – wasn't in attendance.

Late in the evening, I discovered Umberto sitting alone in an old stone alcove taking in the panoramic view of the Dolomite Alps. He invited me to join him – after all, we'd worked together five days a week for a little over four years and he was probably expecting me to gush about how perfect the day had been. And it was – perfect – until I blurted out the fact that I was in love with him. I feared that he might laugh at me, or get angry, but instead he grew silent. I saw that he was unable to speak, and my heart soared. It was the beginning of a year of total enchantment and yet I think a part of me also knew that it was the beginning of the end.

It helps to sob. All those pent-up emotions I keep pushing away don't seem to diminish with time. True love never dies and that's a tragedy when it's not returned. Umberto was my first lover, and I thought what we had was real, until one humid, rainy day he told me that it wasn't.

A rap on the door sends me into a panic and I jump up, swiping at my face and turning away as if I'm reaching out for a file from one of the shelves behind my desk.

'I did call out, but you were a long way ahead of me and you walk fast,' Elliot says.

Squaring my shoulders, I reluctantly turn around and when he sees my blotchy face, he looks aghast.

'Oh, Linzi. I beg your pardon; I seem to make a habit of interrupting you at inopportune moments. I can see now is definitely not a good time.' Being a gentleman, he turns to go, but stops for a second to catch my eye. 'If there's anything I can do to help, you only have to say.'

I sniff, determined to pull myself together and salvage whatever dignity I have left. 'It's not as bad as it looks. No one died and I'll survive. It's quiet up here at weekends.' I give him the warmest smile that I can muster given the circumstances, and his eyes scan my face.

Elliot steps forward and, to my horror, I wonder whether he's going to reach out and touch me. I don't want pity, and certainly not from my boss, even if it is well meant. I've learnt the hard way that it's easy to misinterpret empathy for something more meaningful.

'Well, I am genuinely sorry to have disturbed you,' Elliot replies, awkwardly.

Then I remember the invitation I extended to him on Friday night.

'If you're at a loose end, do you want to take a wander? You haven't inspected the repairs after the deer incident yet.'

He raises an eyebrow. 'Is it something that's expected of me?'

'Let's say it's usual practice.'

'Oh.' He looks at me apologetically. 'That sort of went over my head, I'm afraid.'

'Let's do it now. You can pass on your comments on the sterling job to Gwyn tomorrow,' I inform him rather tactfully.

'Look, I really am sorry for barging in. Maybe another time, Linzi.'

'It's not an imposition,' I reassure him. 'Let's take a leisurely walk-around.' I reach out to open the desk drawer and pull out a tissue and a hair toggle. 'Let's go,' I say brightly.

While I scoop my hair back and pull it up into a ponytail, Elliot opens the door and steps outside. I quickly blow my nose then mutter a long, low rumbling 'argh' to shake myself up before I join him. The look on his face tells me he's not sure what's going on.

'That's better,' I say, breezily. 'Right, let's amble down through the top field and I'll show you how to pinch out a growing tip. Then you can inspect the new gate.'

He nods, keenly. 'Do I get to hear you whispering to the vines?'

I give him a stern look. 'That's like asking a musician if you can watch while he's composing something new. It's a one-to-one experience with nature, I'm afraid. And never walk among the vines if you're feeling negative, it's bad karma.'

'Is that why you—'

'Vented? Yes. It's not often I get upset like that, but I was caught unawares. I'm angry with myself for letting something trivial rake up an old memory, that's all.'

'Strangely enough I know exactly what you mean. It's hard for me to be here and not think about my childhood. In a way I'm glad so many things are different, but I keep getting flashbacks.' His expression is enough to tell me not all of the memories are good ones.

'But it must have been fun having this as your playground,' I comment.

'Oh, it was on occasion, but mostly it was simply a case of doing as I was told. My father saw everything in life as a learning opportunity not to be wasted.'

'Even when you were just a child?'

He begins chuckling softly to himself. 'I remember one time when he was here chopping logs with Granddad. I had this cart I used to drag around for fun, as kids tend to do. My father got me to load it up and left me to move quite a big pile of logs closer to the house. The original one, that is, when it was little more than a farmhouse.'

Elliot's face is animated now, as he thinks back.

'I was probably eight, maybe nine, years old and that was before the forest had the defined pathways I see now. The team was still thinning out the trees and there were roots everywhere. The two of them went off to do something else and left me to it. A couple of hours later, I was still struggling with my first load and only halfway there. When my father saw me he laughed, and it wasn't good-naturedly. He said only I could push a cart and make it hard work. He said, "Don't you even know enough to drag it behind you, Elliot? You'd better start using that brain of yours, my son." It was something I never forgot, but for all the wrong reasons.'

I'm appalled to think how crushing that must have felt to Elliot; a child needs nurturing and encouragement, not constant put-downs. It's that *toughen-up* attitude that can harden someone at their core, teaching them that life hurts less if you detach your emotions. It could be one of the reasons why he's such a successful businessman, but it's sad to think it might affect his romantic relationships, too. 'Kids learn by getting it wrong. Was he always that hard on you?'

'Pretty much. I was a bit of a bookworm, not really sporty in any way, and really skinny for my age. Climbing trees and being adventurous wasn't my thing and I hated getting dirty, which is why I didn't enjoy coming here. I always knew I'd be given a task and I'd probably mess it up. But Grandma made the best cakes and she'd often walk up and ask if I was hungry. Any excuse to rescue me for a little while. I'd end up with my head in a book, getting a sugar rush.' There's a nostalgic smile on his face that is touching to see.

'Don't let those memories put you off. Look around and what you see now is the result of a lot of love that has been poured into this place. It's lush and bountiful and the hotel and restaurant complex is something else.'

'If my father could have loved people as much as he loved this place, both my mother and I would have had much happier lives. What grates on me is that everyone sings his praises . . . Robert this, Robert that. They don't know the mess he made of so many things. He was the one who drove himself into the ground and he could still be here if he'd made better decisions. It sounds scathing but his dream wasn't what Granddad intended. And now I'm stuck with it. But, thankfully, while I know nothing at all about vines, pretty much everything else I can sort. Assuming I can call in some favours.'

I'm shocked at a real sense of bitterness attached to Elliot's words and my heart constricts for him. How long has he been bottling this up? Has it helped talking to me, or simply raked up emotions I'm not sure Elliot is equipped to handle? It's a depressing thought.

12.

Making a Connection

With Elliot a pace or two behind me, I slow to a halt, reaching out to tenderly lift a bunch of tiny grapes the size of pips. Before too long these will start to swell and each day will see a marked difference.

'Look at these little beauties. This is what it's all about, Elliot,' I remind him. 'This sucker here has sprung up almost overnight and it needs to be pinched out. We want all the goodness to go to the fruit, and the rain and the sunshine will do the rest. It's simply a case of giving the grapes enough leaves to provide a little shade and protection. I'd feel proud to own a vineyard like this and stand here seeing row upon row of vines as far as the eye can see. It's quite an achievement and something I don't think you fully appreciate.'

He's deep in thought. 'You're probably right. My walk-arounds have been few and far between. It's something I must remedy. There's a sense of tranquillity out here away from the buzz of the other side of our operation.'

Elliot still isn't getting it. 'Close your eyes and take a deep breath in.'

His eyes widen disconcertingly, but at least he does as I ask. 'Now what?'

'Think about what's different out here. What do you smell? How do you feel? Reach out and touch the grapevine.'

He opens his left eye, cautiously. 'What if I crush something, or snap off a bunch of minuscule grapes?' Now he's laughing at me.

'They belong to you, so what does it matter?'

With both eyes closed he takes a few moments to focus on his surroundings. 'They might belong to me, but you are the keeper of the vines, Linzi. In my hands they'd probably wither.'

'Hmm . . . maybe, but I'm determined to remedy that. Now gently explore the plant with your fingertips. It helps if you slip off your shoes and your socks.'

'What is it with you and this barefoot thing?' Elliot might be having a little moan, but his eyes are still closed.

I stifle a giggle as I didn't mean for him to keep his eyes closed when he was taking off his footwear. I don't want to make him feel awkward by pointing that out, so I close my eyes and do the same in case he's squinting at me. We stand together just living in the moment.

After a few minutes, I'm unable to resist peeking at him. I watch as he tentatively reaches out. His touch is surprisingly tender and respectful. He almost winces when he discovers a cluster of tiny fruits and his fingertips simply airbrush over them. Then he finds a large sucker that has a couple of days growth to it. 'I think this should come off,' he remarks, confidently.

'Then run your fingers down to the point at which it springs from the main stem and gently nip it off. Drop it on the floor.'

'On the floor?'

'Yes, the rabbits will come along and have a chomp. If you notice, we allow a few weeds to grow around the base of the plants. Some self-seeding native plants and grasses give a little shade to the roots, but also feed local wildlife. We still cut the grass strips dividing up the rows, but if I had my way we'd have sheep naturally mowing it for us.'

'Why?'

'Because nature provides for its own and who are we to disrupt that?'

His eyes spring open. 'This is the ethos my grandfather wants me to get on board with. Having talked to several vineyard owners in the past couple of weeks, this isn't the cheapest and most productive method, is it?'

'No, it isn't. But don't underestimate the hidden costs of using chemical-rich products. Not least soil contamination and, as the land slopes away, when it rains the run-off leads straight into a natural water source. That wouldn't be good for the animals grazing in fields on the other side of it. Do you really want our guests eating meat from sheep ingesting pesticides?'

Elliot frowns. 'What you're saying is that short-term profits mean long-term problems?'

'Precisely. And yes, there are times when our yield might suffer if we don't keep a constant eye out for disease or pest infestations, but there are more natural ways to manage that. Not least encouraging the good insects who are higher up in nature's food chain.'

He starts laughing as he watches me with interest. 'That sounds a bit predatory to me.'

'It's nature and it's the circle of life. We're just respecting that fact, grateful for the crops it gives us and acknowledging that even if you own the land, it's a case of living alongside whatever other occupants live there too.'

His smile is one of amusement. 'I get the eye-closing thing. Being a city person myself, the countryside simply has this earthy smell. But when I focus on it, there are lots of subtle differences that come in waves.'

'The wind carries the scent of blossoms and flowers a long way. And the various leaves add different notes, too. Some give off a slightly bitter odour, others give that hint of freshness that I miss when autumn hits. It's often more noticeable at twilight.'

'I have spotted you wandering around at unearthly hours. Do you have a problem sleeping?' He's being serious and I could level the same comment at him if he's awake to spot me.

'No. I love spending time alone among the vines. Sometimes I'll sit on the dewy grass and talk to them.'

'Don't you ever feel uneasy out here when no one else is around?'

'No. I feel safe. It's people who hurt you, not plants. Well, unless they're poisonous and even some of those are also medicinal in tiny quantities. Gaia is so clever.'

'Gaia?'

'Mother Earth.'

'Ah.' He looks back at me blankly, struggling to come up with an apt response.

'Don't worry, Thomas doesn't expect me to turn you into an eco-warrior who worships the land. He simply wants me to show you what we do and why.'

'Is that the reason you stay here? I know for a fact that The Black Ridge Vineyard would welcome you with open arms.'

I do a double take, staring at him. 'How?'

'Because I spent an afternoon there being shown around by the company's assistant CEO.'

'You did?'

He nods. 'It was a personal favour and very informative.'

Wow. Clearly, Elliot's financial background means he has friends at the top.

'Your name came up in conversation and your reputation precedes you.'

'Is that why I'm the only one in the management team not overhauling their budgets?'

If we're talking frankly he can't expect me not to fire back, unless he's trying to catch me off-guard.

'Not really. Having taken some time to look over your expenditure-versus-forecasts for the last three years, there's nothing that strikes me as being out of kilter. Costs tend to increase year on year, naturally, but then in theory profits should do the same thing. The costs are what they are and, thankfully, an increasing number of people are prepared to pay more for an organically certified product. It's a booming market.'

That's the sort of feedback I'd been hoping for and it's reassuring. However, I don't like the way he said 'in theory' when he was talking about profits.

'Your problems right now are centred firmly on finances, aren't they?'

I start walking, belying the fact that his answer could be crucial. I can only hope that he doesn't think I'm being too direct.

'Such an ambitious building project didn't come cheap, Linzi. We will get the return, but we're in that interim stage. Until the hotel is running at a minimum of fifty per cent occupation on average all year round, it's eroding the bottom line.'

'The vineyard is making a loss?' My jaw drops and I quickly snap my mouth shut trying not to look quite as devastated as I feel.

'I didn't say that. The restaurant and our wine sales are doing well, but at the moment that is subsidising the hotel.'

'Everything hangs on the advertising campaign?'

'Yes, and I'm hoping the exposure won't just get people booking for the festive season but encourage them to pop along to check us out in the interim.'

'This is vital, isn't it?'

'Yes, Linzi, it is. The wife of a good friend and business acquaintance of mine is a recognised social media influencer. I've invited them here to stay for the weekend. I'm hoping that, too, will garner us a lot of interest.'

'Oh, I see. Lots of selfies with background shots to entice people here.' I smirk and his eyes sparkle. 'That's a good connection to have, Elliot, and a great idea.'

'I'd rather like you to help me extol the virtues of this place to them when they're here. In all honesty, you'd do a much better job than me all round. Is that asking too much? It would involve some overtime, maybe a couple of hours one evening and a tour of the vineyard on the Sunday morning. Although Penny, Nate's wife, is a live wire and is constantly on the go.'

'It won't be necessary to pay me for that. If this couple end up encouraging their friends and followers to stay here, we'll all benefit. Count me in. And today's little wander around is only the first lesson in your training. Are you good with a spade?'

His laughter echoes out because he thinks I'm joking. But I'm not. I'm racking up the favours and he's a man who understands it's reciprocal. If I ask him to get hands-on to transplant a few of his own vines in the spirit of getting involved, I figure he won't be able to say no.

After a Sunday spent cleaning the cottage, determined to switch off my thoughts, I ended up having one of the best night's sleep I've had in a while.

With my batteries recharged this morning, when the door to the photocopying room opens I know without turning around that it's Sienna. At this time of the morning, she knows exactly where to find me. I'm usually in here copying handouts ready for my teaching session.

'Happy Monday, Linzi. Did you have a relaxing Sunday?'

'I did, thanks. And how was your special evening out with Cam?'

She looks at me, beaming enthusiastically. 'We talked non-stop and even started jotting down some design ideas on a napkin!'

'No second thoughts, then?' I've never bought a property but ploughing everything they have – and more – into what sounds like a wreck of a house seems risky.

'None whatsoever. Cam might not like getting his hands dirty but being in the shop-fitting business he has a lot of contacts. That includes surveyors, as well as builders, and he's commissioned a friend who says he can carry out an inspection on the house tomorrow. As a favour, he'll get his report off to the mortgage company the following day. Things are going to move fast, Linzi, and that's what I love about Cam. When it's time for action, he's on it.'

So it would seem. I've only ever seen the cautious side of Cam, constantly reminding Sienna they still don't have enough in the bank and that she'll thank him later. But the wild-card house seems to have thrown that caution out of the window. I do hope he knows what he's doing – I mean, he ought to, as he's always moaning about clients who want changes and then gripe when the costs come in over budget.

'I hear that you ended up going for a drink with someone on Friday evening,' she continues. 'You kept that very quiet.' The tone in her voice makes it sound rather mysterious.

Honestly, I'm going to have to go out incognito in future. 'Believe me when I say it wasn't planned,' I state, emphatically.

'No wonder you didn't want to join me and Cam.' She flashes me a rueful smile.

'I didn't want to spoil what I hope was an extremely romantic celebration for the two of you.'

Sienna waggles her finger at me. 'Hmm . . . really? Why aren't you keen to share the name of the lucky man who escorted you to The Red Dragon Inn and how long have these secret rendezvous been going on?'

Oh no, she thinks I'm hiding something. 'I'm not joking, it wasn't planned.'

I can see that she doesn't believe me. 'But I have it on good authority you were spotted dining there with a tall, dark and extremely handsome man, and it wasn't the first time.'

There's no hiding a look of guilt and I can't wriggle out of this. Sienna knows everyone, including the waiters at The Red Dragon, who often do the odd shift here at the restaurant during the summer months. 'The truth is that I walked down to the inn because I couldn't be bothered to cook for one. Elliot happened to be there and spotted me.'

'It was Elliot? And you've met him there before?' She looks shocked.

I put up my hands to stop her there before her imagination has time to conjure up all manner of things.

'Once before, for an off the record chat. You know how difficult it is for him, having no history here. He's simply trying to figure out how things worked in the past. He doesn't want to turn everything upside down through lack of a basic understanding of how things operate. I know you have private chats with him, too. Don't pretend you don't, because you're a good office manager and it's a part of your job.'

'I don't divulge the confidential stuff, Linzi, and I know you don't either. But should I be concerned?'

'No more than any of the rest of us, Sienna. We're all worried about the future. And so is Elliot – that's plain to see. But Friday evening was pure coincidence. Elliot wouldn't even have approached me if I hadn't just opened an email which knocked me sideways while I was waiting for my food. It made the blood drain from my face, and I admit that the room began to spin.'

'That's something else you've been hiding from me,' she remarks, sternly. 'I knew there was a problem.'

'Yes, but—'

'Don't make excuses, that's not the sort of friendship we have, and you know it. I tell you everything, but I'm well aware that you hold things back. You have trust issues and I make allowances for that, but it's painful to watch you struggling when I genuinely want to support you through thick and thin. I just wish you'd let me.'

Now I feel awful. 'Not trust issues with you, Sienna, please believe that, my dear friend. I prefer not to dwell on the past – what's the point?'

'Now that's your jaded slant on things. Isn't it about time you confronted your issues?'

Just as I'm about to reply, the door to the photocopying room opens and Sienna rolls her eyes. She hands me a small pile of blank sheets of paper. 'I'll pop in to see you when you've read that report, Linzi,' she says, pointedly.

'Great. Sounds good to me. See you later, Sienna.'

Some things are better off staying in the past. There is nothing at all I can do to change what happened. No matter how bitter the regrets, I can't see the point in talking about it even though Sienna thinks it will be cathartic.

It's been a long day, but the time has come and I can't put it off any longer. My fingers begin typing.

Dear Juliette

I pause. Be polite and apologetic, I remind myself.

I, too, am sorry for the way things have turned out. You felt I abandoned you when I left, but it wasn't like that. I wasn't happy with the way my life was going, but you were doing brilliantly well at school, as we all knew you would. Eighteen was young to take off, but at fifteen . . . well, you were still under Mum and Dad's care.

I wish you well, I really do. And Ollie too. It sounds as if you've found your perfect partner and I'm happy for you. But I'm over being made to feel guilty for being different. I am who I am. And that's the reason why I won't be attending your party.

You know what Dad's like and he can't let things lie. The last thing I want is for my presence to provoke an outburst and risk spoiling your day.

Knowing you and Mum, it will be a wonderful, sparkling event. And that's as it should be. Finding your soulmate is special.

With much love,
Linzi x

I'd be lying if I didn't admit that I suddenly feel lighter and brighter. The awful deed is done. Once the black sheep, always the black sheep and do you know what? I really don't care. Is it living, if you surround yourself with people who want to pigeonhole you, place you in a neat little box and expect you to follow the norm even when it isn't right for you?

I've seen how wonderful life can be. Wonderful and devastating too, but for a short time I lived the dream, and it was well worth the sacrifice. I also came to learn that I have a special gift and when I'm tending the plants I'm in my happy place, where nothing else matters. That discovery was a huge turning point in my life. I wasn't an abject failure, as my father threw at me accusingly when I returned to the UK, and my skills were good enough for Thomas to seek me out. Ironically, I am a teacher, just not in an establishment my father recognises.

I'm on a roll and I text Sienna, next.

Sorry about this morning. I'm over the dip I was in. You've probably guessed it's family stuff sending me off-kilter. Don't stress – I've sorted it. The normal me is back in control! ☺

I wander out into the courtyard, feeling that a huge weight has been lifted from my shoulders. Why do we constantly feel the need to explain ourselves? Or maybe that's just the way I was brought up, always apologising for something or other. Sienna is happy and can't bear knowing that I'm feeling down, but our paths are different, and she must accept that. As for my sister, she simply wants me to forget past hurts so that her engagement party goes without a hitch. Me, I'm happiest when people leave me alone and realise that I was born to do my own thing. That includes making some monumental mistakes, but also finding my purpose in life. And that's to find solace in nature. As I said to Elliot, it's people who hurt each other, but what I should have added is that it's often without realising it. But not always.

147

Elliot

13.

It's Time to Get My Act Together

If I keep eating everything that's put in front of me, I'm going to have to carve out more than forty-five minutes every morning in the hotel's gym. Trips to The Red Dragon Inn don't help, but Linzi has become my go-to source of information and I can't keep going in and out of her cottage. Not without risking some raised eyebrows, and for good reason. Not many women catch my eye, but there's something unique about her that is rather compelling.

Glancing in the mirror as I towel my hair dry, I see I'm in need of a haircut and, as I peer in closer, that my designer stubble is fast becoming a defined beard.

'You're letting yourself go, Elliot,' I mutter, not liking what I see.

Still, this coming weekend I'm off to London. I've already booked a morning session at the spa for a full body massage and then it's off to see my barber for the works. Heading into what promises to be a heavy business meeting in the afternoon, I want to look sharp and not like I'm letting things slide.

When the strains of the theme tune to *Star Wars* strike up, I feel myself sag as I snatch up the phone, pressing the speaker button.

'Hi, Isobel. You're up bright and early on this beautiful Tuesday morning.'

'Beautiful, is it? I wouldn't know, Elliot, because I can't

see the sky from the murky depths of my office. How much longer is this going to continue?'

I grimace at the thought of her expression. 'I'll be back at the weekend, so you can schedule that meeting for any time from two o'clock onwards.'

'It's about time. And come with answers, or don't come at all.'

Ouch!

'Look, getting the vineyard into shape is commanding all my time and there's nothing I can do about that. It won't be forever.'

'And that's supposed to make me what . . . happy?' Her tone is vitriolic, but she has due cause.

'Join the club, Isobel, because I'm not happy either. I assumed that a month would be plenty long enough but in some ways my hands are tied. You know that. It's not a shake-up the company needs, but a bail-out.'

The line is ominously quiet for a few moments as that sinks in. Isobel lets out a sigh of annoyance. 'That's no excuse, Elliot. I love you to bits but you're letting me down – us down – and you're well aware of that. It's crunch time. I know which side I'd walk away from, so don't be a wimp.'

Click. It's all my fault and I've pushed Isobel to the edge. Guess it's time to get Nate on the line. He doesn't pick up instantly and I run my fingers through my hair, nervously. I smile, thinking that I used to spend ages making myself look presentable and now I can't even find my comb. It's time I had a tidy up so that I can let housekeeping in again. I must be the worst guest staying here and if I wasn't the boss I'm sure someone would be taking me to one side to have a word.

I'm not the sort of guy who enjoys hotel living. Ironically, my apartment is orderly and sleek. Everything has a place, and when Isobel stays over it drives me mad because she has this compulsion to move things. She calls it organising me.

'Elliot.' Nate's voice fills the air. 'To what do I owe this pleasure?'

'Two things. Are you and Penny doing anything the weekend after next?'

'I'm free, but I'm not sure about Penny. I'd have to check with her first, naturally. Why?'

'The grand master suite here at the vineyard is available and I wondered if the two of you were free for a weekend sampling some top-notch cuisine and quaffing some excellent wines?'

He starts laughing. 'Have you ever known me to turn down a freebie? That sounds perfect to me, and Penny will be delighted at the thought of a weekend in the country. We haven't been to Wales for several years now.'

'Great! I'll send you the details and the link to the website. I think Penny will want to bring her special lighting attachment for her selfie-stick.'

'Ha! You know my lovely lady so well. You're really going for it promo-wise, then?'

'Nate, the truth is that I have to do something and pretty quickly.'

'Well, I owe you big time. And Penny is always looking for an interesting photo opportunity, so it'll put me in her good books. You know what she's like. You said, uh, there were two things?'

'Yes. It's a heads-up really. There's a business opportunity I want to discuss with you at some point, but I need to do a little more work behind the scenes first. It'll probably take me a couple of weeks at most to thrash out the details, but you'll have first refusal. I think you'll find it an interesting proposition.'

'I'm intrigued. Right, I'd best make sure Penny clears her diary as she won't want to miss this.'

I've sown the seed and the next step is to wine and dine Nate and his adoring wife. They're a great couple and they spark off each other. Not in the way that Isobel and I do . . . no, that's an entirely different scenario. Despite a thirty-five-year age difference, Nate and Penny hooked up almost by accident when a promotional event threw them together. It wasn't long before they became a couple and it's the real deal. Unfortunately, some people assume Penny is after his money, but that's not the case at all as she's doing fine in her own right.

My only concern is Linzi, because she's a very private person and Nate just loves asking questions. He likes to get to know the people he meets and the last thing I want is Linzi feeling uncomfortable. But he'll no doubt have technical questions about the vineyard that I can't answer, and I need her by my side.

As I button up my shirt, my phone kicks into life again but this time it's Grandma and, as I swipe to answer, my heart skips a beat.

'Elliot, my darling. I might have to end the call abruptly as I can't let your granddad catch me. He's fly fishing on the edge of the loch, and deep in conversation with a fellow fisherman, but knowing my luck he'll catch something and seek me out to show me!' Her tinkling laugh is full of love.

'He's enjoying himself, isn't he?'

'Yes.' She lets out a satisfied breath, acknowledging that it wasn't that long ago she was fearful she would lose him. 'But I'm worried about you, Elliot. He knew your expertise was needed, but he has no idea how bad it is. I just wanted to warn you that even though I'm trying to keep him out of the loop, it's obvious he's talking to someone back at the vineyard.'

'He is? I've been dropping hints that he's out of signal and even told Linzi he's avoiding me.'

'I love that lady. She continues to keep his precious dream alive.'

'Yes, Grandma. You've said that a million times already. And she genuinely cares about the vineyard, that's obvious. Do you think he's in touch with Gwyn?'

'I don't know for sure, Elliot. But he said something yesterday that stopped me in my tracks. He said, "Robert had his head screwed on, Katherine. He wouldn't have done anything silly without mentioning it to us first, would he?" I scoffed at his words. Thankfully, Thomas didn't mention it again, but that means whoever he's talking to mentioned finances.'

I throw my head back, letting out a soft sigh. 'I bet it's Linzi. I'm trying to take her into my confidence without letting her know how bad it really is because I can't do this without her, Grandma. People are already taking sides, and my guess is that at least half of the staff are now muttering about job losses.'

'But you're sorting Gwyn's situation, and also Sienna's job share? Ideally, we don't want to lose anyone, but Linzi, Gwyn and Michael virtually run the place between them. Maybe it's time to give them an inkling of what you're dealing with.'

A cold feeling begins to fester in the pit of my stomach. 'Please trust me to handle this, Grandma. I've a few ideas that might turn it all around and I'll deal with Linzi and the phone calls.'

'And your mother? Oh, I so wish we could tell Thomas everything and sort this mess out.'

'His heart wouldn't take it, Grandma. We both know that. Leave me to sort out Mum's problems. I'm working on that right now.'

It's more a case of sorting out the mess my father left behind. A lot of almost worthless investments hasn't made it any easier and I have no intention of seeing her struggle.

Grandma sighs. 'On top of everything else you're juggling, what would we do without you? How's Isobel?'

'Fiery. Exhausting. But I'm on it.'

'Good. I don't want you to give up your whole life for something you never wanted in the first place, my darling Elliot. And you're there on your own sorting out problems that aren't down to you. It makes me sad.'

'Don't worry. Linzi is looking after me – both you and Granddad are right, she belongs here. She's going to be instrumental in us getting through this and if we succeed then I think we should make Red Robin Cottage hers for life.'

'Oh, my dear, what a truly lovely thought. The business wouldn't be where it is today without Linzi's skills. She bailed us out at a time when a failed crop would have crippled us financially. As far as your granddad and I are concerned, if Linzi suggests you do something, then do it without question. That young lady is in tune with nature, and everything is centred around those vines.'

My face breaks out into a smile. 'I know. She reminds me all the time. And she actually had me walking barefoot among the vines on Sunday with my eyes shut.'

Grandma bursts out laughing. 'She did? Good for her. Next, she'll be making you get your hands dirty!'

'Oh . . . not soil. It's full of bacteria and bugs, isn't it?'

'My boy. You might be all grown up and brilliant at what you do, which is saving businesses from going bankrupt, but you're doing this for me and Granddad, and I appreciate that.'

'For my mother, too. I feel bad for what happened.'

'I know and we'll make it right, I promise. Just stop Linzi talking to your granddad and I'll be even more vigilant. Maybe I'll say I want to visit one of the islands. The signal has got to be awful there, hasn't it?'

'Maybe, but with satellite and boosters, who knows these days? Now, if he were to lose his phone—'

'I feel like an undercover agent, sabotaging my own husband,' Grandma complains, sadly. 'He'll be furious with me when it all comes out.'

'But not until we're over the worst of it, Grandma, and I've sorted out Mum's situation. That would break him.'

'I know. If you need to talk, Elliot, text me and somehow I'll find a signal. You've taken on a huge job and it's more than anyone could expect of you. If things don't turn out as we hope, it won't be for the lack of trying, will it? I appreciate the sacrifice you've made for our family.'

'You're the true rock, Grandma, and when this is over I'm

going to remind everyone of that. Behind every successful man is an even more successful woman. My mother, unfortunately, wasn't quite as strong, but I can't blame her.'

'Sadly, your father wasn't an easy man to live with at times. He had a chip on his shoulder and felt he had to go it alone to prove he was good enough. That saddens me even now, Elliot. But I can tell from your voice that you haven't given up yet and that makes me smile. I love you, my darling boy.'

I groan, softly. 'Grandma, I'm thirty-three years old.'

'And whenever I talk to you all I see is the younger version of you who used to stuff all of your food in your mouth before chewing it. You always looked like a chipmunk, and I have the photo next to my bed to prove it.'

All my phone calls with Grandma end on a happy note because that's the type of woman she is. Money and things mean nothing; people mean everything, and I have no intention of letting her down.

I'm usually advising business owners to cut posts and a morning alongside Sienna spent interviewing the three candidates for the office manager job-share role has been a challenge. Reading a well-written and promising CV leads to a certain level of expectation and sadly two of the three people obviously got someone else to do the graft for them. Face to face, it was a totally different matter and the moment I started questioning them, the interviews began to fall apart. Just as I was losing hope, Will Smythe walks in and Sienna does the introductions, then turns to look at me.

'What attracts you to a short-term job-share position, William?' I ask.

'Please, call me Will. I've spent the best part of six years doing a part-time BA open degree and it finishes at Christmas. I've just done a three-month stint with Agri Sure, covering for their HR manager who is now back from sick leave and this looks like the perfect opportunity for me to bolster my CV.'

'The position we find ourselves in, Will, is that Sienna's

role is wide-ranging and we're looking for someone who is prepared to be flexible. There will be a short handover to bring the new person up to speed, then the successful candidate will be required to work five mornings a week.'

'That would suit me just fine.'

At that point there's a little back and forth, and it's obvious that Will is keen to prove himself.

'There might be an option of extending the period by anything from one to three months,' I add.

'I see. Well, that could fit in quite nicely with my own plans.'

'Unless you have any further questions, I'd like to thank you for coming in today and we'll be in touch shortly.'

His handshake is firm, his credentials sound and he answered every question I threw at him with an air of confidence.

After seeing Will out, Sienna reappears.

'What do you think?' she asks, and I notice she's smiling.

'There was only one suitable candidate. Are you happy?'

'I think he'll settle in quickly by the sound of it.'

'Good. You can go ahead and issue the offer letter so we can firm up a start date as soon as possible,' I confirm. 'It's a huge relief. If we'd had to look at another round of candidates, it would probably have meant anything up to a week without any morning cover. Maybe more.'

'You do know I wouldn't have left you in the lurch, Elliot. We'd have sorted something out.'

'And I'm grateful knowing that, Sienna. Before you go . . . I don't suppose Thomas has been in touch with you. Or any of the others?'

'No. I've not spoken to him since you joined us and no one has mentioned it to me. Are you still having problems contacting him?' Sienna gives me a sympathetic look.

'Not really. I'm trying my best not to interrupt his holiday, as it's well overdue. I think he needs this time away to get work out of his system. My grandmother is on a mission and is laying down the law. I just wondered whether he was sticking to it.'

'It seems so,' she replies, without any sense of hesitation whatsoever. 'I'll get that letter for Will sorted and email it over to him.'

'Thanks. It's going to be quite a change for us and for you, isn't it?'

'Yes, but I feel happier having found someone as bright and eager as Will.'

'And your own plans are coming together?'

'They are. On Saturday, Cam and I are meeting the architect at the house to get things started. It's going to be a steep learning curve for me, that's for sure.'

'I think you're exactly the right person to keep everyone on track.' I smile at her. 'I'd have been lost at the start without you constantly thrusting things under my nose when my focus wandered.'

'Saying that, have you agreed the final figure for the advertising budget yet?'

I'm not good at faking it and I'm sure she can tell it had slipped my mind. 'It's the next thing on my list. Promise.'

With that she turns, trying her best to keep a straight face. I'm going to miss having Sienna around all the time. I just hope that once the new house is transformed she'll be eager for things to get back to normal. Now, I'd better pop in to see Michael. Having put him under pressure to make some substantial savings, I'm now adding to his workload with Nate and Penny's visit. Everything must be absolutely perfect and I'm sure it will be, but I can't blame the guy if he's beginning to feel a little resentful. I'm asking for the impossible – keep raising the standards but do it with less resources. It's not easy being the boss when all you seem to be doing is delivering bad news, but at least Sienna walked out of my office smiling. That must count for something.

Linzi

14.

Food for Thought

As July draws to a close, it's Tuesday afternoon and my crew are excited about making a start on transplanting some of the vines from the nursery area to the newly pegged borders at the entrance. It's not an ideal time to be moving plants around but keeping a stock to replace damaged or diseased plants is very opportune.

'Pryce is on the way with the trailer, so we need to dig up a dozen bushy vines and tie the root balls in sacking, ready to load up,' I inform my eager crew.

'They're a bit wild looking,' Gracie points out as we stand looking at the odd triangle of land that, I'm told, was originally a sheep pen.

'I know. I don't often get down here and I quite like to let them grow as they would in the wild. They're mainly to replace anything that gets damaged in the winter storms. We've had the odd tree topple over and take out part of a row. But the boss wants a nice display to welcome our guests and I think the fuller, the better.'

'They're going to take some tying up,' Adam points out.

'But don't they look natural and . . . burgeoning? It's what the public expect to see. They don't think about yield and a mass of pretty foliage might look lovely, but it comes at a cost to the grapes. Anyway, we'd better get digging because I want the first two beds looking perfect by the end of the afternoon.'

* * *

The rumble of the tractor as it gets closer announces Pryce's arrival and I walk over to greet him. The entrance is too narrow for him to drive through, so he parks next to the gate.

'Hi, Linzi. You got a bit of a job on there. And these are going up to the main car park?'

'Yes, as near to the entrance as you can get them will be fine. How are things with you?'

'Good. Gwyn's got the patience of a saint when it comes to helping me get my head around the paperwork, but I'm getting there.' Pryce looks pleased with himself.

'It's good that he can spend a bit more time in the office now, too.'

'I told him straight there's no point putting extra strain on that knee of his before the operation and I'm his eyes and ears for now. It's easy enough for me to report back and get my orders.'

'I'm really glad it's working out for you, Pryce.'

'Just counting my blessings that I have a job for now, to be honest.' He comes closer, lowering his voice. 'It's a bit of a worry, Linzi. The whispers are they're going to be letting a few people go.'

I like Pryce and the concern reflected in his eyes isn't just for himself.

'Let's hope it doesn't come to that. The reality is that we have the best man to steer the vineyard forward and if there are cuts it will be for a very good reason.'

'I know. I've been thinking the same thing, but the idea of it is tough to swallow.'

The sound of laughter, as a few of the group head towards us, fills the air. They're gingerly carrying the plants over to the trailer. It puts a halt to our conversation, but I give Pryce a reassuring smile as he turns to begin loading up.

It won't be good for business if the guests start picking up on the growing level of anxiety that's spreading like wildfire.

'Good job, guys, these are going to make a great first

impression. Get the last of them in the trailer and then grab an early coffee break. I'm just popping into the office. We'll meet in the car park in half an hour.'

I think we're in need of an extra pair of hands.

As luck would have it, as I walk through Reception I spot Elliot exiting the restaurant. He has some papers in his hand and as soon as he sees me he increases his pace.

'I'm glad we've crossed paths,' he says, smiling. 'I was going to ask how the planting is going.'

People are coming and going around us and I incline my head, encouraging Elliot to follow me outside.

'Is anything wrong?' he asks, the moment we're out of earshot.

'Not exactly, but I have an idea that might get the staff talking in a more positive and less gloomy way.'

'Word on the ground is that bad?'

I shrug my shoulders. 'What did you expect? No one knows for sure what's going to happen next, and all eyes are on you. When you're hardly visible, it makes you seem detached.'

'Then they don't know me,' he replies, emphatically.

I roll my eyes at him. 'Precisely!'

'OK. Point taken. What exactly do you want me to do?'

As soon as my crew see Elliot walking towards us dressed casually and with a spade in one hand, a loud cheer goes up. Adam shoots me a glance, walking over to lean into me.

'It's not often you get to see the top man of any company rolling up his sleeves and getting stuck in.'

'Elliot is one hundred per cent behind everything we do here, Adam. I'm going to take some shots for my Rogues' Gallery. As team leader can you show him what to do while I snap away?'

Adam rewards me with one of his cheeky grins. 'Leave it to me!'

Elliot draws to a halt, surveying the results of the last two hours' work and seems impressed. 'Hi, guys, great job so far and I see that I'm just in time. I wouldn't have missed this for the world.'

Stifling a chuckle, I stand back and watch as he interacts with the trainees as if it's commonplace for him to be out here with us. He's a strong man, muscular from all the time he spends in the gym, and the digging part is easy for him. Elliot also asks questions and shows a genuine interest in the answers. He takes instruction well, as Gracie shows him how to start tying up the two vines after he's planted them.

It's funny to see my students turning into teachers, because that's exactly what's happening in front of my eyes. It helps that Elliot knows practically nothing at all about gardening and there's some good-natured interaction.

'Is someone watching Linzi?' Elliot remarks, as he kneels down to start teasing the suckers around the thin wire supports. 'What's her expression like? Am I doing good?'

There's a ripple of laughter. 'Oh, don't worry, I'd let you know if you were doing anything wrong,' Adam quips. 'Everyone is allowed to make a mistake, but if you make the same one twice you'd definitely be in trouble with Linzi.'

'I can hear everything you're saying,' I call out, from the other side of the gravel drive as I get a wide shot of the newly planted beds.

The atmosphere is relaxed and jolly, although it's hard to tell whether Elliot is actually enjoying himself, or just being polite. I turn, noticing that we're attracting an audience of both customers and staff, as people come out to see what's going on.

'Let's have a shot of you all grouped around Elliot. This will be one for the wall!' I exclaim.

Whether Elliot is used to photo shoots I have no idea, but he stands erect, leaning on his spade like a pro as the team gather around him.

'Linzi, you need to be in on this one!' Gwyn appears by my side, offering to take the iPad from me.

'Me? I hate having my photo taken.'

However, they're all waving me over, including Elliot, so I don't have a choice.

'Count to three and then the biggest smiles you lot can muster!' Gwyn states as he takes a couple of quick strides forward and begins clicking away.

After a bit of larking about, I thank Elliot for taking part and the team begin clearing up.

'Thanks, Gwyn. What do you think?'

'You've all done a champion job, Linzi. Nice ta see Elliot out in the fresh air for a change, too. No one can fault his dedication ta the job, can they?'

I trust Gwyn's instincts like I trust my own, and I nod my head in agreement. 'Are you on your way back to the Outpost? I'm heading there myself to download these photos.'

'Yep. Don't feel you have ta walk with me though, as I'll likely slow you down a bit.'

'No, it's fine. I'd like your opinion on where to relocate the shrubs we're digging out. Let me just wrap up today's session and we can take a stroll.'

I turn and gather everyone together. 'The result speaks for itself. If I can leave you to water the vines in and move the shrubs into the shed on the far side of the car park, I'll talk to Gwyn about the best place to replant them. Great job, everyone.' I raise my hand and we all high five before I rejoin Gwyn.

His pace is steady and I fancy he isn't limping quite so much, which is ironic.

'You're on countdown to the operation – how are you feeling about it?'

His left eyebrow twitches as he turns his head to look at me and that means he's nervous. 'All right. Takin' it steadier and not gettin' jostled around on the quad bike so much has made a big different to my pain levels. The doc's given me some tablets that help as the last thing we want is for my blood pressure ta be raised.'

'I had no idea you have a problem,' I reply, frowning.

'Oh, not normally. I'm as strong as an ox, as they say, but prolonged periods of pain send it through the roof.'

'Well, it's good to hear that you're doing the right thing. How's your brother-in-law?'

'Fred sucked it up and gave his daughter a call. She visited this weekend just gone. She was shocked ta see the state he's in, that's for sure. I left them to it, but it sounded ta me like she intends ta sort him out. Guilt's a terrible thing, Linzi, as you can't reclaim the time that's been lost.'

Gwyn sounds more than a little relieved and his words hit home with regard to my own situation, but I shrug it off. 'In times of need we all like to think that family members will step up. It's good to see that happening in this case, Gwyn. Now it's time to focus on you.'

'How many flowerbeds are you lookin' at, Linzi?' Gwyn slows to a halt in a stretch of forest where two big trees were felled last month. It looks bare, the ground still covered with a layer of broken pieces of bark and fine wood chips from the shredding of the smaller branches.

'Three, maybe four. You're thinking here is a good option?' I gaze around. It is sad, even taking down a diseased tree and two such lovely specimens so close together changes the landscape dramatically. The only benefit is that the saplings that were once in permanent shade are now benefitting from the sunshine.

'We've got some great logs that would only need a bit of trimmin' up ta make them the perfect height for people ta take the weight off their feet. If there was a splash of colour to brighten it up, you get a nice view of the lake over there, and a glimpse of the lower field between those cypress trees.'

'That's a great idea.' I gather some stones, marking the outline for a semicircular bed. 'What do you think? Big enough?'

'Perfect. I'll get a couple of the guys on that little job tomorrow morning. You'd best catch up with Pryce early and tell him exactly where you want the logs dropped, as you'll be in class when they sort it out.'

'I will.' We set off again and I realise that I miss Gwyn's company out and about in the grounds. Some of our best landscaping plans came about as a result of ideas popping into our heads while out on routine inspections. Pryce is now taking over that role and I don't seem to have any spare time to seek him out. Life here is changing, for sure.

'Are you happy with the way things are headin', Linzi?' Gwyn asks, out of the blue.

'I'll be happier when we know exactly what the overall plan is, but Elliot is thorough and he's also cautious. I see that as reassuring.'

Gwyn mutters a low 'Hmm.'

'You don't agree?'

'I think he's lost a bit of goodwill takin' so long, if I'm bein' honest.'

As I unlock the door to the Outpost, I stop for a second to look Gwyn in the eyes. 'I'm with you on that one and I'm going to make it my business to point it out to him.'

Gwyn does a bit of a belly laugh. 'Why am I not surprised? If he listens to you he'll have a good ally, Linzi, but if he doesn't, I'm afraid word will get out that all is not well at The Green Valley Vineyard.'

We're in complete agreement on that score and I couldn't have put it any better myself. It's time for action.

'Linzi. You're not still working, are you?' As I press speakerphone, Elliot's voice sounds a tad accusatory. 'I bumped into Gwyn just as he was leaving and he said you were designing a new seating area?'

'Not really . . . I'm just wandering around the forestry trail looking for a couple of good spots to dump some very large logs. The sort you can sit on,' I muse.

'Oh, I see. So, I'm guessing you haven't eaten yet?'

I glance at my watch; I didn't even realise it was gone

seven o'clock. 'No. I was about to head back to the cottage,' I say with conviction. I really need a shower and I'm thirsty, having drained my water bottle a couple of hours ago. But it's peaceful up here and I'm excited about creating yet another little oasis.

'Good stuff. How about I meet you by the Forestry Outpost in, say, about an hour for a picnic?' There's a sense of amusement in his tone: he knows that's the last thing I was expecting him to say. 'Just bring yourself and I'll sort everything else.'

Before I can answer the line goes dead and it leaves me staring curiously at my phone. A picnic? And an hour doesn't give me an awful lot of time, so I guess I'd better get a move on.

It's surprising what standing under a cold shower will do to appease the aches and pains of what turned out to be quite a strenuous day. As I head up to the Outpost, it's true to say I have made a bit of an effort this evening. I'm wearing my hair down and plumped for a long-sleeved white cotton top with a pale blue camisole underneath and navy leggings. I ran out of time, so makeup wasn't an option and I'm glad I didn't hang around when I see that Elliot is waiting for me.

'You didn't carry all that up here by yourself, did you?' I remark, as I get within earshot of him.

There's a hamper from the kitchen, a cool bag, and a small fold-up table. I break into a grin.

'The table was a bit of a challenge, I will admit. I keep forgetting it's a rather long walk.' His eyes smile back at me, warmly.

'So where do you want to eat?'

He shrugs his shoulders, nonchalantly. 'I've brought the food and the wine, courtesy of Deron, and I'm relying on you to lead us to the perfect spot. After all, you know every inch of this place and I don't.'

It's good to hear Elliot being flippant and I'm hoping that means he's had a productive day. 'What can I carry?'

'The table was the killer.' He rolls his eyes at me. 'I don't know what Deron put in these, but they're heavy.'

And judging by the chinking sound as he lifts the cool bag, I'd say besides the food there's more than one bottle of wine.

'Great, because I'm starving. Right, let's head up to the bench at the top of the ridge.'

We chat as we walk, and I tell him about what is affectionately termed by my students as Linzi's Rogues' Gallery. When I let him know that the group photo from this afternoon is now pride of place at the top, he seems pleased.

'It was fun and you were right, I need to be more visible.'

'Well, everyone who was free ended up popping out to take a look and Sienna wants some of the photos to go into our official newsletter.'

'I didn't even know we had one,' he replies, raising his eyebrows. 'There's a lot I still don't know, isn't there?'

I nod my head.

'Actually, you said something the other day that made me stop and think. You know, about not really appreciating what it's taken to turn a modest vineyard into a luxury retreat. We're just lagging behind on getting the word out there. And on that score I have some good news!'

He does sound enthusiastic as we approach our destination but the chatter stops as it takes a good five minutes to get everything set up.

'This is quite a spread,' I muse. Deron has thought of everything. There are several small platters with an array of finger food, two of his famous taster dessert boxes and the chinking sound was a bottle of wine next to two bottles of beer.

'Beer?' I query, pretty sure it's not one of the standard items to be found in the Green Valley picnic baskets.

'I made sure Michael wasn't around to hear my request,' he chuckles to himself. 'And Deron chose this especially for you.'

As I pass Elliot his beer and a glass, he puts it straight down on the table to pop the cork on the wine for me.

'Ah, I didn't realise there were any of these bottles still hanging around. It was a sell-out – takes me back to the summer before last. We had the perfect balance of sunshine and rain at just the right time and the grapes were plump and luscious. It's a little sweet if you prefer our classic dry white wines, but it flew off the shelves.'

I hold out my glass for him to pour and it's a generous one.

'You should try it, too. It was an exceptional year.'

He pours an inch into the bottom of his beer glass and raises it for us to toast, indicating for me to do the honours. Pausing to give it some thought, I smile to myself.

'In memory of what turned out to be a perfect harvest, even though it gave us a major headache!'

'It did?'

'Yes, we ended up filling the empty shelves with a very young wine indeed, something we wouldn't normally do.'

'What's the downside to that?' he enquires, genuinely interested.

'Unless you leave a young wine to breathe before you drink it, the first thing you get when it hits the mouth is the alcohol.'

He has no idea at all what I'm talking about. As our glasses touch, our eyes meet and we watch each other with interest as we take that first sip. I'd dearly love to tilt my glass to check on the clarity, then swirl the pale, straw-coloured liquid around to release the bouquet and breathe it in before the wine hits my taste buds. But I've never been a wine snob and it might make Elliot uncomfortable.

'Actually, I really like this,' he remarks, seemingly surprised.

'Then forget the beer and share it with me.'

I pick up the wine bottle and half fill his beer glass, trying not to wince as I do so. Wine like this should be in a stemmed glass with a bowl to capture each little nuance of the characteristics. But the fact that it seems right for Elliot's palate is promising. I'm guessing what doesn't gel for him is when there's that smoky hint of oak a lot of white wines have, or the sharpness of the dry, crisper varieties.

As we settle back to enjoy the food, the wine and the view, an intermittent stream of cars filter into the car park way below us. The buildings aren't visible from here, but it means business is brisk and that must go some way to reassuring Elliot.

This is a little piece of heaven up here and the picnic is a great idea of his. Thoughtful, too.

After a while, we're done eating and Elliot pours us both another glass of wine.

'I'm beginning to feel a connection again with this place, and you're right, the only way to do that is to get involved. Stuck in my office I could be anywhere. Seeing how enthusiastic your trainees were today rammed home how important it is that we have the right people working for us at every level, not just competent managers. Have you ever recruited from past attendees?'

'No. Jobs rarely come up.'

'But what if we expanded our operation?'

'Then, yes, there are a few I'd reach out to. Adam usually gets the most votes for team leader on various projects and he shows a lot of promise. But now isn't the time to be considering something as ambitious as that, surely?'

'I'm not about to jump into anything, Linzi, I can assure you of that, but I have to look way into the future. It would require additional investment before we could reap the benefits, but it's an option. Admittedly, I've only scratched the surface when it comes to what would be involved as my talks have been mainly with the business managers at the two vineyards I've visited. Next time, I'll ask you to accompany me.'

He isn't joking. 'I see.'

Elliot's eyes settle on the dessert boxes.

'You might need to switch back to the beer,' I warn him.

'When the intense sweetness of the cheesecake and the apricot tart hit your tongue it will affect the taste of the wine.'

'Really?'

'Yes. Don't just take my word for it, though, every palate is different. Try it for yourself.'

I watch in amusement and after a couple of minutes he understands exactly what I'm saying. 'Hmm . . . it's a little too much, but I'm not usually big on desserts anyway. Luckily they're small, as I don't intend to waste that wine. You might have a convert here, but I'm not promising anything.'

As twilight descends, the warm air is dissipated a little by the hint of a breeze. Just enough to get the leaves rustling overhead but not chilly on the arms.

'This is quite a legacy, Linzi, and I'm sorry if I've come across as unduly negative. I've spent my entire working life evaluating businesses and homing in on the problems. I guess what I didn't realise is that when it's a family business with a core of loyal employees who helped to build it, the connection is different. It wouldn't hurt to celebrate the successes, too.'

How can I put this delicately? 'It means a lot to everyone to have their hard work recognised, Elliot. Even my little crew who are only here for the summer. You saw the effect it had when you appeared and worked alongside them, digging. This isn't just another corporate operation, one of many controlled by a board of directors who often have little to do with the day-to-day running. The way you've handled Gwyn and Sienna's situations hasn't gone unnoticed, either. But it's the general lack of communication that is causing the problem. You can't talk about expansion in one breath, and then launch into an exercise paring back the budgets in the next.'

He frowns at me. 'I did say longer term, just now.'

'You did, but everyone knows you took a trip to talk to our suppliers and anyone we have a business relationship with. It was a smart move, but a little feedback would help allay what could be unfounded fears.'

Elliot raises his eyebrows, and just as I'm wondering if that sounded a tad blunt, he swallows the last of the wine in his glass and the bottle is empty.

'Next time I'll definitely go for the cheeseboard. Now this is something I could happily sit and drink.'

As our eyes meet, I give him an abashed look. After all, he's in charge now, especially given Thomas's lack of input. 'Is there any news from Thomas?'

Elliot's expression instantly changes. 'Off the record, he's finally beginning to step back and relax. My grandmother calls me regularly to check in and we've decided it's best to take him out of the loop. Doctor's orders, I'm afraid, and it wasn't that he was avoiding me, but Grandma is laying down the law.'

I can feel my cheeks colouring up and I only hope that in the growing gloom Elliot doesn't notice it. 'Oh, I had no idea. I thought he'd been given a clean bill of health. What a worry for you all.'

'I'm hoping that by the time the two of them return to Wales, we'll have a rock-solid plan in place, and he'll be able to really enjoy his retirement. The warning signs were beginning to stack up again and his doctor said it was down to stress. Lots of fresh air and walking, getting a proper night's rest, and watching what he eats. He'll soon be on the right track because my grandmother is in charge.'

Unwittingly, I've been making it worse by talking to Thomas. I feel really bad, but even so I can't betray a confidence. However, what I can do is make sure next time Thomas calls me I tell him that everything is going well. Because, so far, it is. I'll send him some photos of Elliot with his sleeves rolled up, smiling as he leans on a spade.

'Thanks for taking me into your confidence, Elliot. I really appreciate it and I sincerely hope that Katherine succeeds in getting Thomas's mind off work. After all, he left this place in good hands.'

'Your support and your honesty are invaluable to me, Linzi. I'm trying hard to do the right thing and I intend to succeed.'

'We're all banking on that,' I state, soberly.

'Oh, I nearly forgot! My guests are coming the weekend after next. They're arriving late on Friday night, so will probably have dinner in their room as Penny will have flown back from Portugal earlier in the day.

'I need some help pulling together a bit of a, dare I say, programme to make sure they experience everything we have to offer and some behind-the-scenes tours. We're talking Saturday mid-morning, through to early Sunday evening when they'll head back to London. Are you still on board to help me out with that?'

'Yes. It's no problem at all.'

His eyes light up. 'As our advertising campaign is about to really take off, the task is to get as much social media exposure as we can. Nate and Penny are a dynamic and fun-loving couple. Penny likes to feel confident she knows what she's talking about. She'll be constantly asking questions, so it's not just about the selfies – although it catches people's attention – but whatever insights you can give her ready for when she blogs about her weekend would be most appreciated.'

I can be a charming host when the occasion warrants it and Penny sounds like an interesting lady. If her main concern isn't her eyebrows, or the dreaded pout when she's snapping away, then I'm prepared to be at her disposal both days.

'I have a good feeling about this,' I reply, as we sit together on the bench.

Over the years I've sat here with Thomas, Katherine and Robert. Now Elliot. It's not Italy, but it's the next best thing because we all have one thing in common. This isn't just a job: hopefully, for each of us, it will turn out to be our life's work. And what an achievement, because no matter who owns it they're only custodians – the land and the vines will be here long after we're all gone. I catch Elliot looking at me just for the sake of it and I wonder what he's thinking. As if on cue, he answers the unspoken question.

'Sitting here with you is like stepping out of my life for a moment. Is that what nature does?'

'Yes. It grounds you. No matter how clever you are, what you own, or how much money you have, nature creates this beauty for all to enjoy.'

His eyes search mine and it's a curious moment. 'But it's people like you who nurture it, Linzi.'

I find that comment rather touching as we sit for a while simply enjoying the scenery.

When eventually we make our way back to the complex, at one point I almost stumble as I'm so busy chattering away to Elliot. I miss my footing on an uneven section of path. His reaction is instant and seconds later his arms are around me and he doesn't even acknowledge the sound of shattering glass when the cool bag he dropped hits the ground.

It's an awkward moment and I can't look at his face, so I glance down at the fold-up table that fell into a bush next to the path. 'That was a near miss!' I blurt out, as he slowly releases me.

'You didn't twist anything?' he queries anxiously, as I fuss over retrieving the table.

'I'm fine. Which is more than I can say for the empty bottles and the glasses by the sound of it.'

But he's still looking at me, as if there's something else he wants to say.

'Thanks for helping me to settle in, Linzi. I came here wondering if you and I would fall out, given the way Granddad laid down the law about not upsetting you. The irony is that I don't know what I'd do without you looking out for me.'

The look in Elliot's eyes indicates that he's sincere and this picnic was a nice gesture. But work is always on his mind and I can't allow myself to get lulled into a false sense of security. I have to remember to whom I'm talking at all times, no matter how comfortable I'm beginning to feel in his company.

August

15.

Revelations and Home Truths

'So, how did it go on the walk-around with the architect?' I ask the question, but the fact that Sienna is calling on a Saturday evening means that it's good news.

'He totally understands our vision, Linzi. And the bonus is that if we can put up with the disruption, he says that our plan to use the two bedrooms and the existing bathroom at the front of the house as our temporary sanctuary is doable.'

'Ah . . . the delightful avocado suite has had a reprieve.'

Her laughter is enough to tell me nothing is going to put her off. 'I'll give everything a good scrub and Cam says we'll install a shower over the bath for the time being. When the rest of the house is done, we'll gut it. The two bedrooms are just tired looking, but apparently the plaster beneath the wallpaper is sound, so it'll just be a case of redecorating them to reflect the new contemporary country feel.' Her excitement is tangible and for a second I find myself wishing . . . well, maybe some day I'll be able to afford my little dream cottage in a beautiful forest setting.

'What an adventure. And you get the keys next week!'

'We do, on the fifteenth.'

'If you need help moving your stuff in, you know where to come. And, when Cam's away, if you get tired of the upheaval you can always stay overnight at Red Robin Cottage to have a break.'

'I might take you up on that, Linzi.' She giggles. 'Cam is

a little nervous at the thought of me being on my own for long periods. He's just been put in charge of a four-month contract for a chain of menswear shops undergoing a major refit. It's likely that he'll only be able to get back home late on a Saturday and will leave early Monday morning until it's done.'

Knowing how hard it's been for her in the past when he's away like that week after week, I can't help wondering if the reality once things kick off is going to hit hard. 'Still,' I say positively, 'it won't be forever.'

'That's how we're both looking at it. So, how was your Saturday?'

'I rented a bike and spent four hours in the Brecon Beacons. Seriously, I'm bruised in places I didn't even know I had, but it was fun. I probably won't go every weekend, but they're a friendly bunch and once my muscles get used to it hopefully the following day won't be quite so bad. A couple of them let me try out their bikes but a good one isn't cheap, so I'll see how it goes. For now, I'm content to rent one for half a day. Apparently, it's a lot more fun in the rain than in the baking hot sunshine.'

She laughs. 'It's a good job you're used to getting muddy . . . and wet. But I'm so glad you pushed yourself to do it, Linzi. Don't let what happened with Karl put you off.'

I guess that's a natural assumption, but I'm made of stronger stuff. 'No. I just get tired of being propositioned the minute I'm introduced to a single guy of a certain age and he notices I'm not wearing a ring.'

'There's something bothering you, I can tell.'

I pause for a moment, tempted to dismiss Sienna's concerns but my conscience won't let me.

'My sister is getting engaged, and worrying over whether, or not, I should attend the party is keeping me awake at nights.'

Sienna sighs. 'Oh, I see. Why didn't you tell me?'

'Because Mum and my sister are reaching out as a sort of peace offering, but Dad hasn't changed. It's one thing to explain away my total absence from their lives when I was living in Italy, but not when I live an hour away, and that's why Dad won't want me there.'

Sienna understands there is no easy fix.

'I told Mum I'd think about it, then Juliette sent me an email ahead of the invitations going out. I feel mean not going but it would be the first time I've seen Dad face to face since I went to Italy, apart from a couple of his vitriolic rants on the phone. How awkward is that going to be? A party isn't the best place to attempt to smooth things over, even if he was so inclined.'

'It's a real dilemma, Linzi. If he still won't make you welcome in your parents' house after all this time, he's unlikely to give you a warm reception, is he?'

'Precisely. Instead of making an excuse I just said that I didn't want my presence there to spoil her day.' I'm trying not to get upset because what's the point?

'Take heart, Linzi. You didn't do anything wrong, and you're not obliged to go if you don't want to.'

'I have no idea what's been going on with any of them. Or how long Juliette has been seeing Ollie. It'll look like I'm the one who hasn't bothered with them, when that's not the case.'

'Do you feel better for having made a decision?'

'Yes, if I could stop doubting it was the right one. And at some point there will be a wedding.' I groan. That doesn't bear thinking about.

'If you want to cut all ties, this will probably do it.' I'm not sure whether Sienna is giving me a subtle warning or making a statement. There's no coming back from this, but I can't win whatever I do.

'Do you know if Elliot got off to London bright and early?' Rather diplomatically, she changes the subject. 'He was supposed to travel up late yesterday, but his mother had some sort of problem he had to sort out. As if he doesn't have enough on his plate!'

'I believe so. His car was gone by the time I'd had breakfast and went to put the bike rack on the back of my car.'

'Thank goodness. I'm sure Isobel would have had something to say if he'd overslept! Since he had a word with her she doesn't usually bother me anymore, but he was on the phone for ages to his mother and she only rang me out of frustration. Isobel just wanted confirmation he'd be there for a meeting he had scheduled for this afternoon.'

'It must be important to hold it at the weekend.'

'I thought the same thing. Mind you, at that point she didn't seem to be aware that he wasn't staying for the whole weekend. Anyway, I've left Cam looking at potential finishes for the new kitchen. He's hoping to get a hefty discount from a company he's used a lot in the past but they hand-build the units and there's a long waiting list.'

'Wow, now that's what I call forward-planning.'

'I'm still trying to imagine what the extension is going to look like, let alone the finishes. But as soon as the architect has drawn up the plans we'll get to see a 3D mock-up and that will really bring it to life.'

'Well, have fun. I'm off to the gym. I figure I'll probably have it to myself at this time on a Saturday evening.'

Raffaele looks at me from under his long, dark eyelashes as Bethan places a plate in front of him.

'Ah, there is nothing like a free breakfast on a beautiful Sunday morning!' he exclaims, rewarding her with one of his dazzling smiles. Bethan's lips twitch as she hurries away.

When she's out of earshot, he turns to me, raising his eyebrows and sporting one of his flirtatious looks.

'She's taken,' I inform him. 'They're getting married at Castillo Spa Resort in December.'

Raffaele places his hand over his heart, closing his eyes for a brief moment. 'Such a romantic place. Made for lovers.'

But his memories are fleeting and, seconds later, he's attacking his full English breakfast with relish, forgetting that I have my own connection with the place. We both know I invited him here because I have another favour to ask, and I'd better get on with it.

'I don't suppose you fancy having lunch at the vineyard next Saturday?'

Between mouthfuls he grins at me. 'Now we're getting to the point! There is no such thing as a free meal, *mia cara*, I know that. I'm at your disposal, just like the old days.'

The last thing I want now is to get distracted by talking about our time together at the vineyard in Greve.

As I toy with my delicate crepe oozing with summer strawberries, Raffaele is enjoying what must surely be one of the best organic cooked breakfasts in Wales. Everything on his plate was sourced within less than a twenty-mile radius.

'Before lunch, if you had time to spend an hour doing a private wine-tasting session with two very special guests of Elliot's, I'd be—'

'You'd pack your bags and head to The Black Ridge Vineyard and make my boss the happiest man alive? I don't believe it!'

My resultant laugh at his response sounds girly, even to my ears.

'No. I'd be forever in your debt.'

He flashes me a cheeky grin as he leans forward, lowering his voice. 'You already are, as I am in yours. How can I refuse? Things will get harder here before they get better, Linzi, you do know that. You sense it, don't tell me you don't. You can name your price, you know.'

I shake my head at him, my appetite returning. Elliot is going to be delighted when he hears he isn't the only one who can call in favours.

'That's business, Raffaele, and I'm a realist. What's the word outside of these four walls?'

He grows serious, that almost constant smile of his slipping. 'Who knows what is said behind closed doors? Elliot's visit was kept very quiet, but when the deputy CEO arrives to give someone a personal tour you can bet the discussion has some weight.'

Elliot said he was simply gleaning information from an old friend, and I have no reason to think anything different. I ignore that comment and start eating in earnest, as Raffaele's breakfast is disappearing fast.

'While I have your attention, there is a personal message I need to deliver, and I do that with some reluctance, *mia cara*.'

When I look up, I see a hint of sadness reflected in his eyes and my heart skips a beat.

'Vanna called me and asked for your number. I did not give it, but I said I would ask your permission to do so.'

'Why would Umberto's daughter be calling me? Is there a problem?'

I put down my fork and push the plate away.

'That I do not know, Linzi. She did not enlighten me. But you should know that I have finally made the decision to return to Tuscany to work for the Leone family again.'

'B-but . . . why?' I stutter. 'I thought you were settled here?'

He stares back at me with a look that is half apologetic and half remorseful. 'Because my mother wants me to find a nice Italian girl and settle down. I've known for a while, but I didn't know how to tell you.'

It's not like Raffaele to simply toe the line. He's much like me, or the person I used to be, who saw the world as a big and exciting place. Raffaele has never been short of female company and, sad to say, he has broken a few hearts along the way.

'Vanna is now in charge of the vineyard at Greve, and she's in need of my services. They gave me my start; how can I refuse? Besides, my sister and my brother have been enlisted to convince me I'm needed. They reminded me that our grandparents aren't getting any younger. If I'm lucky I get to see them what . . . twice a year? The time has come, Linzi, as I knew it would. I think you knew that too.'

He reaches out to touch my hand in friendship. Raffaele

knows things about my life that no one here in England does. He held me in his arms until I ran out of tears and then helped me pack my suitcases. He made a trip to the UK some two years after I'd settled at The Green Valley Vineyard, and I happened to mention that The Black Ridge Vineyard were looking for someone to do wine-tasting tours. The rest is history.

'Then if it's the right thing to do I wish you well, Raffaele, but for me the reality still hasn't kicked in.'

'You will come to visit me in Italy . . . won't you?'

I can't lie to him. 'You know that will never happen. But we won't lose touch, as my life wouldn't be the same without you in it.'

Bethan appears to clear our plates and check if we need more coffee. She's a little surprised to see me and Raffaele holding hands across the table and looking emotional.

'*Delizioso*, Bethan, *grazie*!' Raffaele thanks her and Bethan's face lights up.

You can't fall in love with an Italian man and not have it change you forever. Both Bethan and I know that first hand, but it's not something I've ever shared with her.

'*Lo trasmettero allo chef*, Raffaele.'

Being engaged to an Italian, Bethan knows that they are passionate men and that often comes with a flirtatious nature. But it's because they approach everything with a fun attitude, wanting to brighten every woman's life – no matter how young, or how old. Raffaele will bring a rosy hue to the cheeks of someone's great-grandmother just because he can. Oh, how I'll miss his presence. He always lifts my spirits.

When we eventually saunter back to his car, he gives me a fierce hug. 'Next Saturday, then? Text me the time. And . . . Vanna?'

As he releases me, I shake my head. 'There's nothing I want to hear, Raffaele.' Vanna has enticed Raffaele to return home, and she'll snatch him up quickly before he can change his mind. But surely she must know that going back is the last thing I'd ever consider.

Watching Raffaele's car as he drives away, my heart is pounding in my chest. This is another blow on top of everything else and I can't even process the information right now. There are problems that need sorting out here and I'd be betraying Thomas's kindness to me if I didn't step up.

I've talked Raffaele into doing a private session with Nate and Penny and it will certainly put a smile on Elliot's face. That's a small win and all I can do is focus on the positive because it's beginning to feel as if my world is crashing down around me.

And there's another little problem. While I don't intend to be in any of Penny's photos if I can possibly avoid it, I know there's a point in dressing to impress. Instantly glancing down at my hands, I realise I'll never have perfectly manicured nails, but at least they're clean. OK, I'm sure I have some nail polish somewhere. I am a woman who works with the soil, which is the reason why Elliot has involved me, but I'm also one of his management team.

My emotions are in turmoil. Raffaele is leaving and I can't quite take it in. Every time I get a little good news it seems something bad happens. As I walk back to the cottage, my phone pings and it's a text from Reception. Apparently, I have a visitor. Stopping to glance around the car park behind me, there isn't any vehicle, other than staff cars, that I recognise. But as I approach the glass doors leading into Reception I'm horrified. Mum is standing there, handbag over her arm and looking nervous.

'Linzi! Oh, my darling – it's so good to see you!' With that, she dissolves into tears while I look on in a state of complete and utter shock.

I'm not sure what to do, so I steer her towards the door, thinking that at least outside the sobbing won't sound so bad. Now I know where I get it from. I only shed silent tears when I'm, say, watching a sad film. Aside from that, I'm a wailer, just like her.

We're surrounded by a steady stream of guests making their way into, and out of, the restaurant and the noise is attracting attention. Even worse, two waiters pass by carrying room service trays, curious about what is starting to turn into a spectacle.

Grasping Mum's elbow firmly, I give her no choice but to walk with me.

'Please stop crying, Mum. Let's head to the cottage and I'll make you a cup of tea.'

It's unnerving seeing Mum in such a state and the fact that she's alone is odd, as she doesn't drive.

'How did you get here?' I question, as I fumble to get the key into the lock. My nerves were on edge before this little incident and now I, too, am desperately in need of a strong cuppa.

Mum sniffs, foraging around in her bag for some tissues. 'I . . . I . . . got a . . . taxi.' She manages to get the words out.

'From Berkeley to here? That must have cost a fair bit. Please say it's not parked up waiting for you with the meter running?'

She shakes her head. 'I've a number to call when I'm ready to leave.'

At least that's something. What if she'd said Dad was sitting in his car? Gosh, I have no idea what I'd do if he suddenly appeared out of nowhere.

'Right, it's through there. Straight ahead.'

Instinctively, we both slip off our shoes, and Mum places her handbag on the shelf beneath the coat rack. Now I'm worried, because I seem to be turning into my mother, who most definitely is not a free spirit.

I hurry through to open the patio doors and encourage her outside while I make a pot of tea. She prefers tea leaves, but tea bags will have to do. My emotions are literally all over the place and that delightful crepe is now sitting very heavily in my stomach indeed. So much for a relaxing Sunday.

As I take out the tray, I wonder whether I should suggest

we talk inside, then realise I'm being silly. There's enough noise around us from nature as well as people coming and going to mask normal conversation and Mum has, thankfully, managed to pull herself together. That's another trait we share. The tears might flow like a waterfall, but they don't last long. Unfortunately, for me it's often followed by anger – at myself for letting something get to me.

'Why are you here, Mum?' I ask, leaving her to pour the tea.

'Because we all have regrets, Linzi. I regret not standing up to your dad and his nonsense. He's not the only one who lives in that house and I should have had the courage to walk out when he refused to take my feelings into account. Juliette, too, is sorry for some of the things she's said to you in the past.'

'I was touched by her email. I still don't regret leaving home when I did, but I regret the way we've all drifted apart.'

Mum sighs, passing me a cup and saucer. At least she remembers how I like it made. Hers, I see, is still a tongue-curling brown after mashing the tea bags and taken without even a splash of milk.

'When you left so abruptly, it turned our world upside down. Juliette felt she'd lost her sister and that's pretty much what happened, isn't it? She didn't handle it very well and maybe she was also a little jealous to think of you living a wonderful carefree life in Italy.'

Mum has this knack of putting things very succinctly. That's why she makes a good lecturer.

'It's not that I don't get it, Mum. It was wrong of me to just up and leave, but Dad would never have given me his blessing to do my own thing, anyway.'

I watch as Mum puts down the cup she's only just picked up and I notice that her hand is shaking a little.

'When you got in touch about a year ago, the timing was unfortunate, Linzi. Life had become unbearable, and I was at the end of my tether. Juliette gave me the strength to make some tough decisions, but I didn't want to pull you into it. I found out, through a colleague, that your father has, for several years, been involved in a . . . how can I put this? An on/off relationship with another lecturer at the university and she's a . . . she *was* a friend to us both.'

I can hardly believe what I'm hearing. 'After everything he put you through, that's unforgivable, Mum.'

'He blamed me. He said that I'd become distant and he was right.'

I gasp. 'It's not your fault, Mum – it's his! Don't let him get away with putting the blame on you.'

'Your dad told me it was over, but it turned out it wasn't. When I confronted him, he raked it all up about the past. And you.'

'That doesn't surprise me.'

'I didn't just accept the way he treated you, Linzi. At the time your dad and I rowed constantly and, while we tried to keep it out of earshot of Juliette, the atmosphere at home was dire. At one point your dad intended to fly out to the vineyard to talk some sense into you.'

'What?'

'I had to beg him not to. It was then that I gave up trying to convince him he was wrong and pointed out that as an adult you had a right to discover what life had to offer. He lost his temper and said that someone needed to talk some sense into you.'

Thinking back, it's like a little of the puzzle is slotting together. 'And that's why he rang me shortly after I arrived in Italy.'

'I didn't find out about that until much later. I can't even begin to imagine what he said to you.' I can see how painful this is for Mum.

I give a disparaging laugh. 'It was one long tirade, saying I'd humiliated him and what was he supposed to tell everyone? He accused me of being selfish and told me that I'd live to regret my decision. It was as if he thought I was doing it just to upset him, but why would I do that? It was about me, not him.'

'I know. His attitude created a rift between him and me that never really healed.'

Anger courses through me, but it's tinged with an overwhelming sadness.

'You were such a passionate, happy-go-lucky girl growing up, Linzi. There was always something a little different about you. The house was happier with you in it. For me, it was as if the sun had stopped shining, and for Juliette, no more girly chats, or arguments when you discovered she'd borrowed some of your clothes without asking. She was a young girl in a household where her parents hardly spoke to each other at times.'

What a mess. 'Oh, Mum. I never meant to hurt anyone but having toed the line to please Dad for so long, I desperately needed to be free.'

'I know and no one can blame you for that. When you got in touch to say you were returning to the UK I was so happy that you were coming back that I let it slip. The next thing I knew your dad disappeared into his study and when he returned he said you were never to set foot over the threshold again.' Mum's expression is one of regret and frustration.

'Dad called me,' I reply. 'He asked whether I'd been sacked. When I said nothing, he laughed, implying that I'd proved him right. But it wasn't like that, and I tried to explain about my boss, Umberto. My heart was broken, but all Dad came back with was, "Is he married?" and the answer to that was yes. He didn't know anything about Umberto's marriage, or the person I'd become, so how could he judge me?'

'Oh, my darling.' Mum's face is ashen. 'So much pain . . . that man has a lot to answer for. He's not in a good place right now, but that's of his own making.'

'You've had enough?'

Mum nods her head. 'Your dad and I have an arrangement, which is that he won't move out until after the engagement party. No one is aware, except for Juliette, that the brave face we've been presenting to family and friends, that your dad and I are healing a rift, is a sham. We've slept in separate bedrooms for a long time and there isn't a day when I haven't thought about just walking out. But it wouldn't be fair on Juliette to cause a fuss in the run-up to the party.'

'She still lives at home?'

'Up until about three months ago. Ollie and Juliette have now bought a little place together. I'm a woman of my word, even when it's a daily trial.'

We both reach out to pick up our teacups and I look across at Mum. 'The bastard,' I mutter.

'I'm more wounded by the fact that he came between us, Linzi. What a total fool I've been. But not a day has gone by when you weren't in my thoughts.'

'You know, Mum, I was just about to say the same thing.'

16.

The Voice of Reason

I always wake up full of energy and ready to go on a Monday morning. My head is usually combing through that mental tick list of what we're going to achieve in the week ahead. However, this morning I'm still reeling from yesterday's revelations. If Raffaele's news wasn't enough, my mother's arrival pushed me to breaking point.

Even my students can sense I'm not on my usual form and when Sienna knocks on the door and pops her head around it, I'm glad of the interruption.

'Elliot apologises, but can he have a quick word with you?' Her expression indicates that it's urgent.

'Of course.' I turn to face my group, trying not to look as if this could be the final straw. 'Right, um . . . there's a video I'd like you to watch while I'm gone. If I get it up on my PC, perhaps you, Adam, would hit pause at the appropriate places? I don't have a handout prepared, so you will want to make notes of the main bullet points as they appear on the screen. When I have time later this week, I'll do a few screenshots and pop them in your pigeonholes. I think you'll find this will spark a lot of conversation.'

As I hurry along the corridor, I catch sight of my reflection in the glass and berate myself. There's no point adding to the general atmosphere of concern, and I plaster on a smile and push my shoulders back. By the time Sienna ushers me through into Elliot's office, I've decided that nothing he can say can possibly top the gutting disappointments of yesterday.

'Morning, Elliot. I have some good news for you!' He looks up in surprise and I realise that might have been a tad too enthusiastic, given his expression.

'Thank goodness, because I've just opened an email formally tendering Michael's resignation. This day can't possibly get any worse, can it?'

The look on his face shows how devastated he is and I can't believe what I'm hearing.

'That's unexpected and not the best way to kick-start your day. Did you have a good weekend?'

His expression doesn't alter. 'I wouldn't exactly use the word "good". I was hoping to get back late yesterday but ended up staying another night. I was up at the crack of dawn this morning and this is the last thing I need! So please continue, as I'm badly in need of a boost.' His face brightens with expectation.

'Nate and Penny are going to get a personal wine-tasting experience with Raffaele.'

He slams both hands down onto his desk, quite noisily, and it startles me.

'You absolute . . . angel. I hope he likes having his photo taken, as Penny is going to want more than selfies. Women drool over Italian men, don't they?'

Is he asking me for my opinion? This is getting a little weird. 'He's a good-looking guy and he oozes charm, but as I count him as one of my best friends I couldn't possibly comment about the drooling thing.'

At least I've succeeded in making Elliot laugh.

'Oh, come on . . . us Brits are notoriously reserved, and – unlike our Italian counterparts – we have a lot to learn about paying women compliments. Penny is going to love every second of it!'

'What about Nate?'

'Nate knows that Penny only has eyes for him, but the ladies who follow her blog will be enthralled.'

That's rather sad. 'Isn't that like living your life second-hand? I mean, get on a plane and fly to Italy. Experience it for yourself!'

'Oh, they will, in their droves. And they'll also come here. It's a lifestyle she's touting and every click, every booking it generates, grows her income. She's a very astute and successful businesswoman in her own right. Nate, of course, is a millionaire several times over, but her success isn't solely down to him.'

Our vocations are worlds apart and Penny obviously lives a glamorous lifestyle; there's no way I'm going to be able to impress her based on knowledge alone. I need to look the part too.

When I glance up, Elliot is holding out a sheet of printed paper to me.

'This is in strictest confidence, Linzi, but you know Michael much better than I do. It's obvious to me that he doesn't really want to leave but I just don't know what to do about it.'

Dear Elliot

It is with great personal regret that I feel obliged to tender my resignation. As per my contract, the two-month notice period commences with effect from today.

My time at The Green Valley Vineyard has been among the happiest in my career so far, but it's time for me to consider other options.

I'm happy to suggest a few people who might be interested in applying for my position and whom I consider would be an asset to this family concern.

Please do not take this in any way as a reflection on the change in management. I'm sure the coming changes will equip the company well going forward, but the stress of recent events has given me cause to reconsider my future.

I would like to thank you, your late father, Robert, and your grandfather, Thomas, for what has been an incredible journey.
Yours sincerely,
Michael Llewelyn

It's heart-breaking as Michael isn't the sort of person who gives up without a fight.

'What did he really want to say to me?' Elliot asks, with a frankness I can't ignore.

I dig deep, tapping into my gut instincts. If I tell the truth then I might be scuppering any chance Michael has if this is a last-ditch attempt to get Elliot to listen to him. Any boss facing the threat of losing a manager with such a wealth of experience has his own agenda.

'That he understands you have some tough decisions to make . . .' I fall silent, wondering how far I should go.

'And? You can't stop there, Linzi, it benefits no one.'

The look we exchange gives me the heart to go on. 'And maybe you should get around the table with your managers and see if they can come up with some suggestions before you start letting people go.'

Elliot visibly sags back into his chair.

'You think I'm being hasty?'

'No. You're considering every angle but, with the greatest respect, you don't know your team here at the vineyard well enough. We're made of stronger stuff and we won't give up without a fight.'

He raises his hands, forming a bridge upon which he rests his chin as he considers my advice.

'So in your opinion, it's not too late to stop Michael leaving?'

'He has a wife and a young family. They live on the doorstep and every weekend that he isn't working they're at their holiday place on the Gower Coast. If you lose him I'd bet money that he's going to The Black Ridge Vineyard. And, to be honest, they need him because their restaurant

197

is like an afterthought.' It sounds a bit mean-spirited, but it's the truth.

Elliot draws in a deep breath and when he breathes out he looks totally deflated. 'I'd guessed as much.'

'Did you know that they're losing Raffaele?'

A look of shock registers on Elliot's face. 'Not before next Saturday, obviously. But why is he leaving?' He narrows his eyes, peering at me rather intently. 'Is this a rumour, or fact?'

'Raffaele told me when he joined me for breakfast here, yesterday. He's returning to Italy.'

'That will be inconvenient, he has quite a reputation. As has Michael. Please tell me they aren't going to poach you, too, because you've lost your faith in me as well?'

He's serious.

'You can do this, Elliot. Whatever it is that you're grappling with, you'll find a way out of it. But I don't think you can do it alone. We need you and you need us, it's as simple as that.'

'Thanks, I think I needed a bit of a pep talk this morning. I know this is asking a lot on top of everything else, but will you speak to Michael? Let him know how devastated I am after reading his email.'

And just like that something in Elliot's attitude changes. He's not playing the role of the hatchet man, cutting out dead wood to enhance profits, because there is no dead wood and he knows it. His back is up against a wall and that means it's purely financial. I have no idea what Elliot is having to contend with, but the potential here for the future is enormous. We simply need to tighten our belts to keep things going while Elliot finds a way to get things back on track.

'You have a good team, Elliot, so listen to what they have to say. Gwyn has your back while he's getting himself sorted by giving Pryce all the support he needs to cover for him. I'm willing to do whatever I can to raise morale. And, if I'm not mistaken, Michael has a few ideas you might not have considered before you start laying off staff. It doesn't hurt to listen, does it?'

'If word gets out Michael is leaving it could do a lot of damage. Can you pave the way for me with Michael before I speak to him? Let him know that I might have been a bit hasty. I value his opinion and I am prepared to listen if he has any suggestions.'

'I'm off to see him now.'

Elliot heaves a massive sigh of relief. 'Please tell me the time on my PC is wrong. It can't possibly be just gone nine thirty, because I feel like I've been here for hours.'

'Remember, we're all on the same side and you're not alone in this.'

As I exit the office, I'm just about to pull the door shut when Elliot calls out: 'If you can work another miracle, I'll be forever in your debt, Linzi.'

Hurrying away to track Michael down, I'm delighted when I spot him in Reception. He's deep in conversation with the receptionist and I hang back. Loitering and trying not to look like I'm a woman on a mission isn't easy. Michael doesn't even realise I'm here and after grabbing some paperwork the receptionist hands to him, he strides back to the restaurant area.

'Michael, do you have a moment?'

He turns, surprised to see me. 'Linzi! Don't you have a class this morning?'

'Yes, no . . . well, sort of. Can you spare me five minutes in private?'

He raises his eyebrows, indicating for me to follow him out onto the patio area at the rear of the main restaurant. He holds the door open for me but says nothing.

There's no one about and we sit at one of the tables overlooking row after row of glorious vines. It's idyllic, but I'm too busy registering the weary expression on Michael's face.

'I'm assuming Elliot has asked you to have a word with me, Linzi, but I don't intend to change my mind. If he thinks I'm bluffing then he doesn't know me. I've given this a lot of thought and what he's asking me to do is short-sighted. In the long run he'll regret the upheaval it's going to cause.'

If Michael isn't prepared to even listen to me, then it's a lost cause. Instead of plucking words out of the air and hoping it sounds cohesive, I simply sit back in the hardwood chair and stare out without really seeing. The silence is painful, but necessary, and after several minutes I can feel Michael staring at me.

'You think I'm making a mistake. That's obvious.'

I haven't moved a muscle and I still avoid looking directly at him.

'You're disappointed in me.' When I turn to face Michael, his tone is equally as despondent as his expression. 'I've tried to explain to Elliot that he's approaching it all wrong. We won't just lose the goodwill of the staff we let go, staff I'm confident we'll be desperate to get back well before Christmas, but it will sound a warning bell to the others. What if people see this as the beginning of further cuts and start looking to go elsewhere?'

I nod my head, acknowledging the point he's trying to make. 'I know. And it's tough because we don't employ any lightweights. We expect a lot from the people we take on, including flexibility, and it works both ways. It's what we're known for, and that's what makes this a scary time because it's unprecedented. But if you leave now it will be a red flag, Michael. If you don't think Elliot can do what needs to be done, then I won't be far behind you.'

Michael stares back at me, clearly shaken by my statement. 'You'd leave the vineyard? But it's not just your job, it's your home.'

'My home while I'm working here. Together with you and Gwyn, I'm hoping we're a strong enough management team to find a way to get through the next couple of months. The truth is that if we can't rise to the challenge, I can't see any newcomers having even a ghost of a chance.' I watch as he swallows hard, as if he has a lump in his throat that's impossible to shift. 'And Elliot is astute enough to understand what a huge loss it will be when you go.'

All I can do is be honest with Michael. If his mind is made up then that's it, but that email wasn't penned by an angry man intent on walking away to make his point. It was a letter written out of pure frustration because he's worked his socks off managing both the housekeeping and the restaurant teams. He's steered them through the chaos of the building work when it was unbearably dusty and noisy. But he kept things running smoothly, no matter what problems he had to surmount. To walk away now will feel like a defeat to him and I know that.

The silence is agony and, just when I think there's no more to be said, he leans forward, putting his head in his hands. 'I thought it was over, Linzi. Last night I had a decent night's sleep for the first time in ages, having made the decision. I can't go back on it.'

'I understand, Michael, but I'm glad we've talked. Elliot is desperate, naturally, because Thomas wasn't able to sort this out. Elliot has a shot, but he can't do it without us. There are other options, I'm sure. The Black Ridge Vineyard would snap this up without having to pause for thought. Perhaps we're fighting a losing battle anyway.'

I stand, leaving him to it, but as I walk past him he reaches out to put his hand on my forearm, giving it a comforting squeeze. 'It's been quite a journey, hasn't it, Linzi?' he mutters, softly.

'It has, Michael. However, no job is worth having sleepless nights over, is it? You deserve better.'

Seeing how resolute and dispirited Michael is feeling, who could blame him for walking away? I text Elliot, suggesting he gives Michael a little time to let the reality of his decision sink in. When they talk, it's best that Michael has a clear head, but Elliot was right: in his heart I don't think Michael does want to leave.

* * *

I hurry back to the training room to find there's quite a discussion going on and, while it's good to see, I'm feeling empty inside. The topic of the video was about the general wine-making process and additives.

'I don't agree,' Gracie states. 'Sulphites kill off unwanted bacteria and yeasts, so that's a good thing, right? So what if it causes a few people to get a wine headache?'

I'd be letting them down if I didn't do my job. Which is to share what I know.

'Actually, Gracie, that's a myth and probably means the imbiber has drunk more than they should.' This sends a ripple of laughter around the room. 'The problem is that about one per cent of the population are sulphite sensitive. But we'll be doing a much deeper dive into the reasons behind some of the additives and the pros and cons.'

'What about vegans and wine additives?' Adam asks, and it's an intelligent question.

'That's very relevant these days. As we know, for many years both French and Italian winemakers would add egg white to their barrels. Proteins suspended in the wine would bind to it and drop to the bottom. The clear wine would be strained, leaving the sludge at the bottom. The process is known as fining and racking, but there are more modern ways of doing—'

My phone pings and, as I glance down at the screen, I'm surprised to see it's a text from Elliot.

Thanks, Linzi. Michael has already reached out to me. All is not lost, well, not yet anyway. We'll catch up later.

My head is all over the place and I look up to see everyone staring at me.

'I think we'll change things up a little today. How about we tackle creating those new flowerbeds along the forestry trail now that the wooden stumps are in place? If we spend an hour or two either side of lunch, then mid-afternoon we can come back and watch the second video in this series.'

Heads nod. I'm hoping the fresh air will clear my mind. There's no point getting het up about a situation I have no power to change. But to me it's beginning to feel like we're fighting a losing battle.

Curled up on the sofa relaxing after such a tense day, I'm not really surprised when there's a tap on my front door. Elliot stands there looking a little flushed and I step back, indicating for him to come inside. I've been on edge, hoping that he'd come straight here after his meeting.

'What the hell did you say to Michael?' Elliot says as he pushes the door shut behind him and slips off his shoes.

I lead him through into the sitting room and he glances around with interest. In contrast to the kitchen-diner, this room is cosy. The soft furnishings are elegant, with heavy drapes secured with pale grey tasselled tie-backs I sourced from Italy. They match perfectly with the greys in the printed fabric which features flocks of tiny birds flying over the tops of the silhouettes of trees. The silver-grey linen, deep-buttoned sofas are sumptuous. On the far wall a console table holds the small collection of items I brought back from my travels.

'You collect stones?' Elliot asks, raising his eyebrows as he looks at me rather curiously.

'I do. And each one tells a story. The tiny white marble one I picked out of a pile of dirt on a path close to The Parthenon in Athens.'

'I thought you only made it as far as Italy?'

'Italy was my base, but I got away for holidays. Anyway . . . you were saying?'

Elliot frowns, having lost his thread, and as I take a seat, he reluctantly drags himself away from the remnants of my past. Most people collect valuable items, but not me.

'Yes . . . Michael. We spent the best part of an hour talking because of you.'

Is that an accusation, I wonder, as he stares across at me intently. All I can do is tell the truth.

'When I saw the impact making that decision had on Michael, I realised he deserves better. The truth is, Elliot, that I'm guessing there has been some mismanagement, but it's not down to any of your management team. You weren't here to see the impact the building work had on Michael's staff, more so than the rest of us. He motivated his team through the dust, the constant disruption . . . it was sixteen months of hell and for what? This cost-cutting exercise must feel like the final straw.'

Elliot nods his head, as if in agreement. 'You'll be glad to hear he's not giving up just yet, but he has given me an ultimatum.'

'He has?' Good for Michael.

'I've agreed that no permanent staff posts will be cut, but it's time to get everyone together and explain what's going on in the background.'

'But you need to save money.'

'Yes, we do. Even with the measures I'm about to put into place to get as much exposure as possible, it's imperative I keep a close eye on the bottom line between now and the autumn.'

'Which means?'

'Managing with as few casual staff as possible but there won't be any job losses for now.'

'During our busiest period and the holiday season?'

'That's the best I can do, I'm afraid, but it was enough to get Michael to withdraw his resignation. If his staff go for it, then we all know it's asking a lot. Hotel bookings are starting to creep up, and if that continues, then it will put more money into the salary budget to get additional help.'

Gosh, it sounds like we're crawling along.

'If it means Michael stays, I know he'll get the support he needs,' I reply.

'I told him straight I don't intend to let anyone down even though we have a few tricky months ahead of us.'

I'm suddenly distracted when Elliot crosses his legs.

'Are those pheasants on your socks?'

'Yes, they're great, aren't they? They were a gift.'

Ah, Isobel. Maybe she's encouraging him to get into the country vibe, realising the vineyard is always going to take up a lot of his time. I'm sure it won't be long before he coaxes her here for a little break.

'On a totally unrelated matter . . .' He clears his throat, obviously feeling uncomfortable about what he's about to say. 'I hear there was a bit of an upset in Reception yesterday. It was something I overheard, but your name was mentioned. Is everything all right with you?'

There was obviously going to be talk because it was quite a spectacle.

'It won't happen again, Elliot, I can assure you of that.' After my stalker incident last year, this was unfortunate. I can only hope the two weren't mentioned in the same breath.

'My concern is for you, Linzi. I told you that if you have any problems I'm here to help. It's the least I can do.'

He's not going to let this go and I can hardly refuse to talk about it.

'My mum turned up out of the blue.'

From the little I've told him about my family, my reaction is enough for him to understand her appearance came as a total shock.

'Oh, I see.'

'It was awkward to begin with, but we had a talk that was long overdue.'

'You've made up?'

'Unfortunately, it's not quite as simple as that.'

'But it means you're going to your sister's engagement party?'

I glance over at the invite tucked behind the clock on the mantelpiece above the fire. 'I guess I am.'

'You're not going on your own . . . are you?'

The invite says plus one and I was going to ask Raffaele, but he's got a lot to organise before he flies off to Italy.

'Probably.'

'When is it?'

'The weekend after next.'

'You're doing me a big favour this coming weekend and if you're going to need someone by your side to get through this party, I'm at your disposal. From what you've said, it might help to have someone to jump in if there are any awkward silences.'

I look at him as if he's mad. 'You have no idea what you'd be letting yourself in for, Elliot. My dad will be there, and I don't think he knows I'm going. Honestly, I can assure you that I'll be fine. If I say as little as possible and go around wearing a smile, everyone will be happy.'

'You've been good enough to help me fight my battles and now it's my turn to help you out. You can hardly extol your own virtues, so I'll have your back. What did you say . . . two university lecturers and the youngest head of department? I won't take no for an answer. Just tell me what time and where. Oh – and whether it's formal wear.'

I burst out laughing. 'Country formal, not London formal. The setting is very upmarket. In a way it's a pity they weren't talking to me – they could have held the party here.'

Elliot's eyes brighten. 'Maybe the wedding, then? We can drop a few hints while we're there.'

On one hand, I might end up being glad of the support, but on the other, the thought of introducing them to Elliot, my boss, makes my stomach flip over.

He stands. 'I'd love to stay and chat, but I have a spreadsheet that won't populate itself. Once that's done, I'll have everything I need to make an announcement.'

We filter back into the hallway, and I wait as he slips on his shoes. As I open the door and he saunters past, he stops to look at me, smiling. 'That was quite something you pulled off today, Linzi, thanks.' And without warning he stoops a little to plant a brief kiss on my cheek.

Elliot leaves me standing there, feeling a tad breathless. I'm not at all sure that was appropriate, even if he is grateful. And now he's offering to be my plus one at Juliette's lavish engagement party. To say that I'm feeling a little confused is making light of it. Are we friends now? Not just boss and employee? How did that line become blurred? I feel safe around him precisely because he has a significant other. Besides, I'm not the sort of person who steals another woman's man, even if he has a smile that could melt someone's heart. I'm sure it was a one-off and simply reflects the relief it's obvious he's feeling at reaching a significant turning point today. Not least a potential triumph after his negotiations with Michael.

17.

When It's Hard to Raise a Smile

I'm not one for late-night shopping but Tuesdays are notoriously quiet, apparently. It's not really my favourite pursuit but I'm desperately in need of some new clothes. Sienna and I head straight out after work. For her, this is a fun thing to do.

In the car, I tell her all about my conversation with Mum and she glances at me, her eyes gleaming.

'That's wonderful news, Linzi, although sad about the divorce. It's not a nice thing to go through.'

'It's still sinking in, to be honest. I don't think Dad knows that Juliette has invited me to the party.'

'At least things are going in the right direction. It's been ages since we had a wander around the shops, hasn't it?' she muses. I give her the stare.

'This isn't window shopping; I need a posh frock for Juliette's engagement party and something smart casual for this coming weekend.'

I daren't take a peek at her reaction because my focus is firmly on the road ahead. The lanes are narrow in places and, even though we're slowing down for the blind bends, there's always the risk that someone coming in the opposite direction isn't being quite as cautious.

'Where are they holding the party?'

'Wendlesbury Manor House. It's near Berkeley in Gloucestershire. Fortunately, it's an afternoon do starting at two o'clock, so I hope to be back by early evening. It's only just over an hour's drive.'

'I'm free if you'd like some moral support.'

'I really appreciate the offer, Sienna. However, I think this is something I need to do on my own.' Elliot's offer was kind, too, but the best I can hope for is getting through it with my dignity intact. If angry words are thrown around the last thing I want is more witnesses.

'How's Raffaele doing? I was so sorry to read your text. I know how much you're going to miss him.'

'He's nervously awaiting confirmation of the date he flies out. He has a lot of loose ends to tie up before he leaves.' I pull a sad face.

'I did wonder at one time whether the two of you—'

'Stop right there! He's like a brother to me,' I insist, pulling a face.

'What's this weekend thing you have planned?'

'Oh,' I reply. I'd assumed Sienna knew all about it. 'I'm giving Elliot's guests a tour of the vineyard. It's a photo opportunity, really, to get some social media chatter going.'

'This is linked into the big advertising push, I presume?' she questions.

'Not really, it's just something he's arranged. I thought you knew all about it. Nate and . . . uh, Penny, that's it.'

'No, it's news to me and the names aren't familiar, either. It's a bit of a cheek – you were due to be off this weekend, weren't you?'

'It's fine.' I don't like to mention the huge favour he thinks he's doing me in return, or the fact that there's no way I'm taking anyone with me to this party.

'That was a bit of a to-do, yesterday. Elliot was keeping everything to himself. It's the first time I've seen Michael without a frown in a few weeks, so I'm hoping his storming into Elliot's office ended in a positive outcome.'

'Let's keep our fingers crossed we're over the hump.' What else can I say?

'I know you're aware of what's going on, but I do hope it's all going the right way, Linzi. You've not been your normal effervescent self either. I'm putting that down to the stress over this party.'

'Yes, it hasn't been an easy time.'

'I heard a rumour that Elliot took you for a picnic.' There it is again, that hint of mischievousness in her voice.

'Sienna . . . I promised Thomas I'd teach him the basics about viticulture. Elliot is a workaholic and I grab whatever time I can get, given that we're both busy. And somehow we still have to fit in time to eat.'

She gives a little laugh. 'Your Rogues' Gallery put a smile on a lot of faces. No one envisaged Elliot with a spade in his hand, let alone mucking in with the trainees. But all credit to the guy that he agreed to do it.'

Did I bully him into it, though? It's a bit of a stretch to imagine he joined in because he really wanted to.

'Right, that's enough talk about work. I'm in your hands this evening because I don't intend to try on an endless array of outfits, but I do want to look good in whatever I end up buying.'

'You know, Linzi, if you paid just ten per cent of the attention you give to your vines to your attire, you'd be a veritable queen of glamour. This tells me your wardrobe is sadly lacking and that's remiss of you. When did you last buy a dress?'

The silence that ensues seems to stretch out endlessly as I wrack my brains. 'I have no idea. I did order some leggings, T-shirts and jeans online about . . . maybe late last year? In fairness, I don't have a huge wardrobe and it's mostly work clothes.'

'Seriously, Linzi, you need to get a proper life outside of work.'

Is Sienna saying that to stir me into action? If that's the intention it's falling on deaf ears.

'I guess this trip is going to cost me a fair bit then,' I chuckle.

'Linzi – you can afford it. That dream cottage you're saving for isn't in jeopardy because of one shopping trip. And think how marvellous you're going to feel if you know you look the part.'

'The part?'

'Elliot's viticulture and training manager. That's how he'll introduce you when his friends arrive.'

No pressure then, but I'm glad to have my best friend by my side to advise me. 'What would I do without you?' I ask. 'And yet before too long I'll be seeing a lot less of you.'

'Aww . . . I'll be around every afternoon. And you'll be able to pop over to the house as I'll be glad of the company. Cam is going to buy a gas barbecue and he's calling it our outdoor kitchen.'

I burst out laughing. 'Oh, Sienna! I know it's going to be tough on you both, but when it's all done you'll have a lot of stories to tell your kids.'

'Kids? Um . . . I think we still have a wedding to fit in somewhere in between . . . goodness knows when!'

To say that my evening out with Sienna on Tuesday unnerved me is a bit of an understatement. It finally hit me how important this coming weekend is to Elliot. After a chat with Gwyn, he graciously offered to take my trainees on a field trip on Friday. Visits to other vineyards are always informative and leaving Pryce totally in charge for the day was, for Gwyn, a bit of a test.

'Leave it to me. I'll book the minibus if you send me the details you have and the time we're expected.'

'You are a lifesaver!'

'Why are you so nervous about Elliot's guests, Linzi? You've done lots of individual tours before for friends of Robert and Thomas.'

'I know, but this feels a bit different. I think there's a lot hanging on it. The couple are influential and it's free advertising.'

'Elliot isn't tellin' us everything, but he seems ta know what he's doin'.'

I'm not even sure Gwyn is aware that Michael put in his resignation, then rescinded it a couple of hours later. But Gwyn has enough to deal with in the run-up to his operation and helping me out today is an offer I can't afford to refuse. There's a lot to organise to ensure things run smoothly and Nate and Penny are arriving tonight. That means sitting down with Michael for the first time since our frank conversation on Monday morning, to ensure everything is all set up.

It's time to make a quick call. 'Michael, I'm free when you are to discuss this weekend's special guests.'

'Ooh, right. I'm at your disposal, Linzi.'

'I'm in my cottage and I've just made a cup of coffee if you'd like to pop along.'

'I'm on my way, with a pen in my hand and a notepad.' It's good to hear the lift in his voice, because it's more like the Michael of old. Always up for a challenge.

When he arrives, there's no awkwardness between us at all and I'm so relieved I automatically give him a hug.

'Hey, are you getting emotional?' he levels at me.

'Of course not. I'm just . . . pleased to see you!' But words aren't necessary. We've known each other long enough for our friendship to come before anything else.

'Let's go through to the kitchen, the kettle's boiled and the mugs just need filling with water.'

'You're on edge about this couple who are arriving tonight, aren't you?'

He lays his notebook and pen on the table, pulling out a chair and not taking his eyes off me as he eases himself into it.

'I wasn't, but now I am. The less Elliot has to spend on these glossy ads, the better.'

'OK. Tell me what you know.'

'The guy's name is Nate, I'm guessing he's a little older. Elliot gave me the impression that he's known him for a long time. Reading between the lines, I think he's big in the financial sector, but he's also married to a major social media influencer. So, whatever either of them put out there, people take notice. The sort of people who are looking for everything we offer – fine dining, a luxury break and a stunning setting.'

I carry the mugs over to the table and sit opposite Michael. In front of me are a couple of sheets of paper with some notes I made late last night after a brief chat with Elliot.

'They have the best suite – it took a bit of rejigging but reading between the lines Elliot was pleased,' Michael informs me. 'He couldn't give me an arrival time.'

I sigh. 'Same here. All I know is that Penny is flying in sometime during the day and by the time they get here he thinks they'll be too tired to eat in the restaurant.'

'Then we bring the restaurant to them,' Michael states, confidently. 'I'll get everything all set up on their balcony. The full works. White linen tablecloths, flowers and a wine bucket ready to be filled with ice while they're checking in.'

'OK, worst case they arrive quite late.'

'No problem. They'll be hungry and Deron won't leave until they're served.'

'But that's a big ask . . . it's a large menu.'

'Let's do something a bit special. Did Elliot say whether they have any dietary requirements?'

'That was the first question I asked, and the answer is no.'

'Brilliant, that makes life a lot easier. I'll have a special menu printed off for them. Let's go overboard.' His smile is encouraging.

'That's perfect, Michael. Thank you.'

'Right, that's tonight sorted. I'll ask the receptionist to check whether they'd like a room service breakfast. If they're eating late, that might be a good idea. What's the plan for lunchtime?'

'Raffaele is coming in to do a wine-tasting session with them. I figured it's best to have lunch afterwards. The food will soak up the alcohol, so plenty of spring water on hand during a light lunch. I'm assuming Elliot has booked a table for the evening?'

Michael nods his head. 'He said you were dining with them, too.'

'Oh, right. He's been up to his eyes in it recently, so it probably slipped his mind. I'm so grateful you mentioned that, it could have put me in a bit of spot if I hadn't turned up.'

Michael looks at me, slightly abashed. 'And I added to his troubles big time this week. I was convinced Elliot wasn't really taking on board what I was saying, but he backed down and he did it with good grace.'

'It's funny, but when I think back now, Thomas often skirted over the issues. The biggest one being Robert. And I know you had your concerns, too. But in hindsight, I have no doubt that it was the stress Thomas was under that caused his heart attack. That tells me something has been wrong for a while. I fear Elliot didn't really know what he was taking on, but even so, he's like you, me and Gwyn: giving up is not an option.'

'Do you know what my wife asked me when I told her I was going to hang in there a while longer?'

I smile at him. 'Tell me.'

'Whether you were on board with it. When I told her what you said to me, she understood why I changed my mind. She said, "If Linzi walks away of her own accord, I want you to follow her, but don't be the cause of the demise of something you've put your heart and soul into, Michael. I love you too much to see you become a broken man." I knew then she was right. You saved me from making a big mistake, Linzi, and I'm in your debt.'

Instead of making me feel better, it makes me feel worse. I'm disappointed Elliot still hasn't announced when he's getting everyone together, and with each passing day, it makes things more difficult.

'The feedback you're getting is that your staff are behind you?'

'Yes. It's all or nothing. There's too much at stake, Linzi. Elliot will be addressing everyone on Monday morning.'

'I hadn't heard. That's great news!' I'm elated, but what I'm really thinking is why put it off for yet another weekend?

'I gather he's taking his friends for a look around Cardiff Bay after your tour on Sunday morning and I'm assuming they'll be lunching out, as he hasn't made a reservation.'

'That's the plan. They'll take both cars and will head straight back to London afterwards.'

'Right. I think that's everything I need. I'd best go and warn Deron.'

'But he's not working tomorrow, is he?'

'Oh, he won't miss this, that's for sure. He'll rejig the kitchen rota. We can't offer overtime, but we can work together to get around things like this. If you don't mind me saying, you seem a little on edge today.'

'I'll be glad when this weekend is over, to be honest with you. My next task is to meet up with Pryce and a few of the guys to do a walk-around and check everything is looking its best. Have you been up to see the new beds alongside the forest walk yet?'

'No. I'll have a wander . . . when I get a moment.'

We both laugh, knowing time is a precious commodity right now. 'It'll still be there when things calm down,' I point out. 'But it does look lovely and it cost us nothing. This year's trainees will be leaving much better equipped than they came and understanding that the key to any job these days is flexibility.'

Michael raises his eyes to the heavens. 'That's a bit of an understatement.' He laughs. 'Relax, Linzi, you've got this, and The Green Valley Vineyard is nothing if not picturesque.'

I'm not a curtain twitcher, never have been, but this evening I am. Reception is on alert and the moment Elliot's guests arrive they'll buzz him. If I look out of my sitting room window I can keep an eye on the new arrivals, as I'm more or less level with the reception desk. Six o'clock comes and goes, then seven, and eight o'clock is fast approaching when, finally, I glance out and am convinced it's them. Two people arrive and linger in Reception, so it's obvious they're checking in. He's tall with broad shoulders and walks with a bit of a swagger, she's a good foot shorter, slim, and looks rather delicate standing next to him. I can only see the back of them and it's a fair distance away as there's the width of the courtyard and the glass walkway between us. However, seconds later, Elliot arrives. I pull back, not wanting to be seen, just relieved as Deron and Michael will both be standing by, waiting.

Unexpectedly, someone walks in front of my window and the sound of the doorbell makes my heart sink in dismay. Elliot wouldn't spring this on me, would he? He said he'd settle his friends in and I could relax tonight.

When I open the door, to my delight it's Raffaele and I heave a sigh of relief.

'Hey you, this is a lovely surprise. Come on in.'

'I'm having second thoughts.' He grimaces.

'About your wine-tasting session here tomorrow?' I ask, nervously.

'No, it'll be my pleasure. I meant about going home . . . for good.'

'It's only natural, Raffaele. It's a big step.' I know how hard it is to go home after a long spell away. Nothing is quite the same as you remember it. Or maybe that was only true for me, and Italy is one of those places where time seems to stand still.

'My mother, she is already sending me details of the single young women in the area she thinks might make a suitable match.'

I grin at him, but I know he isn't joking.

'And you're not ready?'

I pop open a bottle of wine and grab two wine glasses as we walk through to the garden. I pour him a small one and hand it to him.

'In some ways I am, Linzi. I guess that's why I made the decision, but it's a scary thought. My father always said you know you are a man when you are ready to settle down and have a family. But up until now I've not considered myself to be someone who likes to be tied down. It's all I can do to look after myself, let alone a wife!'

I watch as he instinctively holds up his glass, tilting it sideways to check the clarity and the colour of the wine, then righting it to swirl the liquid around before sniffing the bouquet.

'You're very different to the young man who originally settled here, Raffaele. The experiences you've had have changed you; whether you accept it or not, you've matured. You're stepping into the next phase of your life and obviously it's going to be a little daunting. Every bit as daunting as the day you arrived here, when you rang me in a panic saying you'd make a mistake.'

He tilts his head, letting out a wicked laugh. 'I did, didn't I? My English wasn't that good and I struggled to understand some of the accents around me. It took me a while, but it's been truly amazing.'

'And you have even more adventures to come. If you can't fall in love in Italy, then there's no hope for you!' I giggle.

'Spoken like someone who knows, *mia cara*. But love is not always forever, is it? Even when the connection is overwhelming.'

'You can't make someone love you, Raffaele, and that's the bitter truth.'

My tone is flat as we think about the joys and the pitfalls of love.

'Then how will I know for sure it's not simply another fleeting encounter? You knew without a doubt, but it wasn't meant to be and that makes me feel sad for what was taken from you.'

'Oh, Raffaele, you're such a dear friend to think of me, but I'm happy here.'

'You will never return to Italy? Even to keep me company?'

'I can't. If I ever have to start again it would probably be in France.'

'Monsieur Roussel? He offered me a job, too! Mammina would never speak to me again if I'd taken it. You are thinking about it now Thomas has stepped away for good?' His brow furrows.

'Not really. It's not the first time Monsieur Roussel has contacted me, and I do feel for him. His father died and, rather like Elliot, he's been thrown in at the deep end. Several years down the road he's realising he's made a few mistakes and his yield has dropped considerably.'

'It is sad. But that would not be too great a challenge for you, *la donna che sussurra alle vigne*. A vine whisperer is always in demand, no? They have a lot of old stone cottages in France going very cheap.'

The way he says 'cheap' sounds more like 'chip' and it makes me smile. 'That had crossed my mind, but you know me. I can't walk away in the middle of something.'

He shakes his head, sadly. 'Will you not speak to Vanna? If not your number, let me give her your email address at least.'

'No, Raffaele. If she does have problems at the vineyard, I'm not the one to sort them out.'

We sit for a while and eventually I make some coffee. Dark and strong, just the way he likes it. As the light fades, the mood changes and he begins talking in a more animated way about his future. It isn't until he's about to leave that he tells me he's flying out next Saturday, and my face falls.

'The day of Juliette's party!' I exclaim. 'I was hoping to drive you to the airport.'

'When Vanna sent me the link to the booking, I knew you'd be disappointed. I have so few days left to sell the things I can't take with me, get everything packed up and clean the flat.'

He's avoiding eye contact because after tomorrow I have no idea when we'll meet up again. It's a crushing feeling and, as we hug, I know that tomorrow when we part I will have to be strong. I hold on to him while trying to keep my tears at bay and when he says 'goodnight' his voice, too, is hoarse.

I watch Raffaele walk away. It's true to say he arrived in the UK more of a boy than a man, but the person I'm seeing now is ready to find the one true love of his life. I'm thrilled for him, but it's yet another little dent in my heart.

18.

Coping With the Ups and the Downs of Life

It's seven o'clock when my phone pings, and I'm sitting in the courtyard drinking my second cup of coffee, having been up for over an hour.

Morning. Are you awake?

It's from Elliot.

I am.

I don't suppose you're dressed?

That's a bit of a strange question to ask.

I am. Why?

I've only just woken up, but when I looked out, I saw Penny wandering around. She's obviously trying to grab some photos before people are up and about.

I should have thought of that.

No problem. I'll make my way over to see if I can assist her in any way.

His reply makes me smile.

What would I do without you? You're a lifesaver.

Glancing in the mirror before I head out the door, I'm glad I fussed with my hair, taking the time to straighten it properly. First impressions are everything and I scrub up pretty well, even if I say so myself. Mind you, wearing a pair of tailored navy-blue linen trousers and a white silk blouse falling to mid-hip level, I think Sienna nailed the smart casual look for me. Unfortunately, having only purchased one new dress, that's what I'll be wearing tonight.

As I hurry past Reception, there's no time to stop and chat as I have one thing on my mind: our very special guest. Taking a short cut between two of the buildings, I spot a woman meandering down between the vines, a camera in her hands. She's wearing a pale lilac dress and her long dark hair is pulled up on top and secured with a matching scrunchie.

The birds are singing their little hearts out, but despite that, and the low rumble of Saturday morning traffic from the motorway far in the distance, the sound of my arrival makes her turn.

I greet her with a smile. 'It's the best time of the day,' I remark softly as I draw to a halt next to her. 'A perfect photo opportunity. I'm guessing you're Penny?'

She crinkles up her eyes, curious that I should know her name.

'I'm Linzi, the—'

'The keeper of the vines! My husband, Nate, and I spent an hour chatting to Elliot last night and he's obviously in awe of your skills. All of this is down to you, then?' She scans the long rows of greenery. 'It's all so neat, yet luscious looking. It's enchanting. I feel like I could be in France and it's not something I would have associated with Wales.'

'Oh, there are many vineyards the length and breadth

of Wales, you'd be surprised. We're particularly lucky here because the land slopes away from the ridge behind us. It affords the vines some protection from the strong winds in winter and it's a suntrap in summer.'

'That's why they call it the Welsh Valleys,' she remarks, astutely. 'It's a breathtaking view, that's for sure.'

'You get a great shot from the far corner looking back up towards the restaurant terrace. And if you wander through the gate over there' – I point to the spot that used to be a thick hedgerow before the unfortunate accident with the deer – 'there's a sweeping view of the rolling fields beyond.'

'It couldn't be more perfect. The photos are going to jump off the page. Thank you for the heads-up.'

As I'm about to take my leave, she asks me a question.

'Are there any old stone buildings in the grounds? Anything a little run-down maybe?'

'The Forestry Outpost is a converted stone barn and it has some old outbuildings that aren't in the best of repair, but it's a good mile from here. It's up near the top of the ridge. I was planning to take you up there when we do the tour of the grounds tomorrow morning. You'll be able to snap away to your heart's content.'

'I'll look forward to that. And you reckon I should continue on down here?'

'I can wander down with you, if you like. Keep your eye out for the rabbits – you might get lucky. We also have owls and falcons in this area.'

As we walk and talk, Penny is really animated, appreciative of the little details I point out to her. And the moment we reach our destination and she turns around, she instantly raises her camera. 'Oh, wow! This is truly incredible. And the light is perfect.'

I stand back, watching her do her thing. Never having met a blogger and social media guru before, I'm impressed by the way she knows exactly what shots she's looking for. At one point she has me parting the leaves on one of the vines so she can do a close up of the grapes.

There isn't a selfie stick in sight, but I'm sure that will come later. She's equally excited by the vista beyond the planted areas and, as we take a circuitous route back to the main building, a small copse of trees doesn't escape her attention either.

'I love the nesting boxes. You encourage the wildlife, I see. I wondered whether they'd cause damage and be a constant problem.'

That leads into a long discussion, as I explain our ethos here at the vineyard. We end up sitting on the terrace having coffee as she asks about my background. Penny is a frequent traveller to Italy herself; the conversation flows and before we know it there's a steady stream of guests around us partaking in breakfast.

'I'd better get back to the suite, Nate will be wondering where I am. Although he's used to me wandering off. Well, thanks so much for taking the time to do such an early walkabout, Linzi. I'll look forward to catching up with you later on this morning.'

As we part company, I have no idea why I was nervous about this weekend. Everything is going to be just fine.

I text Elliot as I walk.

Penny is just heading back to her room. She's ecstatic and got some really lovely photos. You can relax!

Just as I'm opening the front door to the cottage there's a ping and I glance at my phone.

As long as she's smiling, I'm happy! Thanks, Linzi. Appreciated.

I'm half tempted to respond saying it's my job, although that might sound a tad sarcastic. But it's been a great start and it bodes well.

223

* * *

'Elliot, Raffaele has just pulled into the car park. I'm on my way to meet him. Do you know where Nate and Penny are?'

'I don't think they've surfaced yet. They had a light breakfast in their suite, I gather, so I'll pop along to see if they're ready. If you want to get things set up in the wine-tasting room, give us say, half an hour?'

'Will do.'

Slipping the phone into my pocket, I hurry forward to greet Raffaele.

'You dressed up just for me?' He asks cheekily, as we hug. 'You look amazing, Linzi.'

'Stop . . . you know I hate compliments. How are you doing this morning?'

He holds up his hand, rocking it from side to side. 'Emotional. It is harder than I thought. But I appreciated our little chat. Change is tough on everyone but you're right, it is time and I am ready for what is to come.'

Raffaele isn't the only one who is feeling emotional. Goodbyes are never easy, but this one is devastating for me.

He stands there, shrugging his shoulders. 'You cannot be sad, Linzi, because no one likes to see a grown man cry, do they?' His grin, though, is half-hearted. Having seen Raffaele cry like a baby on several occasions, it's time for me to be strong.

'Tears have a purpose, my lovely friend,' I tell him. 'But you can count on me. And I'll be expecting regular video calls as I'm going to miss that face.'

'And who will I have to tease in future, if not you?' He looks at me sadly and I chuckle.

'You'll be much too busy to think about me. Now come on, it's time for you to turn on the charm. I haven't met Nate yet, but Penny is going to be captivated by the depth of your knowledge.' To which, Raffaele bursts out laughing.

But I'm right. She is, the moment Elliot does the introductions. Raffaele is so photogenic she's itching to begin clicking away and it's just made her day. I stand back, getting ready to disappear into the background, but after shaking hands with Raffaele, Nate turns to look at me.

Elliot immediately introduces us. 'And this, Nate, is Linzi Patterson.'

I step forward, holding out my hand, and Nate gives me a beaming smile.

'Welcome to The Green Valley Vineyard,' I say, warmly.

'Thank you and what a pleasure it is to meet you, Linzi. After Penny told me all about your early-morning walk, I will admit that I wish I'd dragged myself out of bed to join you.'

'Don't worry, I'll be taking you both on a leisurely tour around the estate tomorrow morning and I'll make sure you don't miss a thing. But the whole point of a break away is that it's relaxing.'

'See, Penny?' Nate says, turning to glance at his stunning wife. 'Someone who agrees with me! The chance to sleep as long as I want rarely happens and I think I've finally found the place to do that within an easy strike of London.'

Elliot is standing there grinning. 'I'm sure it's not just the peace and quiet that attracted you here, Nate.'

Nate laughs, patting his stomach. There must be at least a thirty-year age gap between Penny and him, but unlike a lot of men of his age he hasn't let himself go. He's an inch or two taller than Elliot and sturdily built rather than overtly muscular, but he's trim.

'Yes, it's true. I like good food and I appreciate a decent wine, so I'm really looking forward to this wine-tasting session.'

'You'll be in good hands with Raffaele, I can assure you. Sadly, he's leaving the UK and heading home to Italy for good next weekend.'

'Oh, what a pity!' Penny jumps in. 'Then we're very lucky indeed. Tell me, Raffaele, how did you start your career?'

Seconds later, the two of them walk on ahead, leaving Nate, me and Elliot in a little group.

'Right, I'll leave you to it. If you need anything, Elliot, just give me a call. Enjoy!'

As I walk away, I hear Elliot saying to Nate, 'Raffaele works for The Black Ridge Vineyard. He's in great demand and Linzi called in a personal favour to get him here today.'

'Hmm . . . we're honoured. And thanks, Elliot, because judging by Penny's reaction she's in blogger heaven!'

That's the thing with older men, they don't get jealous just because a woman likes to look at a handsome man. They know that love is about way more than what's on the outside. Nate exudes the air of man who is at a stage in his life where nothing fazes him, he's more or less seen, and done, it all. And he didn't just survive, he's done well out of it.

People often assume the attraction to an older man is financial security, but that's not necessarily true. A good heart and a wealth of experience teaches a man what really matters to a woman and it's not money. Since Umberto, I've never met another man who made me feel the way he did, no matter what their age. Often, the growing pains of a relationship threaten to destroy it because of a lack of maturity. Or worse, not having learnt to grab on to a good thing when you have it because the grass might just be a little greener somewhere else. Hindsight is a wonderful, if galling, thing for so many people. Even Sienna and Cam were on the cusp of potentially ruining what they have, but they were brave enough to take a risk. And fingers crossed it was the right one, because I think they make a perfect couple.

I bow out of joining them all for lunch, saying that Penny expressed an interest in stone buildings. Apart from the part-tumbled-down former outhouses, I know she'll love the Forestry Outpost. But it's a working office and it needs tidying if she's going to be snapping away. Elliot understands, as I've promised him I'll definitely be there for dinner this evening.

The real reason is that sitting around a table having lunch with Raffaele would be agony for both of us. We'd struggle to keep the mood between us light and upbeat, which wouldn't be fair on the others.

It's time to give Gwyn a call. 'Good morning, how're you doing?'

'Linzi, I thought you were entertainin' the boss's guests?'

'They're in Raffaele's capable hands.'

'Ah, me dear, it can't be easy for you.'

Sitting back in the chair and putting my feet up on the desk, I feel a little deflated. 'I hate goodbyes, Gwyn. I really do.'

'I know, but a friendship like the two of you have is a real bond. You'll be there for each other in times of need and that's what true friends are for, ain't it?'

'Yes, I just hope I can keep it together.'

Gwyn laughs. 'I'm bettin' Raffaele won't.'

'The reason I'm calling is that Penny is looking for unusual photo opportunities. Apart from the stone ruins, the Outpost has that rustic, behind-the-scenes charm she's looking for and—'

'—and me desk is a bit of an eyesore. Feel free, but don't mess with the piles. Just put one on top the other and stick it in one of the desk drawers, they're all empty.'

That makes me chuckle. 'Thanks, Gwyn. I feel bad asking, but *rustic charm* sometimes needs a little staging.'

'And she's goin' to be splashin' this all over social media?'

'I reckon so, given the amount of photos she's taken already.'

'Then you'd best get busy,' he declares.

'Now I have your blessing, I will. Do you have anything planned this weekend?'

'Just gettin' things sorted. Besides the bag I need for the hospital, movin' into the vineyard afterwards for a few weeks is like packin' for a holiday. The missus used to sort that for the both of us and now I know why she was always writin' lists.'

Aww. The thought of how he's feeling now tugs on my

heartstrings, sending a little wave of sadness radiating out from my chest.

'Lists are good!' I reply emphatically, in the cheeriest tone I can muster.

'That they are, and I guess I'm not too old ta learn new stuff. There's life left in this old dog yet and the thought of gettin' back into stridin' around the vineyard doin' me inspections is what's keepin' me goin'. Good luck tidyin' up, Linzi. Who knows, I might even like the new look and consider usin' those drawers more often.'

'Amazing . . . was that a pig I just saw flying past the window?' I chortle.

Gwyn does a belly laugh. 'Cheeky! I'm aimin' to surprise you all, Linzi. This is a second chance for me and I'm grabbin' it, thanks ta Elliot.'

It's actually nice to hear Elliot getting some kudos for a change. And yes, I'm doing my bit, but Elliot is the one who created this opportunity getting Penny here, and it's something neither Thomas, nor Robert, had thought to do themselves.

With so many mixed emotions swirling around inside of me, when I'm in the mood to shut myself away, this is the one place I always feel calm. I love spending time here. Not only is it peaceful when I'm here alone, it's also far enough away from the main trails and the hubbub of the complex to feel it's a bit of a hideaway, a sanctuary. Three of the walls are solid stone, at least three feet thick. The fourth side was originally open to the elements when it was used as a barn for storing farming equipment. I'm not sure when the wooden framing to enclose it was erected, but it's beginning to show its age.

The windows are repurposed ones and the cladding below them will no doubt have to be replaced within the next couple of years. But in summer the solid stone walls make it pleasantly cool and in winter with the wood burner going, the area sectioned off as an office is plenty warm enough.

Attached to the barn are three smaller stone buildings we use to garage the big equipment. They all need some serious re-pointing and one of them took a hit when the trailer was backed into it. But we put the stones to one side and one day we'll get around to getting it fixed.

I keep looking at my watch, conscious that Raffaele said he'd give me half an hour's warning before he's ready to leave. When I finally get his text, my stomach starts to churn. Admittedly, it probably doesn't help that I haven't eaten a thing since breakfast, but my nerves are jangling and food is the last thing on my mind.

It's time, mia cara!
I'm on my way.

As I stride out, that little voice in my head is telling me to be strong. Raffaele carved out time today to do this favour for me and I want us to part on a high. *Deep breaths, Linzi*, I tell myself resolutely. *You can do this for him.*

But as soon as I step off the forest path and onto the walkway skirting the main car park, I know I'm in trouble. That firm resolve begins to weaken. Raffaele is leaning up against his car, his arms crossed as he waits for me. There are two vehicles circling, hoping to find a parking space and one of them pulls over, thinking he's about to leave, but he waves them on and begins walking towards me.

'How did it go?' I ask as soon as he's within easy earshot.

'I think your guests were very happy and I look forward to jumping online to see the results. There were a lot of photographs taken. Many of me!' His grin is infectious.

We stand next to the ranch fencing, looking out over the seemingly endless rows of vines and the meadow beyond that slopes gently away beneath the shadow of the ridge far above it.

'You don't mind?'

'Anything for you.'

We lapse into silence, staring straight ahead at the view – anything to avoid eye contact. Then we start speaking at the same time, bringing us both to an abrupt halt. Instead, Raffaele throws his arms around me and I bite my lip, forcing myself to hold the tears back.

Several minutes elapse as we cling to each other. When, eventually, we pull back Raffaele reaches out to cup my cheek in his hand.

'Linzi, look at me! It is not goodbye forever. You won't come to Italy, so I will come to visit you.'

I nod my head, unable to speak.

'I promise.' His gaze holds mine and is only broken when I hear footsteps behind us and someone clears their throat.

'Sorry, I don't mean to interrupt . . .' As we both turn, Elliot is standing there, clearly in need of something.

'It is not a problem, Elliot. I'm late leaving already,' Raffaele confirms. Even so, Raffaele gives me one last, lingering hug before he reluctantly releases me and turns to go.

Elliot waits respectfully, as I watch Raffaele walk back to his car. It takes me a few moments to regain my composure before I force myself to smile. 'Is there a problem, Elliot?'

Seeing my glassy eyes, he quickly looks away. 'Nate is going back to his room to catch up with his emails and Penny asked whether you were free to show her the Outpost? If it's not convenient, Linzi, I understand. I might not be able to give her the history of the buildings, but I can certainly walk her up there myself.'

'No. It's fine. Goodbyes are always hard. It's looking very tidy inside now and ready to be photographed.'

'If you're sure it's not too—?'

'I'm sure. Give me five minutes to pop back to the cottage and I'll meet her in Reception.' Struggling to maintain my composure, I hurry away from him. If I splash some cold water on my face to shake myself up then grab a couple of bottles of water from the fridge, it's business as usual. Life goes on no matter what, doesn't it?

19.

A Surprising Turn of Events

Answering the phone and hearing the lilt of Sienna's voice I could kick myself, as I really did mean to ring her.

'Sorry, it's been a long day,' I sigh. 'All good, well, apart from a heart-breaking goodbye with Raffaele. Neither of us had time to say very much before Elliot appeared. It was my fault for making myself available at a moment's notice, but I didn't even get to wave as Raffaele pulled away from the car park.'

'Ah. Maybe that was for the best, Linzi. It was never going to be easy, was it? So, this was Raffaele's last weekend and he gave up today to please you.'

'I know. I couldn't feel any guiltier if I tried, but Penny's eyes lit up when they were introduced.'

'Gosh, how did that go down with her husband?'

'Oh, Nate's fine. He's an old-school gentleman. Besides, Penny sees everything through the lens of her camera and she's more of a workaholic than Nate is.'

'Some of these bloggers earn seriously good money, I hear,' she points out.

'Oh, that isn't a problem for this power couple. Nate's in the multimillionaire category. He drives a red Ferrari. It's parked in the staff car park and most of the guys have popped out to have a look at it.'

'Nice for some! It makes our renovation budget look like peanuts.' She laughs. 'How do you feel about tonight, making up the foursome?'

I'd just taken a mouthful of water and end up spluttering it everywhere. 'Sienna! I'm representing the vineyard, not going on a date. You wouldn't believe the amount of questions Penny has asked. Nate's easier, very laid-back and determined to relax. But Penny is constantly on the go and, between us, I think Elliot and I are beginning to tire. Michael's tour of the facilities sparked more interest from Nate, judging by what he said when I bumped into him just now. I suppose as they have the best suite with the best view already, Penny's looking to balance her photo spread for the article. She loved the Outpost this afternoon.'

'Really? Oh well, whatever gets the most attention, I suppose. Still, just get through this evening and help them walk off all that food tomorrow morning, then you can relax.'

'Once I hand them over to Elliot tomorrow I fully intend to put my feet up and watch a film to keep my mind occupied. It's going to be a long week leading up to the dreaded party and it won't help if I dwell on it. How's it going with you?'

'We're whittling down our stuff ready for the move. There's no point living surrounded by a sea of boxes of things that won't fit in with our new sleek contemporary theme. My temporary wardrobe will be a hanging rail on castors.' She groans, but I can tell she's excited.

I know it's an exaggeration, but it feels like everyone around me is packing up ready to move on. I hope that's not an omen. If things come in threes, with Raffaele, Sienna and Gwyn, fingers crossed everything is going to work out just fine.

As soon as I'm off the phone, it's time to slip on the new dress hanging on the back of the bedroom door. The sales assistant called it Tiffany blue, but to me it's a pale turquoise. I'm a little worried the colour is a bit too summery for a business dinner, but my other options aren't suitable.

Beautiful, well-off people like Penny exude a level of confidence a lot of the rest of us simply don't have. I know that I'll feel self-conscious walking into the restaurant, worried that I won't carry it off because I'm not used to dressing up. Even though it's plain, it's the most I've paid for a frock ever. It's the exquisite cut that turns a few metres of fabric into something elegant and I like to think that it's not too over the top. Although, it did put a smirk on my face when I caught my reflection in the changing room mirror and I muttered to myself, 'Not too shabby, Linzi!' As I'll be wearing it at least twice, I suppose it was a bargain.

I'm never sure whether you do makeup first, but for me that's the worst bit. I'm used to a sweep of eyeshadow, a hint of mascara and a quick swipe of lipstick but tonight I want to look my very best. Using the fine eyeliner brush the women on the cosmetics counter assured me was infallible, I end up scrubbing it off twice and starting again. The clock is ticking and now I'm beginning to sweat a little as I still have my hair to sort out. It's also extremely warm tonight and the temperature probably won't drop for another hour or two, at least.

Realising I'm going to be late if I don't leave in the next ten minutes, I give up. Going in search of a black comb I bought ages ago and have never used, I twist my hair up and fasten it. I give my head a quick shake to check that my updo is firm enough and then I tease out a few little wisps to soften the look.

OK, I'm done fussing. Let the evening commence.

As if I'm a guest, Michael escorts me to the table. And, naturally, he's reorganised the layout especially for tonight. Elliot, Nate and Penny are busy talking, but as we make our way across the entire width of the restaurant, my legs feel a little shaky. The table has a generous corner spot that looks out over a part of the terrace that is an oasis of planters filled with bright red geraniums and a profusion of white petunias. Beyond that is an unobstructed view diagonally across the vineyard. Thoughtfully, Elliot has taken the seat with his back to the view.

'I'm terribly sorry for keeping you waiting,' I apologise, as Michael pulls out the chair next to Penny and I sink gratefully down into it.

Nate waves his hand in the air dismissively. 'A lady shouldn't feel hurried, and you've been at our beck and call since early this morning, thanks to my eager wife getting up at the crack of dawn.'

As I turn to Elliot, he looks thrown. He was deep in conversation as Michael and I approached, and now I've interrupted his flow.

'I was just . . . um . . . saying that um . . .' Elliot falters, and I couldn't be more embarrassed.

Although I'm not late, I am the last to arrive, but the timing was unfortunate. And now I realise that I'm staring at him, too. Elliot wears a suit well, but tonight he must surely be one of the most handsome-looking men in the room. Navy blue suits him and with a white shirt and a sleek silver-grey paisley tie, I have to drag my eyes away.

'You were talking about adding wine-tasting sessions as a permanent feature,' Nate reminds Elliot.

'Yes. Given your feedback it makes perfect sense. What do you think, Linzi?'

Michael has already summoned a wine waiter and I don't get to answer, as Nate and Penny are required to show off their newly acquired tasting skills. Even Elliot seems to have the knack tonight and I mirror them in a low-key way, determined to take a bit of a back seat.

'So, what do you think, Linzi? Is that a good idea of mine?' Elliot's eyes sweep over my face, as if he's studying me. Is my lack of an instant, positive reaction a problem to him? I wonder.

'I know that Raffaele makes it look easy, but a competently trained wine steward with a good nose and the right personality and charisma isn't easy to find. Anyone who has that superior sense of taste and smell will be eager to advance themselves and top sommeliers can command their own price. I've met a few of the big names and, believe me, they're characters in their own right.'

'Yes, I agree. Formidable, comes to mind,' Nate joins in. 'There's a lot of wine snobbery, but I will admit that if we're planning a big dinner party, I have an expert who orders the wine for me.'

'Spoken like a man who knows what he enjoys, but also wants to please his guests. It's like asking an electrician to choose the light fittings.' I laugh, but when I look at Elliot he's not amused. 'I'm trained to the level I need to be in order to make sure the grapes are picked at just the right time, but it's not where my interest lies.'

Penny has already quaffed half of the wine in her glass, in between trying some of the speciality breads on a wooden platter in the centre of the table. 'I suppose you never know who your audience is going to be,' she joins in. 'Raffaele had the ability to make us both feel extremely comfortable, but it was also fun. When he asked if we could taste a hint of concrete after a sudden downpour of rain, Nate and I looked at each other and burst out laughing. The strange thing is that the minute Raffaele said that, it was there – that weird, almost damp taste with a distinctly mineral twang to it.'

'As you can tell,' Nate interrupts, 'neither of us are fans of a really dry white wine. Now this one is very pleasant indeed. All credit to The Green Valley Vineyard and we'll also be ordering a few cases of last year's award-winning Sparkling Blush. Penny loves a bit of fizz, don't you, darling?'

'I do.'

Elliot waves away the wine waiter, who has been hovering, and tops up Penny's glass himself. He's been listening intently, but his eyes keep wandering in my direction. Have I let him down? Or maybe it was the words I chose. I was simply trying to explain why someone like Raffaele is always going to be in demand. If I apologise, that's going to be equally as awkward, and I could kick myself for not just agreeing with Elliot in the first place. After all, recruiting someone would be his problem not mine, but at least I've explained why it's not something I'd consider taking on. Not least because I don't have the patience to deal with difficult people who love the sound of their own voices. Raffaele has had some tough customers in the past and he deals with them professionally and diplomatically. But there's no doubt he's an expert and he could go head-to-head with a top wine buff and still garner respect.

'I'm looking forward to a tour of the grounds tomorrow morning, Linzi, before we visit Cardiff Bay. And Penny is keen to capture some of those far-reaching views.'

Penny gives me an enthusiastic smile. 'There's a lake, too, I believe?'

'There is and I'll take you up to the top of the ridge where there's a shady spot to sit and take it all in. How are the photos looking?'

'Unbelievable. It's going to be difficult to choose and that's not a problem I get very often, I can tell you.' It's obvious that Penny has enjoyed every minute of her visit so far. 'And Raffaele very kindly gave me permission to use the photos I took of him across all my platforms. Some people like to approve each individual photo beforehand or have their favourite apps and aren't prepared to give me blanket approval. As I have an assistant who helps me, I've had the odd occasion when something has been posted and we've had to take it down very fast.'

'It's fairly quick to do, isn't it?' I ask, genuinely interested.

'Yes, but with well over a quarter of a million followers on my most popular account, it doesn't take long to rack up twenty-thousand plus views before the mistake is discovered.'

'Gosh, I had no idea. I'm on two apps and I know every single one of my followers,' I admit, my eyes widening at the thought. 'If I get a new follower, I assume it's a spam bot and I don't follow back.'

Penny chuckles. 'I'll take the bots as well as the real people. I'm not fussy as long as the figures go up and not down.'

Michael appears with two waiters in tow, standing back to watch with a look of satisfaction on his face as they serve our starters. He then steps forward.

'Chef has created a twice-baked blue cheese soufflé with truffle. Enjoy!'

'Well, eleven out of ten for presentation,' Penny says, grabbing her camera and taking a few shots. The small ceramic ramekin showcases a mouth-wateringly golden-brown mound that rises up to twice the height of the dish. The truffle sauce is a series of dots that lead up to a sweeping swathe, like a delicate feather. We all hold back, waiting for Penny and I'm hoping they can't hear my stomach grumbling because I'm starving.

No one makes a soufflé like Deron, and this was an inspired choice. I can see Elliot is a little on edge and trying not to show it.

Nate teases out a forkful and the look on his face needs no words. 'Well, that's heaven on a plate!' he states, emphatically. 'I've had a few of these in my time but never have I tasted anything so light, and the truffle sauce is a perfect accompaniment for the blue cheese.'

Penny and I glance at each other, smiling. 'If he could get half as excited about my photographs, he'd be the perfect husband!' she declares.

'I'm not perfect?' Nate makes a face.

'Well, when you're actually listening to me you are, dear heart. When you're in business mode then I might as well leave you to it because your head is somewhere else.'

'In my defence, unlike my lovely wife, sometimes I find it almost impossible to switch off. Does your partner accuse you of the same thing, Linzi?' Nate asks and I freeze, as he immediately glances in Elliot's direction.

'Oh, no . . . I'm married to my work,' I reply, trying to laugh it off. How lame was that?

'Between you, Michael and Gwyn, who I understand is the estate manager, what's left for Elliot to do? You all seem to be very competent to me,' Nate continues. He looks directly at Elliot again, humour reflected in his expression.

'Not a lot,' Elliot murmurs.

Nate turns to look at me for an answer. The thing I'm puzzling over is that if Nate and Elliot are such good friends, why doesn't Nate seem to know about the problems? I realise he's only bantering, so it calls for an answer in similar vein.

'I'm sure Elliot will earn his keep,' I reply, to which we all burst out laughing, including Elliot.

'If anyone is going to keep me on my toes, it's Linzi. As my grandfather told me, I need Linzi more than she needs me.'

Ooh, that didn't sound quite right, and it could be misconstrued. I look at Elliot, widening my eyes.

'Viticulturists with Linzi's level of knowledge are thin on the ground,' he adds. 'It's reassuring to know that the vines are in good hands.'

Behind us, the restaurant is filling up and our conversation feels a lot less exposed with a little more background noise.

'Just as well, Elliot, eh?' Nate continues.

'Let's just say that it's an area in which I won't be dabbling. But' – and Elliot turns to look directly at me this time – 'Linzi did have me planting vines the other day.'

'And I have the photos to prove it,' I gloat.

Penny's ears prick up. 'Really? Oh, Elliot, please convince Linzi to let me have one for my blog. Was it staged?' she enquires, seemingly not sure whether we're winding her up.

'No. I have a few where's he's actually shovelling soil.'

'Now come on, ladies. Stop ganging up on me!' Elliot declares, sounding miffed, but he's definitely feeling more relaxed now and I'm glad.

Nate chuckles. 'Know when you've been outsmarted, Elliot. Just say yes and be done with it.'

Elliot groans. 'It seems I don't have a choice.'

'Are you kidding?' I respond. 'How often do you see the man in charge rolling up his sleeves like that? It's social media gold.'

Penny puts up her hand and we high five. 'Linzi's right, Elliot.'

'Oh, for goodness' sake . . . just make sure you choose one that at least makes me look a little dignified.'

'With a spade in your hand?' Penny giggles. 'Don't worry, you can thank me when the hotel is full and you're turning people away.' With that, she gives Elliot a wink.

'My wife knows her stuff, Elliot. Seriously, you've got something very special here.'

Is Nate expressing an interest? Please, don't let this weekend be about . . . and then an awful thought creeps into my mind. Is Elliot looking for a buyer? Swallowing the lump that is now firmly lodged in my throat as our plates are cleared, I can only hope I'm wrong. Besides, Thomas wouldn't allow it, surely? I take a large sip of wine to calm my nerves, hoping Nate is just speaking his mind not sizing the place up.

As we sit out on the terrace drinking our after-dinner coffees, we're all feeling mellow. If I did upset Elliot earlier on, he's forgiven me and to the people around us we do probably look like two couples dining together.

When I watch Nate and Penny interacting, I can't help but be reminded of my time with Umberto. Albeit I was a lot younger than Penny, and Umberto was probably around Nate's age at the time, or a little older. I don't know why people fixate on an age difference, but they do. The couple before me have a rock-solid relationship and it's wonderful to witness. They banter, but it's the way I've caught them gazing at each other when they're totally unaware. It's a look of utter contentment. Anyway, who needs words when you're in love? If it's the real deal, then nothing and no one can come between you.

'I know that look, Nate. You promised me . . . no business this weekend.' Penny points a finger at her husband.

Nate looks back at her, guiltily. 'I know, but you'll be bored to tears sitting here for the next couple of hours because you'll want to wander. It's what you do. The light at this time of the evening is amazing, you're always telling me that. See, I do listen!'

Penny rolls her eyes and Elliot starts to fidget in his seat.

'I know we're doing the lake tomorrow, but with that soft pink hue in the sky it might be a shot worth taking. What do you think, Penny?' I hope I'm reading Elliot's body language correctly. Is Nate a part of his rescue plan and he's hoping to talk him into investing? I wonder.

It's an offer Penny can't refuse. 'If I can slip into some comfortable footwear first, I'm in!'

All evening I've been mulling over whether Elliot has a hidden agenda. If he's struggling to make the finances work here, even in the short term, then Nate might be the answer to get us over the hump.

'Let's do it, then. I'll meet you in Reception in ten minutes, Penny?'

'Perfect. And we'll leave you guys to it for the next hour, but I don't want a single mention of anything the least bit work-related tomorrow, so be forewarned.'

I'm slightly amused, as isn't that precisely what Penny is doing? Taking photos is her business, she's selling a lifestyle and the pursuit of a perfect setting. I guess I'm equally as guilty encouraging her. But the vineyard means everything to me, and if Elliot is in a hole, I have his back.

Elliot

20.

Treading on Eggshells

'Look, Nate, it's time to level with you. The business opportunity I mentioned is close to home and I'm hoping it will solve all my problems in one go. It's an exceptionally good deal and, in all honesty, it stings a little for me to walk away from it. I know you recognise a good thing when you see it and I think it's perfect for your portfolio.'

'Problems? You? It looks to me like you're growing your empire here, although this is a bit of a diversion for you. I am a little surprised you're not thinking of offloading it and making a nice profit to reinvest.'

'Believe me, I had no intention at all of getting involved with the family business, but I had no choice. And, yes, that was one of the options I came up with, but you can imagine how that went down. My grandparents consider this to be their legacy and hope that future generations will continue to keep the dream alive.'

Nate narrows his eyes, peering at me as if looking for an angle.

'Families, eh? Before you get around to telling me what exactly the deal is that's on the table, what are you battling with here?'

I wave my hand in the air and minutes later two double whiskies arrive. I'm going to need this. I take a hefty slug and launch straight in.

'My grandfather inherited the farmhouse and nine acres,

in total. Seven acres of fertile farmland and two acres of dense forest. He had a vision all right, but in the beginning it was just him and a small team of men. The transition hasn't been without its pitfalls.'

'It looks like a thriving business to me. Your managers obviously know what they're doing and the standards here are exemplary.'

'Yes, the finishes are top-notch too. Except that when it was handed over to my late father his ambitious building project exceeded the budget and some.'

Nate leans into me, a grim look on his face. 'Now I'm with you. How much?'

'He re-mortgaged his house and my mother didn't find out until after he died.'

Nate and I both pick up our glasses. I down the rest of mine in one.

'And the pot's empty?'

I nod. 'Pretty much. He drained every budget he could, then unbeknown to my grandfather he began putting in his own money. Of course, when Granddad stepped back in . . . well, he couldn't understand why the vineyard had cashflow problems, and that's when he reached out to me.'

'Poor Thomas. You're not telling me that he doesn't know what Robert did, are you?'

My face tells the story.

Nate raises his eyebrows, almost as horrified as I was when I found out. 'No wonder Thomas had a heart attack if he couldn't get a handle on the finances. And you've inherited a can of worms.'

'What choice do I have? Grandma says if my grandfather finds out the truth, it'll finish him off. There was a stacking loan structure that hid the real picture. If my father hadn't done what he did, there would have been creditors knocking on the door. Once there's a proper return coming in on the investment, this place is going to do well. In the meantime, I have to make sure we can keep everything ticking over.'

Nate grimaces. 'That's a real shame, Elliot.'

'It's been tough. Going through probate, my father's financial affairs were a bit of a mess. He was quite a heavy investor and, as we know, with high risk can come high rewards. It became increasingly clear he was obviously hoping to make a quick killing and put everything straight. I thought at first he'd taken out the mortgage to buy some more stocks and shares, but that wasn't the case as it turned out. My mother went to pieces. The thought of losing her husband and her home was too much. I calmed her down and I've been handling her finances until I can find a solution.

'When I started going back through the vineyard's previous years' financial statements, it all became a lot clearer. He'd transfer in a lump sum to pay off a loan early, allowing him to take out a bigger loan to give him extra working capital. But he was never in a position to pay himself back because he was spending more than was coming in. My grandfather came in at the tail end. At that point, all he could see was that every penny that was coming in was more or less going straight out each month. Obviously, the bottom line improved once all the work was complete, but there's still a sizeable loan to service.'

'It's a sorry state. However, I'm interested if you do decide to sell up. It could be a goldmine once the place is marketed properly. Quick and easy, no other parties involved. You know I don't mess around.'

'Thanks, Nate, and I really appreciate the offer, but I promised Grandma I'd find a way to sort the short-term cash flow problem here and pay off my mother's mortgage.'

Nate curls up his lips and lets out a low whistling sound. 'That sounds expensive.'

'It is, but it's a price I'm prepared to pay.'

'The dutiful son and grandson, eh?' He sighs. 'Will it wipe you out?'

'Not quite. But Isobel has finally accepted that I have no choice but to bow out of our partnership.'

Nate looks stunned. 'But you've worked your socks off building that business and it's on the cusp of making you a small fortune.'

'Tell me about it, but the timing isn't doable. I need cash now and a lot of it. The problem is that Isobel is fussy about who she's prepared to work with. She's mad at me because initially I thought I'd come to Wales for a couple of months, make a few changes and then get back to London. I knew there was a good team here; it had to be to keep things going while my father ploughed ahead with his plans. I was going to spend a few days at the vineyard each month and everyone would be happy, including me. And Isobel.'

Nate frowns. 'Isobel isn't one to upset, Elliot.'

'I know, but it's a good . . . no, it's a brilliant deal, Nate. The consultancy has grown phenomenally and, as difficult as Isobel is, you couldn't ask for a better partner. Our team of business consultants are expert at what they do. As you well know, carrying out expenditure audits, identifying savings and increasing profits is the only way to turn an ailing company around. We're at the stage now where we have an excellent track record, and a lot of our business is word of mouth.'

His amusement is plain to see. 'When it comes to Isobel, tenacious springs to mind. I've seen her in action, and I think I'd rather take on a Rottweiler than I would Isobel when she's full throttle. But you're right and I appreciate you giving me first call.'

I know how his thought processes work and I can almost feel his mind ticking over.

'This is just between us for now, naturally,' I add. 'I can give you a few days to think it over, but I need to act quickly. In the meantime, I'm going to sell a few shares I have which will make me a nice little profit and that should keep things ticking over.'

'How soon can you send me over some figures to look at?'

The seed is sown. It's true that Isobel has a reputation

for getting straight to the point, and to a businessman like Nate that's an asset because she's also a fearless negotiator.

'It's all ready to go, and I'll get something off to you in the morning.'

'It'll mean saying goodbye to everything you've worked for, Elliot. Just like that.' Nate clicks his fingers in the air. Even he can't believe I'm doing this. 'Although I have to say, once you get the books right here, you're on to a good thing. If I were in your shoes, I'd probably have come to the same conclusion. It's fine to be hard-nosed in business, but when family are involved it's tricky. I lost a fair bit on the deal I did with my brother and I said never again. He thought he could make some quick money, but sometimes you have to wait for your return, don't you? Your situation is . . . unfortunate, to say the very least.'

I stare down into my glass. Another six months and I could probably get double what I'm asking in return for my share of the partnership, but at least I won't be skint. And the future here is bright.

'There's something you're holding back and that's not like you, Elliot. It's not money related . . . I'm a good listener, you know.'

Yes, and he's very astute. I think I might have made a bit of a fool of myself tonight. The moment I turned around and saw Linzi in that dress, I knew I was well and truly sunk. Nate knows what's up, as it blew everything else out of my head. I shrug my shoulders at him.

'It's a first for you,' he says and then, rather uncharitably, he starts laughing. 'Don't worry, my boy, I've been there myself and look how happy I am now.'

'Nate, please. I feel embarrassed enough as it is. Do you think Linzi noticed? Or Penny?'

'Who knows? If I could read women like I can read men, I'd have the world at my feet.'

My face brightens. 'Well, Isobel thinks like a man, Nate, so I think she's the perfect business partner for you. She never backs down if she thinks a deal can be squeezed just a tad more and her reputation precedes her, which is opportune. All she'll want from you is your money and you can sit back as a silent partner and wait for a big return on your investment.'

Which is the truth because everything is set up and running sweetly now. I've spent four years networking and reaching out to my contacts and Isobel made sure the contracts got signed. The business is heading to the moon.

'A little tip from me, Elliot.' Nate leans in closer, a wary expression on his face. 'Don't live to regret the one that got away. And I'm not talking about deals here.'

It's good advice and I know it. It seems that money is the least of my problems. How can I compete with Raffaele? Linzi was devastated this afternoon. How long will it be before she quits and follows him to Italy? Then what will I do?

I've been here, what . . . thirty-one days and probably ten hours and from the first moment I saw her I had this weird feeling that I could be in deep, deep trouble if I didn't watch myself. However, my life was in London and I knew I'd be heading back there as soon as I'd sorted out the mess my father had left this place in. I had bigger things going on in the city and I wasn't about to let anything get in the way of that.

'The problem is, Nate,' I confess, 'I'm not entirely sure I know how to handle this emotional roller coaster I'm on at the moment. It's uncharted territory and that scares the heck out of me. Suddenly, nothing else in my life matters except the thought of being here with Linzi, and that was most definitely not a part of the plan.'

'That's love for you, Elliot. It's how you know it's for real.'

Linzi

21.

No One Makes a Fool Out of Me – Not Again

'Thanks for bringing me up here this evening, Linzi. The Outpost is unique and the view from here, particularly in this light, is magical.'

'It's my pleasure, Penny; I knew you'd appreciate it. It's a bit of a hidden gem because, surprisingly, not a lot of our visitors walk up this far. Where the path forks, the lower track leads down to the lake and that's the main attraction.'

Personally, it's the forest that calls to me every time. The breeze coming through the trees as we sit here is refreshing and I feel I can breathe easily again. I've been on edge all evening after a disastrous start that went downhill before it evened out and, hopefully, ended on a bit of a positive note.

'Would you mind if I sneak in a shot of you by the vines?' Penny enquires. 'Not to put out there; I sense you don't like being in the limelight. I know it's the first visit here of many for Nate and me, but I have a catalogue of personal travel photos and you've totally made this weekend. Oh, Elliot is lovely as ever, but you've got your work cut out there when it comes to lecturing him about viticulture.'

My heart sinks in my chest. Even Penny thinks that around the dinner table I was a little harsh, dismissing Elliot's idea. I'm so used to talking to my students, I probably sounded a little disrespectful given that he pays me well for my expertise.

'It's kind of you to say that. And as for Elliot, he'll get

there. I really hope some of your followers are tempted to pay us a visit too. The one thing that lets us down is a lack of marketing skills, but Elliot is addressing that and it's equally as important to the running of the vineyard.'

'He has a stellar track record; I can vouch for that. He wouldn't be one of Nate's closest confidantes if that weren't the case. Nate, too, knows a lot of people and he'll be spreading the word about the vineyard. Naturally, when businessmen get together it's hard to keep the conversation off work. But I feel bad, because you gave up what could have been a couple of hours alone with Raffaele. I caught sight of you saying a brief goodbye in the car park and even then Elliot was striding towards you to get your help with something or other.'

I heave a little sigh. 'I'm not good at goodbyes and neither is Raffaele. He's a man who can't hide his emotions and we have a tendency to set each other off.'

Penny smiles at me with her eyes. 'That's sweet. Will you end up following him?'

'Oh, no. Not at all. We're friends, he's like family to me. He'll end up marrying a beautiful Italian woman and having lots of chubby-cheeked, dark-haired babies. I knew he'd eventually go back, but I thought he'd stay another year or two.'

Penny picks up her camera again, unable to resist the chance to snap some ducks flying in formation over the lake.

'Wow – this is so peaceful. I could happily live here,' she mutters, softly. 'Sadly, it wouldn't suit Nate. He likes to be in the centre of things. Elliot was saying that you have a cottage here.'

'Yes, it's opposite Reception. My job is my life – well, for the foreseeable future. Every day there's a new challenge and it's the only thing that makes me feel happy and fulfilled.'

'The only thing?' Penny questions, her mouth twitching at the edges. 'Elliot's eyes nearly popped out of his head when he saw you in that dress.'

I can feel the blood rushing to my cheeks.

'It was more to do with being late and interrupting his

flow, which was unforgivable. And I think I might have unwittingly said a couple of things that didn't go down so well. But I couldn't do what Raffaele does, that's for sure. It's probably not wise to put it quite so bluntly though, given that Elliot's the boss.' I grimace, awkwardly.

'I should imagine there are lots of reasons why Elliot would forgive you if he did take what you said the wrong way. And not just because you're the viticulture and training manager.' For some reason there's a hint of amusement in her voice. 'I notice that he registered every man in the room who glanced at you this evening.'

'He was probably checking to see if the tables were full.' I laugh, dismissively. 'Besides, I'm sure his girlfriend would have a thing or two to say if he had a roving eye.'

'Oh, Elliot isn't with anyone. He has the odd date, but Nate says Elliot won't ease up until he's made his first million. Then, maybe, he'll have some fun. Unless someone catches his eye in the meantime, of course.'

I look at her unable to hide my surprise. 'But Isobel—'

'—is his business partner. You didn't know that?'

It's funny that often it's what people don't say that's meaningful but, having made the assumption, it's enough to throw me into a state of confusion.

Instead of replying, I change the subject. 'Shall we head back? If we go full circle, then I'll pose for you in the private area of the vineyard that I call the nursery. And if you wouldn't mind sending me a copy, I'd be very grateful. I don't have many photos with me in them.'

Penny is eager to set off. Thankfully, it kills the conversation about Elliot and, having spotted a tawny owl, Penny asks about the local birdlife. But even as I'm speaking, in the back of my mind I'm reeling over the fact that Isobel is Elliot's business partner.

When we eventually saunter back to the main building it's later than we initially planned. Penny and I part ways in

Reception. Penny goes in search of Nate and I ask her to say goodnight from me. I figure I've more than done my bit for today. A leisurely two-hour walk around the grounds tomorrow morning and my job is done. It has been enjoyable in parts, stressful in others. I am puzzled though, because Elliot was acting rather bizarrely this evening and I think Penny was wrong. On reflection, I might even have come across as a little condescending, and that thought makes me cringe. If Elliot was solely focused on impressing Nate, I might have well and truly put my foot in it.

As I'm about to shut the front door behind me, I hear my name being called and suddenly my heartbeat quickens. I still can't get my head around some of the things Penny was saying earlier on and what I need now is time alone to think.

'Linzi!' Elliot calls out, as he hurries over to me. 'I'm so glad I caught you. It's been an incredibly successful day and I want you to know how grateful I am for the huge part you've played in it. I've left Nate and Penny alone together out on the terrace and I wondered whether you'd consider joining me for a nightcap.'

I'm guessing he's had a couple more drinks as he seems merry; it's obvious he's buzzing and in the mood to celebrate.

'It's a kind offer, but not tonight – I'm starting to flag.'

Elliot's face falls. 'I was rather hoping to get some um . . . general feedback from you. Just so I have some sort of direction for tomorrow.'

I thought it was all planned out, but he does sound disappointed. 'Sorry, I'm in need of coffee, not alcohol.'

'Ooh, yes. That's a great idea, thanks.'

That wasn't an invitation and mentally I sag.

'It'll only be a quick one, as I'm all talked out.'

'Of course, I understand.'

He follows me inside and I notice that he has sheep on his socks today.

'Nice socks – your girlfriend has good taste,' I remark, waiting to see his reaction.

'Oh,' Elliot replies nonchalantly, 'my grandmother sent a package from Scotland. She has a wicked sense of humour and says when I'm in a meeting and it gets boring, it's a topic for conversation. Funnily enough, you're the first person ever to notice them.'

I make a beeline for the kettle, my heart pounding in my chest.

'Is that a way of avoiding the question of whether you have a girlfriend or not?'

'No, I don't. Why would you think that anyway?'

Now I feel silly. 'Because of Isobel?'

Elliot starts laughing and instead of taking a seat, he comes to stand behind me.

'What's going on in that head of yours, Linzi?' He sounds genuinely perplexed, and I turn to face him. 'Admittedly, we're two people caught up in a difficult situation and doing the best we can to pull together to work through it, but there's something else going on between us. Don't pretend you can't feel it, or that I didn't make a bit of a fool of myself at dinner. Graciously, Nate and Penny made light of it, but I owe you an apology.'

'I think it's more the other way around. I'm sorry if I spoke out of turn, it was just nerves.'

'You didn't look nervous to me, you looked . . . wonderful. Stunning in fact.'

His tone is gentle, and I don't know quite what to say.

'In the very beginning it was purely work,' he continues. 'The truth is that I've hung in there because you were prepared to join forces with me. Why would you do that if there wasn't some sort of attraction between us? I'll level with you; I'm putting everything on the line now, but I think . . . I mean, I hope you can see that you're the one inspiring me.'

Elliot's words leave me feeling bewildered.

'I was merely trying to help.' My voice sounds small, apologetic even. 'It was a labour of love for me nursing the vines back to health and that creates a very special sort of bond. I would do anything to help if it guaranteed the future of the vineyard.'

He looks shaken as he stares back at me.

'But we have this special connection and I thought that today something between us changed. We . . . you and I, presented a united front and Nate and Penny could see that.'

'We did?'

'When you relax in my company, we're so in tune I feel I can say anything to you, then for no reason I can fathom, you clam up. Like now. Unless . . . is it Raffaele? You told me he was just a friend, but from what I witnessed you were pretty torn up earlier on.'

Elliot is standing in front of me holding his breath, fearful of my response.

'Because he's flying out on Saturday. Of course I'm going to miss him.'

'The day of the family party. Now I understand. But I'm falling for you and I'm not afraid to admit that, Linzi. Are you telling me that when I open up and you suddenly go icy cold on me, it's because my feelings aren't being returned? Did I misread what I thought – hoped – were subtle signals? I get that you've had a big disappointment in the past and I, stupidly and rather naively, thought I was dealing with that sensitively.'

My throat goes dry and my pulse quickens. *Thud*, goes my heart. Just when I think it'll never beat again, there it goes and it's painful. 'I thought I was safe around you, Elliot, because you were with Isobel.'

'Safe? Of course, you're safe with me, Linzi. I don't understand.'

Sometimes, neither do I. It's not easy to explain the sense of panic I'm feeling right now.

'I gave my love to a man who ended up rejecting me. I can't do that all over again.'

'You can't what? Trust me? And all this goes back to Umberto, the man you put on a pedestal, and it turned out that he was only human after all.' In his desperation, Elliot's words sound mocking to me and I lash out.

'You're used to getting exactly what you want, Elliot. And, yes, it's probably my fault. I should have said something when you kissed my cheek. My experiences ever since Umberto have taught me to be cautious for a reason. You've not exactly shared very much about your personal life with me, considering your little speech. I was shocked to the core when Penny informed me that Isobel isn't your girlfriend.'

He looks at me, genuinely puzzled. 'I never said she was my girlfriend. We're business partners. Oh . . . you thought . . . you assumed . . . or were you beginning to think that I'm the sort of guy who cheats on his girlfriend? In which case, I'm surprised you're still speaking to me.'

Umberto broke my heart and then my stalker made me feel vulnerable all over again, just in a different way. And now, is Elliot implying that I've been leading him on?

'I don't have to explain myself to you. What I do outside of work is my business,' I reply flatly.

'You think I'll give up on you just like that? I'm lots of things, Linzi, but fickle isn't one of them. If you come out and admit that Raffaele is the man for you, then it will tear me up, but I care enough to want what's best for you.'

'You're so convinced that you're right! Do you know how much I long for a man to come in and sweep me off my feet like they do in the films? Someone who is going to tell me everything will be OK? But that man doesn't exist. Two people, two agendas and who can say for sure if it will last, because nothing is guaranteed.'

'Are you telling me that you're not prepared to even give me a chance to prove to you that I'm serious? You closed your heart a long time ago, I understand that. A hurt like that must leave a permanent scar, but I'm no expert when it comes to falling for someone because this is a first for me. If you feel anything at all in return, I'll prove to you that my feelings are strong enough to keep us going until you're ready to let go of the past. I'd rather be alone than with the wrong person, Linzi, and believe me when I say this isn't exactly convenient. But I understand what commitment means, which is precisely why I've steered clear of it so far. And then there you were. What confuses me is that we get on so well and if we take it slowly—'

'I live here in a cottage you own, Elliot,' I remind him, flatly. 'Everything I own would fit into a small van. My savings are significant to me, but probably less than your annual expenses budget. You're in finance and I'm a gardener. How does that make us compatible?'

Elliot visibly crumples, closing his eyes for a few seconds before letting out an agonising breath. He looks defeated and it's gut-wrenching to witness.

'I'm guessing that Umberto chose his family over you, Linzi, and he made a huge mistake. I'd know for sure if you sat down and told me the entire story, wouldn't I? Our situation is different. You're even more invested in this place than I am, and I'll tell you something you didn't know. While you might think the vineyard was handed to me on a plate, I'm more heavily invested in it than you can possibly imagine. I didn't plant the vines or commission the building programme, but since I've been here I've given it my all. I think I've proved myself worthy of a little respect, if not of your affections. I have feelings too, and you're trampling all over them.'

Disparate thoughts are whirling around inside my head, and I can't even think straight. 'I can't do this now, Elliot, I'm exhausted, totally exhausted. I'm sorry, but I think you should go.' And with that I turn my back on him again.

When I hear the front door slam, my entire body sags. My life is, once again, in tatters and I stand to lose everything. I know that in some ways Umberto wasn't just my lover: he filled a gaping hole in my life. What was missing was a strong man who could influence me, and he taught me so much about vines, life and how to love unconditionally. I can't make the mistake of falling for my boss again; it's like a sad cliché.

I have no idea how to handle this. Still in shock, I go in search of my phone to make a call. I'm on edge as I wait for Sienna to pick up, hoping it doesn't go straight to answerphone. Then I realise it's late and she's probably sleeping.

'Linzi?'

'I've messed up and—' My words peter out as I'm too choked up to talk.

'Whatever has happened? Do you need me to me come over?'

Trying not to sob out loud is hard. 'No . . . I just need . . . to talk.' I'm angry with myself and it takes a couple of minutes of awkward silence for me to get it together. 'Sorry, I . . .'

'It's Elliot, isn't it? I dropped hints, more than once, because you were refusing to see what was happening. Oh, Linzi!'

'He only thinks he's falling in love with me because, foolishly, I wanted to help him. I felt sorry for Elliot and that can hardly be construed as forming an attachment, can it?'

'Do you want the truth?' Her words seem to be amplified as they echo down the line.

I curl my legs up under me, sinking back into the sofa for comfort.

'What truth?'

'He can't hide the way he looks at you and we've all noticed it. Every time you talked about Elliot you kept on with the "feeling sorry" thing and I didn't like to point out the obvious,' she says, her voice full of empathy. 'Was that wrong of me? I mean, aren't most people simply hoping to find someone to make their life complete, even if they don't realise it?'

Hearing that comes as a total shock. Is Sienna right? Have I been kidding myself all along?

'Even if that's true . . . Elliot might need me now, but in a year's time things will be fine here and he'll probably return to London. That's what's creating this special bond between us. It's often the reason why people have affairs, but it usually ends in tears. Having fallen for the boss once before, I know it doesn't work, Sienna. This is history repeating itself. Elliot is simply feeling vulnerable and for a man like him it's not something he's used to dealing with. He's confusing gratitude for the fact that I've been here to fill in the gaps for him and make suggestions, for something more meaningful.'

Sienna tuts. 'Elliot hasn't exactly been keen to keep running back to London and into Isobel's arms, has he? Doesn't that tell you something?'

'She's not his girlfriend, she's his business partner,' I reveal.

'Really? I didn't see that one coming.'

'Penny mentioned it to me in conversation and I asked him outright this evening.' And Penny also said a lot of things I didn't want to hear about the way Elliot was acting during dinner.

There's a loud rap on the front door. It's almost eleven o'clock and that means something is wrong. If those sheep have found another way in again, Gwyn is going to be cross because they did a good job of replacing the fencing.

'I must go, someone's at the door so there's obviously a problem. Thanks for listening, Sienna. Sleep well.'

I don't give her time to respond before I click end call and hurry into the hallway. When I open the door Elliot stares straight at me, a heart-rending look in his eyes. And then, before it even registers what he's doing, he stoops to kiss me very softly on the lips. As he wraps me in his arms to draw me closer, suddenly, I find myself kissing him back. When he releases me, he turns and walks away without saying a single word. What he leaves in his wake is a quivering wreck as the reality of the situation hits home. My body is confirming what my head can't seem to process. The attraction between us is real, very real. Even if I'm not ready to face up to it, it's something I can no longer deny.

22.

The Past Comes Back to Haunt Me

An unexpected tap on my door early on Monday morning makes me open it cagily. When I see that it's Sienna, it's a huge relief.

'Who were you expecting?' she whispers, as she steps inside.

'No one. Not even you. It's only just after six thirty, why are you so early?'

She stares at me pointedly. 'Because my bestie is in a fix and I'm worried about her. How did it go yesterday?'

I can't tell her about the kiss, she'd read too much into it and I want to keep things simple. 'Elliot didn't join Nate, Penny and me for the tour, thank goodness. And I managed to avoid him for the rest of the day. They had lunch at Cardiff Bay and a walk-around before Nate and Penny returned to London.'

As we take a seat on the sofa, she's frowning. 'So, how do you feel about what happened on Saturday?'

'Confused. Embarrassed. When we talked, you said Elliot can't hide the way he looks at me. It's not a topic of conversation among the others . . . is it?'

I can tell from her expression that she was hoping it's a question I wouldn't ask.

'Linzi, why do you think Michael wasn't running to you every two minutes? He thought that maybe your trust in Elliot was a little biased.'

It's crushing. 'I see.'

'Look, don't retreat back into your shell. If you switch off now, then—'

'Then my future isn't here, is it?'

'Please don't say that, Linzi. If you leave, then Michael won't hang around for long. It'll be like the domino effect. And I'm going to be working part-time for more or less nine months, there's no point kidding myself. The further we get into what we've taken on, even Cam has now accepted that. If you and Michael aren't here when I'm looking to return to full-time, it won't be the same place.'

'Sometimes change is good. Look at the situation with you and Cam. From what I'm seeing it's bringing you even closer together. Who would have thought?'

'I know and I can't dispute that. But what about Gwyn? Hopefully he'll have his operation and be back on form, but will he want to stay? The three of you control the day-to-day running of this place, and if you're right about Elliot going back to London at some point, I'm betting Gwyn will look elsewhere too. His loyalty lies with Thomas, and yes, Elliot has stepped up for him, but Gwyn will have no history with the new people coming in. Instead of a cohesive team, it could end up being a case of each new manager defending their own territory and that doesn't bode well.'

It's not falling on deaf ears, but what can I do?

'Linzi, please tell me what you're thinking.'

'I'm beginning to realise that nothing is going to be the same going forward. And in my situation it's about way more than just the job. It's getting complicated in ways I didn't expect and I can't handle that. I spent hours yesterday mulling over my options, because living and working here puts me in what is fast becoming an untenable position.'

Sienna stares at me, clearly devastated. 'But where will you go?'

'Maybe France, but it's too soon to say for sure. Once Elliot has put in place whatever he's planning, I'll let him know. I'll see the season through and leave after the harvest, at the end of October.'

'Even before you've set something up?'

'There's a job ready and waiting for me, all I need to do is send the email. It's a family vineyard in the Loire Valley, close to Nantes. I don't intend to leave The Green Valley Vineyard, or my vines, during growing season. I owe Thomas that much for what he's done for me over the years. Next time, though, I'll buy a little place close to where I work. Seeing you so excited about renovating your new home has made me stop and think about my long-term future. I want something of my own; it's time to put down some roots.'

Sienna's sharp intake of breath is painful to hear. I'm thinking on my feet here, because if the events of this weekend hadn't happened I'd still be clinging on to the hope that everything will come right in the end. However, if Elliot stays it's going to become increasingly awkward between us and if he sells up, I'll have no affinity with the new owners, only for my precious vines. The sad truth is that they never were mine anyway, and if I've learnt one lesson in life it's not to take anything for granted.

'This hasn't come totally out of the blue, has it? You've been considering it for a while.'

Monsieur Roussel from Le Vignoble de la Maison Faure, in the Loire Valley, has reached out to both Raffaele and me several times over the past year.

'I'm glad that Elliot has taken over but I can't risk getting hurt again, Sienna. Even if we are attracted to one another, Elliot and I hardly know each other; imagine how difficult it would be with everyone here . . . watching our every move.'

Sienna utters a sorry-sounding sigh. 'So, you're going to run away.'

'It's self-preservation time. I know that sounds selfish of me, but you have Cam and you're happy, Gwyn will have choices because he'll be good as new. As for Michael, he should stay if it's the right thing for him to do, not because

I'm here and that gives him the impression it's all going to turn out just fine. What if that's not the case? Elliot could be out of his depth and longing to return to what he does best, in London. Even though I don't want to move on, not least because I think of this as my home, the things I love about this place are already beginning to change and I fear that it's only the start.'

My friendship with Sienna deserves, at the very least, my total honesty after a night spent facing a few harsh truths. If I make the same mistake again I have no one to blame but myself.

'Oh!' she exclaims, sounding tired and weary. 'Why is life so complicated? And Will's arriving this morning to start the handover.'

'Just in time for Elliot's pep talk with the staff, as well. What time has he scheduled it? Talk about a double whammy.'

'Eleven o'clock. Why?'

'I don't think it's appropriate for the trainees to attend, Sienna. This is in-house stuff and, potentially, commercial in confidence. We have a heavy session anyway, so if my absence is noticed please make my apologies and, when you get a moment, can you let me know how it goes?'

'Of course. After all the effort you put in this past weekend, I'm sure Elliot will understand. You've more than demonstrated your good intentions, but he's going to be shocked, Linzi. Everyone will be surprised and puzzled by your decision to leave, because it will be a huge blow. Not least to Elliot.'

'I wish . . . oh, I don't know. The old days were good, Sienna. But for the last few years it's not been quite the same, has it? It's only now that I'm realising it. No one is indispensable, including me. Come on, there's time for a quick coffee before you start work.'

'Make it a strong one. Will is going to wonder what he's walking into today. Fingers crossed Elliot will be on form because he'll need to convince everyone that he's got his finger on the pulse.'

Elliot knows how to put forward a proposal and I have no doubt at all it'll restore everyone's faith in him. What he'll leave out is that if it doesn't work, Nate is probably already standing in the wings ready and waiting. Yes, he'll pump money in, but he won't have the same sort of connection, or loyalty, that you'd expect from someone with a family connection. But at least Elliot will have tried and be able to walk away knowing he did his best. I can't knock him for that.

'Morning, Linzi, I'm sorry to interrupt when you're teaching,' Bethan apologises, 'but there's a delivery for you in Reception. I wasn't sure whether you wanted me to pop it down to the training room?'

Glancing around as I talk, I see everyone is head down writing as the brief today is cost-saving ideas. 'No, it's fine. I'll come and collect it. Thank you.'

I stand and they all look up at me. 'I'll be back in a bit, guys. Keep those ideas coming. You have another twenty minutes.'

In truth, I've been nervously clock-watching while pretending to be reading some papers. It's only half an hour until Elliot's announcement. A part of me wants to be there, but another part of me doesn't. As Bethan comes into view I can't see any parcels in front of her, only a huge bouquet of flowers, peeking up over a substantial box.

'Someone has an admirer,' she declares. 'I can't remember the last time I received a bouquet as a surprise.'

'The flowers are for me?'

'Yes. And aren't they gorgeous?'

'Yes, they are. I'll just . . . um . . . pop them over to the cottage and put them in a vase.'

'They're in a vase inside the box,' she points out.

'Yes, right. Well, it's cooler over there and they might get tipped over in the training room. Thanks, Bethan.'

Raffaele has never sent me flowers, why would he? Oh

no . . . this is Mum making sure that now I've finally RSVP'd, I won't change my mind.

However, when I put them down on the kitchen counter and open the card my hands begin to tremble.

I'm sorry, forgive me. Too much, too soon. Please, give me another chance. You need some time to think and I don't intend to rush you.
Elliot x

Think about what? The joy when you pull off the seemingly impossible, Elliot, and then as time moves on you become bored with the vineyard because it's not your passion. And it never was, you actually admitted that. It's *my* passion, though, and I think I'm finally realising my worth. If you return to London at some point because this isn't enough, I won't fit into your world of high finance. And maybe that's what's stopped me letting go and falling head first for you, because you'll never truly fit into mine, either.

By mid-afternoon my stomach is churning as there's been no word from Sienna. I was hoping she'd give me at least a little feedback on how Elliot's pep talk was received. However, when I go in search of her she's in an HR meeting with Elliot and Will. Instinctively making my way to the tearoom, I'm feeling dispirited, and I notice that everyone I pass seems in a hurry today. Or are people avoiding me?

Instead, I turn around and increase my pace as I cross the car park. Perhaps a little fresh air will clear my head before the trainees get back from their break. The sound of a wood saw makes me turn my head and I spot Pryce, who immediately waves in my direction.

'Hey there, Linzi,' he calls out.

Do I wave back and scurry off, or do I see what sort of reaction I get from him? But he's a nice man and we usually stop for a chat when our paths cross.

'Goodness, that's a sturdy-looking repair,' I remark.

He grins at me, looking pleased with himself. 'It's been on my list for ages to replace this stile and I'm trying to whip round and do a few things so Gwyn can grab a bit of time to sort his desk.'

It's hard not to chuckle, as that usually means moving piles of paper from one spot to another. 'Hmm . . . Gwyn might need a while in that case,' I reply, light heartedly.

I don't intend to hang around, but as I turn Pryce lowers his voice. 'You missed the boss's communication meeting, Linzi. Everything's all right . . . is it?'

Inwardly, I groan. The last thing I want now is for people to begin monitoring my reactions as the changes start happening. I'm battling with what feels like a twisted knot of emotions that I'm scared to untangle because at my core I'm feeling fragile.

'It's all good, I'm just busy with the trainees. We're spending more and more time outside, but the classroom work still has to be done.' I give Pryce what I hope is a reassuring smile, intending to leave it there.

'Seems we have the right man for the job at last,' Pryce states, pressing his lips together. 'I had my doubts, Linzi, I'll be honest. But Elliot said if we can tighten our belts for the next three months, he'll have everything shipshape in time for the run-up to Christmas. That was a bit of a relief for the housekeeping team who were expecting job cuts, until Quinn piped up.' Pryce rolls his eyes.

Quinn is one of those people who seem to have a permanent chip on their shoulder and he had it from day one, so it's not something any of us have done. 'He did?'

'Yep. Interrupted Elliot to announce he was handing in his notice.'

'Huh.' I shake my head, sadly. 'How did that go down?'

Pryce grins from ear to ear. 'Elliot was cool as a cucumber. He said he was sorry to hear that, but he understood. And he went on to say that for those who were willing to be flexible through this next period there'd be a special bonus to come at Christmas. Ever since Robert passed we've all been worried something isn't right, Linzi. I was even thinking of moving on myself as I've a family to think of and a mortgage to pay, but Elliot wasn't just saying what we wanted to hear, he meant every word he said. It's good enough for me and I know you were on his side from the start. In my book, that alone is worth giving him a chance.'

I can walk away from The Green Valley Vineyard, but am I capable of letting go? The vines are my babies, the vast majority of the staff are my friends and then there's Elliot and he's . . . a complication I wasn't expecting to have to handle.

'How are you, *mia cara*?' Raffaele's voice as I raise the phone to my ear instantly lifts my spirits.

'Hanging in there. Are you all packed up and ready to leave in the morning?'

'Only just. It's been a hard week and everything takes longer than you think it will. And are you ready for the big family party tomorrow?' He makes light of it, knowing that in reality I'm dreading meeting up with them again after so long.

'As ready as I'll ever be.' I'm grateful my working week is over and it's only now, as I'm relaxing with a glass of wine in the cottage, that I'm starting to dwell on the party.

'Word is that Elliot has great things planned for The Green Valley Vineyard. Those frowns have turned into smiles, apparently. Are you happy?'

Good news travels fast. The advertising campaign is already beginning to pay off and with Penny having posted a whole stream of photos, the phones seem to be constantly ringing.

'It's nice to feel a change in the atmosphere; the tension is easing, and everyone seems determined to pull together. Come Christmas, Elliot promised them that it's going to be a whole other story and it sounds like they'll be ending the year on a high.'

'They'll? Where will you be?' Raffaele is frowning, I can hear the change in his tone.

'I meant . . . Elliot's family. I'm fine. Really.' Except that I'm not, fine that is, but he's about to fly off and I don't want to unsettle him.

'If you ever need me, Linzi, I'm just a phone call away. And I always have your best interests at heart, you do know that?'

Now he sounds apologetic, but he has nothing to apologise for. 'I do. Just travel safe, text me when you get there and then catch me up with your news when you're settled. I miss you already.'

'Me too, *mia cara*. Me too.'

As I put down the phone, I realise he wasn't his usual, exuberant self. In fact, it was an odd call, but then our goodbye was interrupted on Saturday. I was half expecting him to get in touch but I'm not used to him sounding so dispirited.

Then a random thought pops into my head. I know Monsieur Roussel has been in contact with Raffaele – he wouldn't have mentioned our recent discussion, surely? I'm sure Monsieur Roussel will know by now that Raffaele is returning to Italy anyway, so I'm probably being paranoid. Raffaele is simply feeling sentimental this evening.

When my phone rings again and the number is unrecognised, I answer it hesitantly.

'Hello?'

'Linzi? It's Vanna. Please, please do not put down the phone.'

'Did Raffaele give you my number?' I question, raising my voice out of sheer disappointment.

'No. I had to get it from someone else because I need to talk to you. Please do not hang up, my father instructed that I get in touch, and I cannot let him down. Not when it was his last wish.'

His last wish? 'Umberto is . . .' I can't even say the word, as the room seems to be closing in around me.

'He died in his sleep, having had a massive heart attack, Linzi. Life here without him will never be quite the same again. I did not want you to hear this from anyone else, as that is what he would have wanted. My father talked about you often and he wanted you to have his *diario di giardinaggio*.'

I bow my head, unable to speak. It's finally over, his life is done.

'As you know, his gardening journal meant everything to him, Linzi.' There's a sadness in her voice that is difficult to hear. 'He wrote in it every single day; sometimes a line, or two. Often, a reflection on how he was feeling. Sometimes offering up a prayer for rain during a dry spell and other times thankful for yet another bountiful crop. He put a bookmark in one of the pages which contained a special message for you. As you know it is a big book and if you text me your address I will wrap it carefully and send it special delivery.'

'I am so sorry for you and your family, Vanna. I had no idea and my heart weeps for your loss.' A solitary tear trickles down my face because it's my loss, too.

'The vineyard is in my hands now. Raffaele, as you know, is returning and it will be a comfort to me. My father taught him well and this is where he belongs. If you ever . . .'

'There are too many sad memories for me, Vanna. And how is your mother?'

She makes a disparaging 'pff' sound. 'Still shaming the family, living with my uncle as if they are husband and wife. She didn't even attend Papà's funeral.'

When I pressed Umberto for the reason why he was sending me away, he said that his wife had expressed regret for having left him. If she returned then the family would, once again, be complete. Even though it made no sense to me from what I'd witnessed going on, I couldn't argue with that, and he knew it.

'Perhaps that was for the best, Vanna, but it's sad to hear. And you are well?'

'Yes, Linzi. My husband and I have been running the

vineyard for a while. Papà wasn't the same after he sent you away. Even his precious vines couldn't console him. But you must read the message for yourself. It will take probably a week for the book to arrive, so I will go now and take a photo to send you. That would make him happy. I wish you well, Linzi. You brought a lot of joy into his life and for that I thank you. *Arrivederci!*'

It hurts. The pain in my chest is so intense I can't even shed the tears that are welling up inside of me. I begged Umberto to let me stay and I ended up making him angry. He knew it was the only way he could get me to leave. And it broke both our hearts.

It feels like forever until there's a ping and, while a part of me wants to ignore it, the other part of me longs to see Umberto's beautiful handwriting once more. I thank Vanna profusely, adding my address, and then I click on the photo.

It was written the day after I left and unlike much of the sections above and below it, it's mainly in English. Now the tears fall as I picture Umberto sitting there with his morning coffee, scribbling away.

Cuore mio, *my English rose, Linzi*

Today I sit alone and wonder how I could have let you go. But I knew I must. Not knowing where you are breaks my heart into little pieces. One day you will meet a young man who will match your passion, your intensity and your goodness. And that's what inspires me to go on.

I will thank God for each day as it comes, for the sunshine and the rain to make a good harvest. And I will ask him to do one thing for me. That is to bless you with a happy life with someone at your side who deserves to be there. Because that will please me.

Always in my heart, amore mio. *Always and forever.*

A moaning sound makes me look around and then I realise it came from my own lips. Umberto loved me, he really loved me. He didn't discard me in the hope that his wife would walk away from his brother and return to him for Vanna's sake, or because he was pining for her.

'Oh, Umberto,' I groan aloud, 'you turned my life around. You helped me to grow into the woman I was destined to be, and I ended up breaking your heart.'

I was ready to face a future together, but he wasn't. He thought I was too young to know what I wanted. Was that true? I reread his note over and over again, until I fall asleep on the sofa. It's a fitful sleep, filled with the sound of cicadas, as I'm transported back to the hillsides of Greve, in the heart of Chianti country and wonderful memories that will never leave me.

23.

Understanding the Meaning of True Love

'There,' Sienna says, standing back to admire her efforts. 'Your hair looks amazing, Linzi. Let me see those nails?'

I hold out my hands, and she screws up her eyes, scrutinising my fingertips. 'Stop fussing, they're fine and I'll do.'

'Hmm . . . that's not quite the right attitude for what you're walking into, is it? Come on, stand up. Lighten your mood, put on your brightest smile. Head high, shoulders back – you're looking pretty damn good to me, girl!'

After all that I've been through, it's taught me that no matter what happens, or how broken you feel, there comes a point when you have to say *enough is enough*. I'm only human, and if my family don't think I measure up, then this is it, because it's their last chance.

'Are you sure you don't want me to come with you?'

'No. And I didn't mean for you to dash over here to sort me out, either. I just wanted to tell you everything.'

She rests her hand on my shoulder. 'I'm glad you did, Linzi. And learning what happened and what a wonderful, gentle man Umberto was, at last I understand.'

'Right. You'd better get back to Cam and I'll prepare myself to be all sweetness and light.'

Sienna scoops up her bag and her curling tongs, and I see her out. It's a beautiful day and perfect for an afternoon tea party. I've been avoiding Elliot and it's time to make a quick exit. Because we're not speaking, he has no idea what time I'm leaving so with a bit of luck he'll be at lunch and won't surface until after I'm well on my way.

'Linzi, darling,' Mum calls out. 'Let me introduce you to Ollie's parents. And this is Terence Belvedere, the owner of Wendlesbury Manor House. We were just saying how beautiful the grounds are. Anyway, this is my eldest daughter, Linzi.'

I smile and shake hands, but my focus is elsewhere. Juliette is walking towards me, hand in hand with an attractive, blond-haired guy, and she's absolutely glowing with happiness.

'Linzi!' she calls out, and they quicken their pace. 'I told you she'd come.' I think that remark was directed more at Ollie than it was at Mum.

Maybe arriving without a plus-one was a mistake. Gazing around, I see that it's mainly couples. But it's a little sad to turn up with a girlfriend, unless you're a couple too, I muse to myself.

'Ollie, this is my big sister Linzi.'

'Are you a hugger?' he asks and, without waiting for a reply, continues, 'Because I am!' With that, he throws his arms around me. 'It's great to finally meet you. Thanks so much for coming, it's made our day that little bit more special.'

In Juliette's email when she said Ollie was really looking forward to meeting me, she wasn't joking: he's obviously delighted and so is she. But my nerves are jangling. What if I inadvertently say the wrong thing?

'You work in a vineyard, I hear,' Ollie enquires, sounding genuinely interested. 'That's an unusual job. What exactly do you do?'

Keep it simple, Linzi, I tell myself, *and keep calm*. It doesn't work and I open my mouth but nothing comes out. Then, seemingly out of nowhere, a familiar voice looms up from behind me.

'Linzi is our viticulture and training manager.'

I turn around, my head in a tizzy. 'Elliot, oh . . .'

'Sorry I'm a bit late, I hope I haven't missed anything. Terence' – he thrusts out his hand – 'it's been a while. How are the family?'

'Fine, thank you, Elliot. And Linzi, your reputation precedes you, it's nice to meet you. Elliot is a lucky chap! I'm hearing wonderful things about The Green Valley Vineyard. I had a phone call from Nate Richardson this week. The wife and I intend to pop along to the restaurant for dinner one evening as soon as we can get a reservation.'

'Just let me know a convenient date and it will be my pleasure to arrange that for you, Terence,' Elliot says, much to Terence's delight.

'Sterling!'

This is awkward as Mum is staring at Elliot wondering what on earth is going on.

'Elliot, this is Ollie and his parents, Susan and Cliff, and my mum, Harriet.'

The thing about Elliot is that he mixes easily, and the fact that he knows Terence seems to have impressed the others. There's some amicable chatter and then suddenly Dad appears, looking sheepish.

'You don't all have drinks,' he mutters and then heads off to the bar situated on the patio. No *hello, Linzi*, and no puzzled glance at Elliot, who is standing next to me looking intrigued at the lack of acknowledgement.

I turn to Elliot, giving him a warm and engaging smile. 'I'll give Dad a hand. I won't be long.'

Elliot leans in and I let him kiss me softly on the lips. 'Your knight has arrived,' he whispers under his breath, and as I pull away, I start laughing. It seems I'm being rescued whether I like it or not. I could certainly do with the support, because I was feeling like the odd one out before he turned up.

As I saunter over to the bar, Dad is busy looking around even though he's aware I'm walking towards him. He can hardly ignore me when I stand next to him.

'Hi, Dad.'

'You came then.' He glances at me for the briefest of moments.

'It's a big day for Juliette and Ollie, why wouldn't I?'

'She's doing well. I'm very proud of her.'

That's so Dad and I'm over it. 'They make a lovely couple and she's obviously very happy. I'm pleased for them both. Does it really upset you, the fact that I'm here?'

He almost drops one of the glasses he just picked up off the bar. I lean forward to grab a couple more as he gives me a sharp look.

'Keep your voice down, Linzi. If you've come to cause trouble you can leave now.'

'I have nothing on my conscience, Dad. I was once young and foolish, I hold my hands up to that, but I never hurt anyone – not intentionally.'

'What do you want, Linzi?'

'Nothing, Dad. I came to please Mum and because I want Juliette to know that I'm delighted she's found a man who makes her face light up. That's it. There's no agenda for me. I don't find other people's happiness a threat. And I've no axe to grind.'

'So, who did you bring with you?'

'My boss, Elliot Montgomery.'

Dad turns to look at me, his curiosity piqued. 'He's not related to the late Robert Montgomery, is he?'

'Yes, Elliot is his son.'

'I went to school with Robert. I read about his accident in the paper.'

Just when I think Dad is going to express the sadness he felt at the time, or tell me how shocked he was at Robert's passing, he fixes me with one of his accusatory gazes.

'Sleeping with the boss didn't get you anywhere the first time around, Linzi, and it seems it's a lesson you're determined to learn the hard way. Nothing changes with you, does it?'

To say that words fail me is an understatement, but when we arrive back the little group has grown and when I turn around a few moments later, Dad is nowhere to be seen. It's another round of introductions and even though I'm gutted my father isn't prepared to let go of the past, I'm determined to join in and be merry. Mum gravitates towards Elliot, but Ollie's mother is keen to tell me about the wedding plans. It's almost as if someone is conspiring to keep me and Elliot apart, and I am a little anxious about what he's saying.

Half an hour later, I glance across at Elliot, widening my eyes and tilting my head in the direction of the buffet located inside a smart marquee. As I turn to walk away, he's quick on my heels.

'What's going on?' I demand, keeping my voice low.

'Remember that day you said that you were longing for a man to come in and sweep you off your feet? Well, I'm guessing you didn't mean that literally, but I couldn't think of any other way to show you how much you mean to me. I just couldn't bear the thought of you being here all alone and maybe regretting your decision.'

'That's very thoughtful of you, considering my behaviour this past week. It's all been a little too much to cope with and my gut instinct is . . .' I pause.

'To run away?'

'You're not far wrong there.' I can't deny it had crossed my mind.

'Should I stay, or would you rather I made myself absent?'

'It's funny, but just before you arrived I suddenly felt very alone and began to wonder what I was doing here.'

'You're here because it's time to reconnect with people you care about, who also care about you,' he says, encouragingly.

'I know that now. Dad is a lost cause, but not everyone feels the same way. And I owe you an apology for pushing you away. I panicked and needed a little space.'

Elliot turns to grin at me. 'The fact that I sent you an

enormous bouquet of flowers and you still haven't said thank you was a bit of a slap in the face.'

I grimace, awkwardly. 'That was rude of me and they're lovely.'

'Did you read the card? Can we start over again, Linzi?'

We draw to a halt in the middle of the vast lawn and suddenly I'm oblivious to what's going on around us.

'Only if you promise to tell me everything.'

'Everything?'

'The past, the present and your ambitions for the future. I don't really know very much about you, do I, Elliot?'

'I can say the same thing. And,' he sighs, softly, 'there is something I need to confess and you aren't going to be happy. Can it wait?' He gives me a hopeful look.

'No. You tell me now before we go any further.'

He hesitates and I find myself holding my breath.

'I gave Raffaele a call to thank him, and the conversation strayed a little.'

'You were talking about me behind my back?' I peer up at him, my annoyance plain to see.

'Calm down, it wasn't really *about* you. I just said you needed closure . . . you know, Italy. I asked if there was anything he could think of that might help.'

In the midst of everything that Elliot has going on, he approached Raffaele because he was worried about me.

'And?'

Elliot looks at the floor, apparently checking out his shoes. 'He said that Umberto's daughter was desperate to speak to you but you refused his request to let him pass on your telephone number. When I explained how I feel about you, he put me in touch with Vanna. She told me the reason why she wanted to speak to you. It wasn't what I was expecting to hear, but I could tell Raffaele mentioned it to me because he sensed something was wrong.'

'It was true what Vanna said, then. It wasn't Raffaele who gave her my number, it was you.'

'Yes. But for all the right reasons, Linzi.' Elliot's voice is emotional, as if he's pleading with me. 'I knew I was risking you hating me for getting involved. I just didn't know what else I could do to show you that I'm prepared to be patient. You needed closure, or you were destined to always be alone, always wondering *what if?* I wouldn't wish that on anyone and now my fear is that if I can't convince you that I'm serious, one day that will be me, too.'

Impulsively, I step forward, sinking into Elliot's arms. He holds me close, and I can hear his heart thudding in his chest. Just knowing in his own, rather clumsy, way that he was only thinking of what was right for me is more than I deserve.

'If you hadn't intervened, I'd never have known the truth about Umberto. He wrote me a note; a special one, letting me go. It was in his precious *diario di giardinaggio*, his gardening journal, which contains everything he learnt over the years.'

'Then I'm forgiven?' Elliot asks, softly, as he buries his head among the mass of curls that took Sienna almost an hour to get just right.

'Not really – it was wrong of you, but somehow . . . I don't know. What I do know is that we're making a bit of a spectacle of ourselves.'

As I pull away from him, Elliot catches my hand. 'No more surprises going forward, I promise. Any sudden ideas I get, I'll run past you first. Are you OK with that?'

'Agreed. And if we're being honest with each other, you are beginning to grow on me. There's just one question I want to ask and it's an important one.'

'Fire away.'

'Am I really the reason why you're so determined to make it work at the vineyard? I suspected that you were trying to get Nate to invest so you can get back to London sooner, rather than later.'

'The truth is, Linzi Patterson, rescuing the vineyard is costing me a lot of money, but I'm not going anywhere now.

And, by the way, it's worth every single penny just to know your precious vines will always be in safe hands.'

'Then you're forgiven.'

Seeing Juliette and Ollie together today gives me hope that I, too, can grab some happiness. And why not? Maybe that's what inspired Mum to press for a divorce, and good luck to her. Putting your trust in someone isn't easy, but if you don't take the risk you'll never know what might have been.

I think I've finally found the one and knowing that would make Umberto happy means the world to me.

September

24.

Our Own Forest Retreat

It's the last day of September and we're all looking forward with great anticipation to the coming harvest.

Sitting here in the twilight, on the pinnacle of the ridge, and looking down over the sweeping landscape, this is everything to me. I can't imagine starting over again anywhere else. And yet I remember saying that once before to Umberto.

Now I know that it wasn't only my heart that was breaking as we sat holding hands across the small bistro table that night. The flickering candlelight illuminated our tear-filled eyes, and I should have realised the real reason why he sent me away. With the sound of the chirping cicadas and the air filled with the heady scent of jasmine and perfumed roses, I remember feeling angry. I'd been given a glimpse of paradise, only to have it snatched away as if I wasn't worthy. That wasn't what Umberto was saying, but his words fell on deaf ears. He instinctively knew that somewhere, out there, was the man I was destined to spend the rest of my life with. Sadly, it wasn't him.

Elliot pulls me closer, sensing where my thoughts are and ready to offer the comfort and reassurance I so badly need. That's a selfless act and one I appreciate, because if he was jealous of my feelings for Umberto, I'd know Elliot's love wasn't strong enough.

'Your dream of one day living in a cosy cottage in a woodland setting sounds idyllic,' he murmurs.

I turn my head to look up at him. 'It is to me.'

'What do you consider to be *cosy*?'

Staring up at the twinkling stars overhead, I give it some serious thought.

'Hmm . . .' Elliot interrupts my reverie. 'Does this pause mean you have a particular property in mind?'

I shake my head. 'No, but I'll know it when I see it.'

'OK, come with me.' As tired as he is, he jumps to his feet, taking my hand and pulling me up into his arms. 'I have a proposition for you.'

'I bet you have.' I grin at him.

'No, not that sort of proposition. Step this way.'

I sincerely hope he's not going to take me on a walk through the narrow lanes at this time of night, although there is a rather lovely cottage for sale a stone's throw away from The Red Dragon Inn.

Instead, he leads me over to the Forestry Outpost and I stare at him blankly.

'I promised you that I'd make your dreams come true. I've been talking to the local planning officer and I've submitted a change of use application to turn the barn into a residential property. We'll likely have to keep the same footprint, but the stone outbuildings are attached and can be developed too.'

I'm speechless as he leads me inside.

'We could double the space if we install a second floor.' Elliot walks over to the dividing panels that enclose the office area. 'Come on, let's venture into the cave.'

It's a door that gets little use because beyond it is a huge empty space that in the past has been used to house hay and farming implements. Elliot disappears and I follow him, thinking that he can't be serious.

He's standing looking up at the large void above our heads that goes right up to the rafters.

'But it's huge. It's too big for a home.'

He shrugs his shoulders. 'Is it? I mean, let's say three bedrooms with en suites and a main bathroom. Then down here, once the temporary walls are taken down, a big open-plan kitchen with a dining area looking out onto the woodland. Floor-to-ceiling bifold doors at ground level, so the view is unobstructed along here.' He indicates with both arms spread wide. 'Are you warming to the idea?'

'Maybe,' I reply, my head buzzing as I do a complete 360-degree turn. 'And what about all that space over there?'

'A utility room and a study, maybe even a *cosy* winter snug – whatever you want, it's your dream. Mine has already come true, and as far as I'm concerned, everything else is simply a bonus. As for the outbuildings, our own private spa would be nice. And a games room, definitely a games room.'

It's hard not to laugh, as he's obviously given this a lot of thought and already has a wish list.

'My dream wasn't this big, Elliot, you know that.'

He hurries over to wrap his arms around me. 'Then we'll start small. Maybe just convert the outbuildings into a two-bedroom cottage, with a sitting room and a kitchen-dining room. Judging by how lovely you made Red Robin Cottage look it'll be a perfect start for us to begin our life together.'

I'm on board with that, but as he turns me around I'm imagining those bifold doors. It might just take me a while to get my head around it.

'There's a problem, though. Guests can walk up as far as the vista point, and they'd be able to look in.'

Elliot's face brightens and his eyes gleam with enthusiasm. 'No, because we'll re-route the path so that it snakes away from here and this area will be fenced off. We'll make a new seating area because the ridge view is ours. The first time I sat next to you on that bench I realised somehow I had to make the impossible happen. How on earth was I going to make you fall in love with me? I knew that wasn't going to be easy, but Grandma told me that I'd figure it out, along with everything else.'

'Oh, Elliot. Your grandma knew?' I can feel the blood rushing to my cheeks.

'And her belief in me didn't waver. She said you were no fool and if it was meant to happen the chemistry would be there.'

And it was. Elliot has no idea how hard it was for me to keep telling myself I was only helping him because it was my job to do so. The real reason that I couldn't stand back and see him struggling was because he touched my heart in a way that I never expected and it threw me. In the end it wasn't until I read Umberto's message that I understood my heart was simply leading me where it wanted to go. It was guilt that stopped me acknowledging my attraction to Elliot. Knowing Umberto loved me so much that he was prepared to let me go changed everything. And in embracing his wish, I instantly knew Elliot was the one I'd been waiting for all along and that he was going to be mine forever.

Sweet dreams are truly made of this . . .

Epilogue

October

Elliot

Over the last couple of months my life has become one incredible round of firsts. It began when I moved into Red Robin Cottage with Linzi, a few weeks after that life-changing afternoon we spent together at Wendlesbury Manor House. It's a day I will always remember because it was *the* turning point.

I instinctively knew that I couldn't hurry Linzi for fear of losing her; she needed a little space to come to terms with everything that had happened. Even though we were working so closely together every day, the transition from boss and employee was slow – it had to be, because in a way I was turning her life upside down. And now here we are, another first is almost in the bag as the last day of the grape harvesting has arrived.

Peering out of my office window, I see the clouds are gathering, and it seems the Indian summer is over and more typical autumnal weather is upon us. One more email and I'll be pulling on those wellington boots to join the team.

When my phone rings, I smile to myself, expecting it to be Linzi, scolding me for running a little behind, but to my delight it's Nate.

'Elliot, my boy, you've been on my mind. How is the harvest going?'

'Pretty darn good, apparently. We won't know until the weigh-in, but Linzi is convinced it will eclipse last year's record and we're hoping to produce probably in excess of twenty thousand bottles.'

'That's quite a result, Elliot. I knew you'd turn it around, but Linzi is the real star of the show, isn't she?' he chuckles.

When it comes to a business deal, Nate doesn't cut anyone any slack, but over the years our friendship has become rock solid. Having rescued him from a few tricky financial situations, to say that he – and the vivacious Penny – saved the day, is putting it mildly. They really helped to put The Green Valley Vineyard on the map and I called Penny to thank her profusely when her photos of the wine-tasting session with Raffaele went viral. After that, we haven't looked back, and we've had to turn so many people away for the Christmas and New Year period that some of them went ahead and booked for next year before we even have a draft programme of events.

'She certainly is, Nate,' I admit. But I'm also well aware that I'm back in his debt and happy to honour that, as I'm sure he'll get himself into a scrape again before long. 'And how's Penny?'

'She's in Andalucía.' I can hear the smile reflected in his voice as he talks about her. 'She was invited to stay in a former monastery that is now a hotel and, by the sound of it, is having a fabulous time.'

'Penny is living her dream and all credit to her, she never stops.' And now I'm living my dream, too, it just isn't the one I'd envisaged. 'How's Isobel?'

Nate groans. 'Tireless. That woman never runs out of steam, but in all honesty you were right – apart from effecting some new business introductions and attending a few strategic meetings, I don't get in her way. It's the perfect partnership for me, Elliot, as it doesn't distract me from my other interests.'

'Like playing golf when Penny's away?' I laugh.

'There is that. Everyone needs to relax, Elliot.'

'Well, Linzi recently surprised me when she bought two mean-looking mountain bikes. Seriously, some of the trails are more of a workout than a long session at the gym, but I'm beginning to get the hang of it.'

'Mountain biking? Hmm . . . she's going to keep you on your toes, Elliot, and it's just what you need. How are the plans coming along for the house up on the ridge?'

'Work begins in about a month's time.'

'Did you manage to talk Linzi into converting the barn?'

'No, of course I didn't. It's the outbuildings first and, to be honest, building over the winter it makes perfect sense to do it that way round.'

'Well, you have the rest of your lives to work on it, don't you? And you've no regrets?'

'None at all, Nate. I wake up each morning looking forward to what the new day is going to bring, although I've still got a lot to learn in many ways. The irony is that life has never been better, and no one is more surprised than me that I feel like I've come home.'

'That's quite a thing, Elliot.'

'Damn it!' I exclaim, as rain suddenly begins to lash at the windows. 'The heavens have just opened. I'd better pull on the waterproofs and get out there to help or I'll be in serious trouble.'

'I won't stop you, but when Penny returns she's going to earmark a date to spend a weekend at the vineyard early in January so we can all catch up.'

'Ask her to email me when you're both free and I'll get that sorted, Nate. It'll be good to meet up. And give my best to Isobel, won't you?'

'I will. The mention of your name no longer invokes that look of intense annoyance, you'll be relieved to hear. Anyway, happy picking. I can't wait to head to Wales and crack open a bottle of the new vintage.'

It's funny; I thought I'd miss the buzz of city life, the contacts and the power trip, but here, life is more grounding. A problem for us is a fallen tree, or a bit of subsidence in the car park. And now it's a downpour with the last field of grapes still to be picked.

'You're right,' I inform Linzi, and it's a phrase I seem to use a lot these days. 'The rain does get into every little nook and cranny.'

We're standing under the temporary shelter in the far corner of the furthest field.

'Yes, but all that will be forgotten when you hold the first bottle in your hands, knowing the effort that went into it. And what a turnout this morning. I reckon we'll be done by lunchtime.'

Pryce has just dropped off a dozen large thermos jugs and some trays of bite-size Glamorgan sausages fresh from the oven. Made predominantly with Caerphilly cheese and leeks coated in crispy golden breadcrumbs, Deron's version is seasoned with nutmeg and thyme. On a drizzly day like this they certainly hit the spot. As I begin dispensing the coffees and teas, Linzi grins at me, happily.

'Come on, everyone, grab something hot!' I call out and people start to make their way over.

'This is mightily welcome Elliot, thanks,' Gwyn states, piling a heaped spoonful of sugar into a steaming hot mug. 'I've been watching and you're definitely getting the hang of it out there.'

Gwyn nudges Linzi and she tries her best to keep a straight face.

'I know the rest of you put me to shame, but we can't all be a tour de force.' I leave them to tuck in, as it's hungry work and everyone is glad of a little break under the shelter.

It's good to see Gwyn back to full health. Linzi was delighted when she called in to see him shortly after he returned home following his convalescence and found him busy decorating.

I walk over to the flap, popping my head out. 'Grandma, Granddad – coffee!'

Watching them walk towards me, seemingly oblivious to the rain, there is a sadness I feel for never having joined in with the harvesting. As a young boy when the vineyard was still in its infancy, I fondly remember helping Grandma in the kitchen once, baking biscuits for the workers when the grape picking coincided with half-term. But I freely admit that I felt no affinity whatsoever with the land, or the vines. Aside from the enjoyable times I spent with Grandma in the farmhouse kitchen, my memories of being outdoors weren't particularly happy ones. I was either getting in the way, or my father was telling me off for not listening when I was given a task to do.

Even into my teen years, Grandma was the only person who ever really listened to me. Granddad worked long days and was often preoccupied. By the time my father gave up his day job to join the family business permanently, I was at university. What saddens me now is that if only my father had reached out to me when he lost control of the finances, I could have steered things back on course.

'Come on, you two, get inside and dry off a little!' I hasten my grandparents.

'Stop your fussing, Elliot.' Grandma's eyes sparkle as she leans in to kiss my cheek. A little rivulet of water runs down her face and drops off her chin. 'A shower never hurt anyone.'

'Yes, but this isn't exactly a *little* shower, is it?'

'Elliot thinks we're too old for this, Thomas.' She leans into Granddad and his face lights up.

'Too old? Never. Haven't missed a single harvest since the day we arrived. It's the highlight of the year,' he replies.

And it is. I stare around at the damp but smiling faces – many I know, as everyone who's free mucks in. Some of the casual staff are new to me, but nothing seems to dampen their spirits. I beckon to Linzi and she hurries over to join us.

'The two of you put us all to shame,' she quips, beaming at Grandma and Granddad. 'You need to slow down a bit and let the rest of us catch up. We're nearly there and it's a good feeling, isn't it?'

Granddad returns her smile and I know exactly what he's thinking. That having passed over the entirety of the business to me, once Linzi is my wife these will officially be her vines and they couldn't be in safer hands. 'It most certainly is, m'dear. And it always seems to rain on the final day, it's funny that.'

Linzi's forehead puckers up; no doubt her mind is harking back in time. 'You're right, Thomas, it does. I guess it's a good omen.'

Grandma puts her coffee mug down to link arms with Linzi. 'I like to think of it as nature washing away the dust.'

'It makes the grapes shine like jewels, doesn't it, Katherine?' Linzi replies.

'Oh, I love that analogy. And it's going to be a bumper year, which is an equally good omen as it's your and Elliot's first one together. What a blessing! It's a pity Sienna couldn't make it, but I gather the building work is going well for her and Cam.'

'It is, and she is gutted not to be here, but there's a lot happening at the house this week.'

'A bit of a working holiday for her, eh?' Granddad joins in.

'Let's just say she's getting really good at troubleshooting the annoying little problems, but they're still on target.'

'Have you heard from Raffaele?' Grandma asks Linzi.

'Yes, he settled in well and is, he tells me, being kept very busy both at work and outside of it.' Linzi raises her eyes to the heavens.

'He was never destined to be a single man forever.' Grandma gives her a pointed look.

It's obvious that Linzi agrees wholeheartedly; I'm just relieved that it's going to be with someone else and not the love of my life. 'I know, but he just hasn't met the one yet. He will, I'm sure of it.'

As I listen to them chatting, I remember saying to Linzi that I'd rather be alone than with the wrong person. In hindsight, my parents weren't terribly well matched; my mother worried about my father overworking and it irritated him. He couldn't see that by nature she's a nurturer and he saw that as a weakness, especially when it came to my upbringing. His ethos was that you toughen up because that's what life demands, but a little kindness at the right time goes a long way. And he was rarely kind.

'Have you heard whether your mother exchanged contracts on her new house this morning as hoped?' Grandma turns her attention to me.

'Yes. The completion date for the sale and purchase is a week on Friday, she texted me about an hour ago.' It will be the end of an era and a fresh start with no financial burdens to hold her back. It's the least my mother deserves for what she's put up with all these years.

Grandma gives Linzi's arm a squeeze. 'It was lovely to see your mum, Juliette and Ollie here yesterday giving a hand – that must have been a special moment for you when they arrived.'

'It was. It made my day, thanks to Elliot.' Linzi glances at me, happiness radiating out of her.

I didn't know for sure how she'd take it, but my gut instincts were proved right. Even so, Linzi is hiding a hint of sadness I know she feels now that her parents are getting divorced. But it's for what could have been, not for what was. Now there's a time of healing ahead for them all.

Linzi's mum took me to one side yesterday and thanked me for inviting them. She realised that it will help to cement their bond going forward and it certainly looked like it was mission accomplished.

'I hope you've left some grapes for me to pick!' Michael's voice makes us all turn around. He's fully kitted out and looking eager.

'Just in time,' Linzi confirms. 'Another hour, maybe two,

and the grapes will be on their way to The Black Ridge Vineyard. Right, I don't know about you lot but I'm ready to get back to it.'

Linzi walks over to me and, while we like to maintain a professional distance when we're working, the look we exchange is full of love, hope and optimism for the future. In the background, I notice that Grandma has walked over to Granddad, and they link hands. In passing on the vineyard to me and Linzi, they're finally able to sit back and have a little fun. It's given them both a new lease of life and, with Linzi by my side, their dream continues in us. And, hopefully, future generations to come. ☺

Acknowledgements

A virtual hug to my wonderful editorial team on this project – the inspirational Hannah Bond and Anna Perkins. It was a fun collaboration.

Not forgetting the other incredible driving forces behind the Embla team – Jane Snelgrove, Jennifer Porter and Emilie Marneur, and Bonnier Books – because our lives are built on stories, and each book does matter! It's a thrill to be a part of it.

A special mention goes out to Denise at Llanerch Vineyard, Hensol, for a fabulous and informative wine-tasting session. Her extensive knowledge and love for the vines was inspirational. I can't thank you enough!

Grateful thanks also go to my wonderful agent, Sara Keane, for her sterling advice, support and all those long phone calls putting the world to rights. It's been an amazing journey since the day we first met, and your friendship means so much to me.

To my wonderful husband, Lawrence – always there for me and the other half of team Lucy – you truly are my rock!

There are so many family members and long-term friends who understand that my passion to write is all-consuming. They forgive me for the long silences and when we next catch up, it's as if I haven't been absent at all.

Publishing a new book means that there is an even longer list of people to thank for publicising it. The amazing kindness of my lovely author friends, readers and reviewers is truly humbling. You continue to delight, amaze and astound me with your generosity and support.

Without your kindness in spreading the word about my latest release and your wonderful reviews to entice people to click and download, I wouldn't be able to indulge myself in my guilty pleasure – writing.

Wishing everyone peace, love and happiness.

Lucy x

Lucy Coleman

Lucy Coleman always knew that one day she would write, but first life took her on a wonderful journey of self-discovery for which she is very grateful.

Family life and two very diverse careers later she now spends most days glued to a keyboard, which she refers to as her personal quality time.

'It's only when you know who you are that you truly understand what makes you happy! Writing about love, life, and relationships – set in wonderful locations – makes me leap out of bed every morning!'

About Embla Books

Embla Books is a digital-first publisher of standout commercial adult fiction. Passionate about storytelling, the team at Embla publish books that will make you 'laugh, love, look over your shoulder and lose sleep'. Launched by Bonnier Books UK in 2021, the imprint is named after the first woman from the creation myth in Norse mythology, who was carved by the gods from a tree trunk found on the seashore – an image of the kind of creative work and crafting that writers do, and a symbol of how stories shape our lives.

Find out about some of our other books and stay in touch:

Twitter, Facebook, Instagram: @emblabooks
Newsletter: https://bit.ly/emblanewsletter